MONKEY BUSINESS
all that

All That MONKEY BUSINESS

CHIP HAYNES

All That Monkey Business
Copyright © 2024 Chip Haynes. All rights reserved.

4 Horsemen
Publications, Inc.

Published By: 4 Horsemen Publications, Inc.

4 Horsemen Publications, Inc.
PO Box 417
Sylva, NC 28779
4horsemenpublications.com
info@4horsemenpublications.com

Cover & Illustration by Niki Tantillo
Typesetting by Autumn Skye
Edited by Tabitha Saletri

All rights to the work within are reserved to the author and publisher. No part of this publication may be reproduced, stored in a retrieval system, or transmitted in any form or by any means, electronic, mechanical, photocopying, recording, scanning, or otherwise, except as permitted under Section 107 or 108 of the 1976 International Copyright Act, without prior written permission except in brief quotations embodied in critical articles and reviews. Please contact either the Publisher or Author to gain permission.

All characters, organizations, and events portrayed in this novel are either products of the author's imagination or are used fictitiously.

All brands, quotes, and cited work respectfully belongs to the original rights holders and bear no affiliation to the authors or publisher.

Library of Congress Control Number: 2024938241

Paperback ISBN-13: 979-8-8232-0559-7
Hardcover ISBN-13: 979-8-8232-0560-3
Audiobook ISBN-13: 979-8-8232-0562-7
Ebook ISBN-13: 979-8-8232-0561-0

This book is dedicated to everyone who could never say what they really did. Like my dad.

CONTENTS

Roswell Explained ix
Chapter 1 1
Chapter 2 12
Chapter 3 24
Chapter 4 35
Chapter 5 45
Chapter 6 56
Chapter 7 68
Chapter 8 79
Chapter 9 90
Chapter 10 101
Chapter 11 111
Chapter 12 122
Chapter 13 132
Chapter 14 143
Chapter 15 154
Chapter 16 166
Chapter 17 177
Chapter 18 188
Chapter 19 198
Chapter 20 210

Epilogue 222
Roswell Revisited 225
Author's Notes 227
Chip Haynes 229

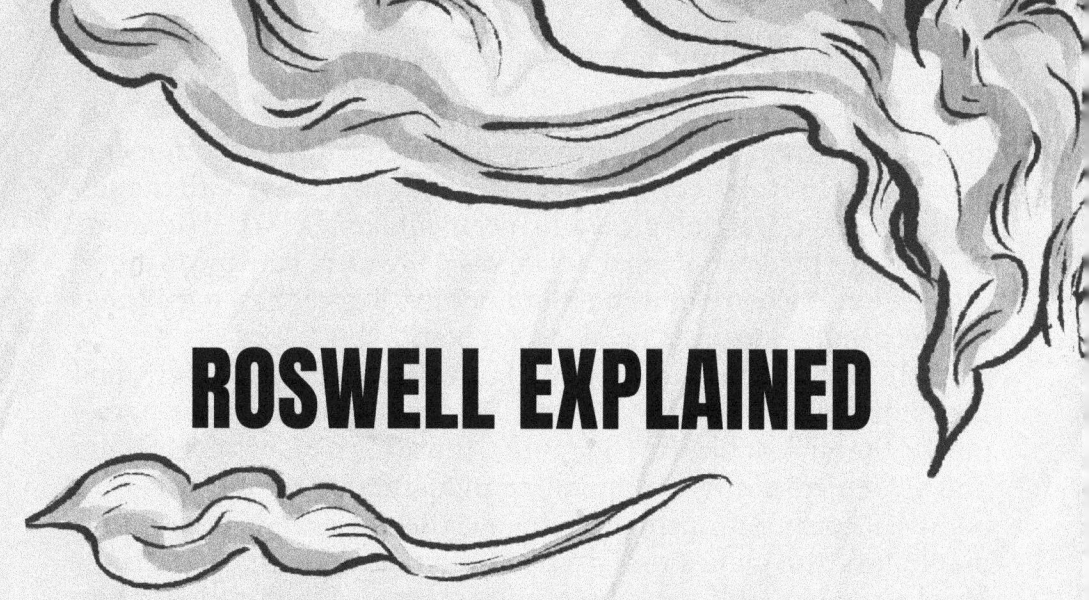

ROSWELL EXPLAINED

IN JUNE OF 1947, SOMETHING ODD CRASHED ON A RANCH outside of Roswell, New Mexico, and over the years, much has been said and written about what (and who) it might have been. The most popular public theory is that it was an extraterrestrial craft being piloted by aliens, and that their small, oddly shaped and badly burned bodies were recovered from the wreckage as the wreckage itself was hidden by the government in a poor attempt to cover up what they knew, that we were, by then, being visited by creatures from another planet possessing advanced technology the likes of which the public had never seen. To this day, that is what many people still believe. But that might not have been what really happened. Not even close.

A little *real* history here: By the summer of 1947, the U.S. had used up all three of its nuclear weapons (one at the Trinity Site near Alamogordo, New Mexico, and the other two over Hiroshima and Nagasaki, Japan, to end the war in 1945). The U.S. would have no more nuclear weapons at all for quite a few years, but they were certainly working on it. The U.S. Air Force was still a part of the U. S. Army at the time, and would be until September of that year, and the first B-52 would not fly publicly until April of 1952. Most of America, the military included, was still operating on pre-war technology. But maybe not everyone. The war gave science and technology a serious boost and a kick in the pants. It was time to get moving!

Advancements in nuclear weapons technology were moving right along after the war. Indeed, advancements in nuclear weapon

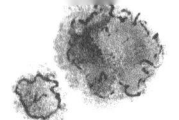

design and strength were seriously out-pacing any advancements being made in American military aircraft design, even with the suddenly acquired technological advancements made by the Germans in jet engine design during that last war. We were starting to see jet planes, but we were making atom bombs bigger than even those first jets could outrun. This was a problem.

Both bombs used during WWII were dropped by specially modified (stripped out and lightened) B-29s, and both planes barely outran the nuclear blasts. They surfed those blast waves out of town, and those were not, by the rapidly changing standards of the day, big bombs. It became immediately obvious that the next (bigger) bombs would take the planes that dropped them with them, and missile technology had still not advanced to the point that it would be a reliable delivery system for anything that heavy for that great a distance. The U.S. government was going to need much faster planes... Or maybe not. Maybe not at all. Maybe quite the opposite.

Maybe what the U.S. government really needed were much *slower* planes, much simpler planes, planes so easy to fly that a monkey could do it. Specifically, a well-trained chimpanzee. They were certainly trainable, worked cheap and few of them had lawyers. Or families. All those chimps needed was the right plane to fly. A simple plane. One so simple that a monkey could fly it. And one that might not fall right out of the sky if he couldn't. Something like a neutral buoyancy aircraft, halfway between a blimp and a fixed-wing aircraft. Neither lighter than air nor heavier, but balanced just right to simply float along. Big enough to carry a nuclear bomb, a monkey or two and some bananas. And yes, I *do* know that chimpanzees are not monkeys. They are primates. Great apes. Work with me here...

Various modified balloon designs were tried (yes, "weather balloons"), with the thick, round, disk-shaped design working the best, offering both the stability for easy flight control and the lift needed for the larger (and much heavier) nuclear weapons. Using hydrogen instead of helium improved their lift capacities immensely, and the flash risk of using that hydrogen hardly mattered. Chimpanzees were being carefully groomed to fly these slow aircraft out over the then-remote desert in New Mexico, over restricted government land, and it was all going well until it wasn't. In June of 1947, one of the Army Air Force's NBAs (Neutral Buoyancy Aircraft) came down, crashed and burned (actually, it burned and *then* crashed) outside of

Roswell, New Mexico. The chimps flying the thing were killed in the explosion before the crash. And the whole idea went down in flames right along with it. Well, maybe. Much time, money and effort had been invested in this top secret project, and no one wanted to give it up without a fight. They still had all of those other monkeys to feed.

    The local ranchers and a few of the curious people (perhaps not *all* local) gathered up some bits and pieces of the strewn crash wreckage that they found on the ground, while the small burnt bodies in "space suits" (specially tailored pressurized flight suits) were quickly taken to the closest military base hospital, and the guys in uniform said it was just a weather balloon. Nothing to see here. Except that it was a mighty fiery crash for a weather balloon (they could blame the hydrogen gas for that), and someone *saw* those weird little burnt bodies. They had to be aliens! So it had to be a UFO! And the fact that the government *denied* that it was a UFO seemed to lend credence to the idea that it *was*. Especially when the government couldn't seem to prove that it *wasn't* a UFO. So it had to *be* a UFO, right? Yeah, well, about that pesky public denial thing...

    Take a look at the situation from the government's unwanted publicity point of view: Their top secret nuclear weapons delivery project just crashed and burned in full view of the American public. People saw stuff. Now, would *YOU* want to stand there, facing a room full of reporters, and tell the whole world that you were training monkeys to fly nuclear bombers? The correct answer here: No, you would not. In the harsh light of the now very public day, the idea of having monkeys fly nuclear bombers suddenly looked exceptionally ridiculous, even for the government. And dangerously so, from their point of view. So what do you do if you're the government trying to hide the really embarrassing truth? You give 'em the lie they want to believe anyway! Let the world think you're trying to hide something else. Like maybe a UFO? Sure, yeah, why not? *That's* what it was! A flying saucer! And those chimpanzees in flight suits? Now burnt hairless and extra crispy? Hey, little green men from outer space! Why not? That sure beats the crazy bad embarrassing truth, now doesn't it? Yep. Now you have to wonder if that was where we got our almost universal (no pun intended, I assure you) visual concept of what an alien looks like today: Something short with two long arms, big eyes and a flat nose. Add hair and whadda ya got? Yep.

And so it was that, over the months and years that followed, that the U.S. government quietly nodded and smiled and let the world think that it was hiding crashed UFOs and extra crispy little green men on a secret base somewhere outside of Roswell, New Mexico. The idea that a burnt chimpanzee in a pressurized flight suit might look a lot like what we thought aliens might look like (and still do) never occurred to anyone, because, honestly, what idiot would let a monkey fly a nuclear bomber? I mean, honestly...

Yes, well, there ya go. Roswell explained.

CHAPTER 1

THE MOOD IN THE ROOM WAS MELLOW. THEY ALL KNEW WHAT they were doing, and it was all going well. Each man had the dials he had to watch, and everyone had a small radar screen to plot their success. By now, the serious was merely routine. The only man standing up and walking around the room was the man asking all of the questions.

"Altitude?"

"Even at ten thousand."

The walking man, the officer in uniform, nodded his approval in silence as he kept walking.

"Air speed?"

Another voice spoke up. "Steady at one twenty."

Still nodding, still walking, still not smiling.

"Point?"

"They're headed straight down One Thirty-five."

The officer stopped walking, turned and leaned in to look at the closest radar screen. Yep, there was that white dot, moving steadily to the southeast. The man in uniform stood back up. Still no smile.

"They're headed for the edge. It's time to bring them home."

Now the quiet room made a little noise as everyone shifted in their chairs and went into action. Everyone knew what to do. One man in the front row moved a microphone closer and pushed the button. No one else said a word.

"It's time to come home, Sammy. Time to turn around. Turn around. *Come home.*"

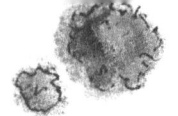

The man who spoke those words released the button on the mic and looked over at the man to his left. A button was pushed, and then another. Nods were exchanged, but it was too early to smile. For as many times as they had done this, they all held their breath every time at this point. All eyes were on the radar screens, and all they could do was wait and see. And hope. Western Witch Flight 84 was going well, but now they had to get that wicked witch home. Getting them back was the true test.

The Western Witch Project was proof that the government had a sense of humor when no one was looking. Named for a certain wicked character in a certain movie who had her own flying monkeys, the name of the project was never spoken out loud in front of any civilian ever. They made sure of that. The unofficial catch phrase, however, had been known to slip off the tongue from time to time.

"*Son of a witch.*"

The officer in charge heard that, sped up and walked right over to the source. "Do we have a problem?"

The poor guy looked up, suddenly aware that he had spoken out loud. He blushed. "No, sir, we do not. Just me. My pen peed."

The pen in the flight technician's shirt pocket had indeed let go, and the dark blue ink stain on the khaki shirt was getting larger as they looked. No one smiled. This was serious business.

"I just washed this shirt last week."

Now the officer smiled, glad that was all it was. "Well, I guess you'll have to dye it blue and join the Navy."

The unlucky technician unbuttoned his shirt to find that he, too, had been dyed blue by the faulty pen. There was some quiet laughter all around, but not too much. They all knew it could have been any one of them. Cheap government pens. The lowest of three bids. All he could do was sacrifice his handkerchief to the cause and get on with the job at hand. They still had a flight to finish. Everyone got back to what they were doing, and the room went silent. Back to work.

In the back of the room, standing in the doorway, Colonel Gorton Baden had been silent all along, and he would remain so. He didn't need to be there at all, but he was the officer over the officer in charge. And he did enjoy watching this team work. It took him back to happier times in another life, in another country. Before it all went so very bad. He kept his hands in his pockets, his one bad habit in uniform. He had to break that habit ... and hide his accent. Both would

CHAPTER 1

take time. It hadn't been that long. Two years. Little changes in two years. Gorton had changed a lot, but his smile still looked more like a grimace. He needed to work on that, too.

The officer in charge of the Western Witch Project was the one roaming around the room, trying to take it all in at once: Captain Eli Lewis, U.S. Army Air Force, age 41. He had gone through the war, and he would get through this. He had flown B-24s in Europe, and he could teach monkeys to fly. He was that good at it. He missed his old flight crew, but this ground crew was coming right along. He was used to them by now, and they all knew what to do. He made sure of that. These guys had taken teamwork to a higher level, and the results were somewhere overhead. Somewhere out there, monkeys were flying planes. All because of these guys in here. All because of Capt. Lewis.

The room itself was less than no big deal: One door, no windows. And there was no window in the door, either. That Col. Baden was standing in the open doorway during a flight was a direct violation of security, but no one was going to mention that to the colonel. He was big enough to block the door, and no one on the other side was any less secure than they were before. It was a tight base. And a very tight building.

The desks in the room were all lined up in rows facing away from the door, but there was nothing to see on the wall they were facing but a large map of New Mexico with a single red dot to mark their spot. A thin red line delineated the boundaries of the base and the restricted land the government controlled all around the base. That was their flight zone. All they had to do was keep their flying monkeys inside that red line.

Capt. Lewis spent those flights walking slowly around the flight control room, watching each man do his job and wanting each flight to be less exciting than the one before. All he wanted was boring. No trauma, no drama, and no surprises. And no leaky pens. Was that too much to ask?

"Heading?"

"We've got them coming back on Three Fifteen."

Capt. Lewis allowed himself a small smile and looked over all of the men at their desks to the back of the room where Col. Baden was still guarding the open door. The colonel gave the captain a small

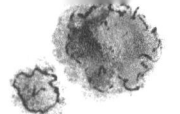

smile and an even smaller nod. Now all they had to do was get them home. And down. They had to get them back down on the ground.

"Bobo, bring the plane down, Bobo. Bring the plane *down*."

Dials were watched and breathes were held. It took some time to register, but after a minute or so, yes, the altitude numbers did begin to drop. Too early to cheer, but the monkeys really were coming home. All they had to do was get back to the base and land the thing. How tough could that be? Everything had been done to make it as easy as possible for them. Those monkeys were not flying a B-24. Not at all.

What those two chimpanzees were flying had been dubbed a Neutral Buoyancy Aircraft by Col. Baden, who had come all that way just to oversee the thing itself. Two years earlier, Captain Gorton Baden, in a pair of filthy coveralls that were not his, had stolen a bicycle and pedaled west as hard and as fast as he could, just ahead of the advancing Soviet army outside Berlin. As it turns out, you really can outrun a tank on a bicycle, given the proper motivation. Gorton was that motivated. Seriously so. He made sure that the English captured him, the Americans wanted him, and deals were made. He got traded like a hot baseball player. Smiles all around. Now Gorton Baden was living the dream, his dream, the American Dream. Some place warm. New Mexico.

With his background in aircraft design, Herr Baden was now Colonel Baden and assigned to the Western Witch Project, which had to be explained. They showed him the movie. Bought him popcorn. All we have to do, they said, was teach monkeys to fly. At first he thought they meant they were giving them wings, like in the movie, but no. *He* was giving them wings—something to fly. It was up to him to design an aircraft so easy to fly that a monkey could do it. Something simple. Something slow. Something safe? Well, two out of three ain't bad. He understood the *why* of the thing, too.

Baden looked at what they had to work with at the facility and what could be brought in if he needed it. He saw all that had gone before, and he knew what he had been working on through that last war. There had been some great advancements made in aircraft design over those last ten years, but this was something in a whole new direction. He thought of it as a flying ground trainer. That helped.

The design took shape as a large, thick, disk-shaped bag. There would be a lightweight internal structure to hold the craft's shape,

CHAPTER 1

with the motors and cockpit mounted underneath for both the stability and the view. Tough to see much of anything from up on top of something like that. The small-diameter props, twin motors and fuel tanks were all behind the small B-29-styled cockpit that gave the chimps an unrestricted view of the world in front of them. As it turned out, they were not afraid of heights. Good thing.

Where it got tricky was the gas, hydrogen. It had to be hydrogen. Nuclear weapons (and all of that fuel) weighed quite a bit, and they needed every bit of lift they could muster to get that bomb delivered. They did save a little on the weight of the fuel, as they only needed enough to just get there, but don't tell the chimps that. Everybody working on the project tried not to think too much about that … or loan the chimps money. This was war. Or would be if it came to that.

With the obvious exception of an atom bomb, the NBAs would be unarmed. That is, no on-board defenses. No machine guns. Because, well, it didn't seem wise to give a monkey a machine gun. Yeah, I know, let it go. Besides, they needed to save as much weight as they could. So, no guns, one bomb, two chimps. And bananas. Lots and lots of bananas. That kept the chimps happy. And by now, the entire ground and control crew was munching bananas as well. They were free, but watch your step. That got funnier every time. Yes, it really works.

From almost two miles up, the New Mexican desert was a wonderful scene of stark colors and blinding white sand, with those gorgeous mountains out on the horizon. What a view! An abstract painting of nature's grand contrasts and man's indelicate hand. Not that the chimps were much into art, but the view up there *was* spectacular. They tolerated it. They'd look at anything if there was a banana in it for them. And there usually was. That's how the plane flew—on bananas. Every time they did the right thing, they got a banana. In that regard, evolution hadn't budged in quite some time. What's your banana?

Sitting side by side in what really was the scaled down nose of a B-29, the two fine primates were clothed in shiny, custom-tailored, high-pressure flight suits, complete with matching small helmets. No goggles, though. The ground crew never could get them to wear those things, and they went through quite a few trying. No bananas there. So they tinted the top glass panels over the cockpit instead

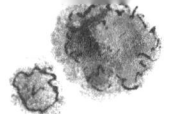

and let it go at that. You do what you can with what you've got. The chimps didn't mind the sun.

The chimps in charge for this flight were Bobo and Sammy. They were a team. The project team knew to pair chimps that got along, and these two got along great. No dominance, no fights, no worries. Bananas all around. They were about the same age, both males, and neither one wanted to be in charge of the other. There was some question that they might be brothers, but no one could prove that one way or the other, and the chimps never said. That did explain the easy teamwork between the two. They even shared their bananas.

In the earlier days of the project, in-flight chimp fights had been a serious problem. The project team did their best to work it all out in the on-ground flight simulators, but sometimes that didn't let you see the problem ahead of time. Lowering the oxygen level in the cabin helped solve some issues, but that was a tricky solution at best. The best chimps were focused on their work, not the other chimp. Getting them paired correctly, and keeping that pair together, helped. And the bananas helped, too. Lots of bananas.

Bobo and Sammy had always worked well together, both on the ground and in the air. If they were brothers, then the project team wanted more chimps like this. More brothers. Keep it in the family, if that's what it took. The older chimps, like these, had been working together in the Western Witch Project for almost two years. This was their A team, no doubt about it. They had done this before, flown free flight, many times. And now the ground crew was talking them back to base, one banana at a time.

"Go to port, Sammy. Go to port."

The ground crew heard a gentle monkey noise over the open mic two-way radio, and the base radar screen showed the NBA start to turn to port.

"Good, Sammy. *That's good.*"

Little by little, one short command at a time, the ground crew in the control room was talking the chimps back to base, and several of them were outside with binoculars, hoping to spot the odd, shimmering aircraft as it came into sight. That big silver gasbag would be tough to miss, as it did reflect the sun no matter the time of day. Where? There! There it is!

One of the men with binoculars pointed, the other men looked and everyone smiled. Yep, there it is. No mistaking that thing. One

CHAPTER 1

of the crew picked up the phone they had hauled out with them and told the crew in the control room that Western Witch 84 was in sight and looked right. Well, maybe a little high. Dials were checked and monkeys were told.

"Bring it down lower, Bobo. *Go lower*."

No one said a word as the altitude dials were watched. Up and down were tougher than left and right, but these chimps were professionals. The NBA began to descend. Number 84 was coming home, but it wasn't there yet. The crew outside walked over to the runway, not only to handle the odd craft once it landed, but to give the chimps a view of their friends on the ground, a target to aim for. The guys all held bananas and waved big waves. The chimps saw that, and they knew what to do. They were comin' home!

Now, in truth, there was really no reason to train the chimps to land the craft. The whole idea of the thing was a one way trip, but still, these things cost money. So did the chimps, and it took years to train them to do what they had to do. It was a complex job, even with such a simple craft. So yeah, they wanted them back for now. They wanted them safe at home, and they wanted that weird aircraft hidden fast. This project was still classified as top secret, and not even everyone on the base knew what was going on. That weird thing? Just a weather balloon. "Weather balloon" had become "govspeak" for "Don't ask." So don't.

They could hear it now, that distinctive high-pitched whine from those lightweight engines and odd small-diameter, seven-blade props. They didn't sound like normal gas aircraft engines, and that was all part of the plan: Confusion. What was that? By the time you figured it out, it was too late. Boom. Gone. But no boom today. The NBA was coming in low and slow, fighting a headwind but winning that fight. Bobo was having to work harder to make the craft go lower, to land, but he could see the ground crew waiting for him, so he knew what he had to do. It was almost banana time!

Aside from the most welcome breeze, it was a beautiful, bright, sunshiny day in the desert. Just a few wispy white clouds up there, and nothing but desert warmth down on the ground. The runways hosted great shimmering mirages of lakes that never were. The ground crew could see them, but the chimps in the NBA, at their higher angle, could not. Those mirages had worried the ground crew at first. They worried that the chimps might not want to land on

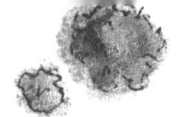

"water," until it was pointed out that they'd only see the not-really-there water images after they landed, so it was no big deal, right? The training team had made a point of walking the chimps toward those mirages many times, making sure they understood that those lakes would go away as they came closer to them. That helped.

Breaths were held as Western Witch Flight 84 fought the headwind and came in for a bouncy landing, but it did land! There were some small cheers from the ground crew outside, and they phoned the guys in the control room. Eighty-Four is down! Big cheers in that room as they all raised fists, each fist holding a banana. That was their end-of-flight tradition. Then they shut everything down and ate those bananas. They were done. At the back of the room, Col. Baden smiled, nodded politely to Capt. Lewis and then he was gone. He would do a silent walk past the ground crew dealing with the aircraft, look at the aircraft and the chimps and that would be the last they saw of him for a day or two.

Capt. Lewis made a careful walk around the room, checking with each of the men at the screens and consoles, making sure everyone was happy with how it had gone that day. He did not eat a banana. He was over bananas. There would be a follow-up staff meeting on another day to go over any problems and for the crew to offer up any new ideas. How could they make it better? Just because it worked didn't mean it was perfect. Given the project's purpose, perfect every time was the goal. After a slow search around the control room for problems that weren't there, Capt. Lewis joined the ground crew outside to watch and listen. He'd get home late, but that was okay. It was a flight day, and late was the norm.

The ground crew outside was far from done. Their game had just begun. As the craft touched down on the runway, two jeeps raced out, one to either side of the thing, and cables were attached to the outer edges of the big, round gasbag. Gotcha! As those two jeeps helped bring the craft to a soft, gentle stop, a third jeep raced in front and snagged the nose wheel strut. Tow boat! With a motion to the chimps inside, the craft's high-pitched motors were shut down and the rotors began to slow. And now more jeeps were on the way.

Now two more jeeps rolled up on either side of the NBA, both of them towing a massive rolling canopy, a great big dark green tent to cover the entire NBA. To hide it and, more importantly, to hide the chimps. No one sees the chimps. They made sure of that. As the NBA

CHAPTER 1

came to a halt and those wicked little black props finally stopped spinning, the ground crew popped the canopy open and pulled their small friends out. It was a party! They made sure of that. Keep the monkeys happy. That was Job One, because everyone knew that if the monkeys weren't happy, people got hurt. These chimpanzees were strong, and they could easily be dangerous if they were mad. So keep 'em happy. They were happy. They were home.

An unmarked green sedan with blacked out windows joined the bustling activity under the canopy around the front of the plane, and the two chimps wasted no time at all in running over and jumping in the open door at the back of the car. This was the crew car, dubbed the "Banana Wagon." The back seat had been removed and the back of the car was full of fresh fruit. It was a monkey's dream machine. They were ready to go! With both of the chimps safely inside, the car door was shut and the car rolled away slowly, off to where the chimps were kept, safe and unseen. They'd clean the car out later.

The craft itself, the Neutral Buoyancy Aircraft, was headed to the same place as the chimps but at a slower pace. No need to rush this, every need to hide it. The jeep drivers all worked in unison, and they kept the NBA under the rolling canopy all the way to the hangar. All the way inside. Only then did everything shut down, and it all came to a quiet halt. The hangar doors were slid shut and locked. There were no windows, not even sky lights. The lights were on in broad daylight, but it was as dark as night in there without them. No photos, please.

The NBA was put in Shut Down Mode, locked in place and the hydrogen very carefully removed from the bag. This was the most dangerous part of the mission, the gassing and degassing of the bag. One stupid move and the whole hangar would be gone, along with everything in it. The crew moved slowly and deliberately, double-checking themselves every step of the way. No mistakes. Their lives depended on it. Scaffolding was rolled out to hold the sagging gasbag up off the hangar floor, to allow the crew to work beneath it as they did their job. The monkeys, on the other hand, were in Party Mode. They knew they had done well.

The chimps, all of them, lived in a complex of rooms that were *under* the hangar. The whole training and housing facility was underground and out of sight. Job One was very simple: No one sees the chimps. They, more than the NBA itself, were The Big Secret. Top

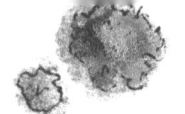

Secret. They had everything they needed in that underground complex, including places to just hang out and play. (Even the chimps got time off.) And even the chimps liked to party.

Did they miss the real outdoors? Did they want to go outside? If they did, they never said. And they never tried to make a break for it if they had the chance. There were those brief moments, before and after every flight, when the chimps were not, in fact, strapped into a seat, and maybe they *could* run if they wanted to, but they didn't want to. Was it because of the desert? The brilliant sun, no trees and blazing heat? Maybe so. It was not what they wanted. It didn't look like home to them, and it wasn't where they wanted to be. Their hidden underground home was cool and quiet and not so very blindingly bright. No reason to run from that. There were no bananas out there in the desert. And this flight was done. They knew that. They knew the routine.

With the NBA safe in the hangar and all of the doors shut, the dark green monkey machine—the car with the chimps inside—was already inside that same hangar. It was opened up and the chimps were brought out. The chimps said hello to everyone. Loudly. Their handlers kept them occupied as the ground crew dealt with the plane they never gave a second glance. They knew they were done with that plane for the day. The crew let them eat their bananas from the car before it was time to go. Then, hand in hand, each chimp still wearing that silvery tailored pressure suit, they were led by their favorite trainer to a door that led down to their underground home. It was where they wanted to go. They were home!

Capt. Lewis had stood back and silently watched the whole thing. He always did. He didn't want to see any problems, and he didn't. The monkeys never ran. They landed happy, and they were glad to be home. It wasn't the only life they had ever known, but it was the one that suited them now. They knew what they were doing, and they were happy to do it. And no one thought about why they were doing it. The captain was more worried about the trainers and the crew. Could they do this for real if they ever had to? Could they smile and laugh and strap those chimps into a nuclear bomber, knowing they would never come back and be gone, quite literally, in a flash? Captain Lewis silently shook his head as he watched the crew secure the craft. Maybe it would never come to that, but yeah, he thought, if he had to, he'd do it himself. But not tonight.

CHAPTER 1

Tonight was Friday night! The flight was a success, the chimps were home and the plane was secured. The ground crew was happy about all of that. They knew all they had to face now was the weekend. No hydrogen, no monkeys, no secrets. They never flew these things on the weekends; there were too many eyes out there. Everyone was off work, everyone was outside, and these shiny things really showed up. The fabric was tough to paint, but they had tried.

At one point, they had tried to make them look like regular airplanes, but that just looked stupid. Good thing the paint fell off. The NBAs were all a dull silver, perfect for reflecting the desert sun in every direction. It was a lousy secret, but everyone kept it as best they could. And everyone had the weekend off!

Col. Baden was long gone before the ground crew was done, and Capt. Lewis finally called it a day. He was the last man out of the hangar and made sure it was locked as he left. He gave a nod to the guards outside and told them they could go. Everything was in lockdown, and the base was secure. It was Friday night for them, too.

Capt. Lewis didn't take his hat off until he was in his own private civilian car. He was now officially off duty, but he kept the tie intact until he got home. Even alone, he smiled at that. It was Friday night for officers as well. It was time to go home to his family, off the base and away from all of those khaki-colored secrets. Time to wear comfy clothes and easy shoes and smile much, much more. And no monkeys. Eli Lewis was looking forward to a monkey-free weekend. And no bananas. That was a Lewis House Rule.

Gorton Baden had a small apartment in town. He had no family. He had lost everyone he knew in that last bad war, but somehow, he had managed to keep his accent. He would spend the weekend reading popular magazines, listening to the American radio and walking around town, working on his English. He liked his new world. It was warm. Gorton found that he liked warm very much. The desert suited him just fine, but still he had to wonder: What about the coast? What about Southern California? What about Hawaii?

And were there monkeys there?

CHAPTER 2

IT DOESN'T MATTER WHERE YOU ARE, WHETHER YOU LIVE IN THE biggest city or on the smallest farm (even if you live on a restricted air base out in the desert): Saturday is Saturday! You wake up and you smile and you can't wait to see what that wonderful, magical day has in store for you! It's time to get up, get going and get away! And to *not* wear the uniform, no matter what uniform you wear. And maybe not even a hat. So there.

Eli Lewis (no "Captain" today) woke up relaxed and happy. For a while, he just lay there and smiled and watched the ceiling not move at all. He smelled the air. No monkeys, no bananas. Yes, it was going to be a good day. He could tell by the smell. The sun was shining, and the world was out there, just waiting for him to join in the fun. It was time to relax his way through the day! Eli got up and got going and never gave his uniforms so much as a first glance, let alone a second. The base (and the monkeys) could wait until Monday. The base never relaxed. Come to think of it, neither did the monkeys.

And yes, of course the base was still there, still staffed and still operating, if only a little bit on weekends. There were guards at the gate and people to answer the phones and officers in charge and all of that, just not so much of that today. Everything was still a big secret, and everything was still under wraps. Literally so on a Saturday. But even the chimps had their weekend handlers. There were still people there, watching over those monkeys. You just never saw them. Not very relaxing.

CHAPTER 2

So what do you do on your day off if your day on is a secret? Eli thought about that as he got dressed for the day, for his big day off. What to do? What to do? What he knew not to do: Go into town. It was best if you didn't. Too many people, too many questions, and no answers allowed. Eli never liked having to answer those questions he couldn't answer. He never knew what people knew, or what answer they expected. So it was best to stay away from people as much as possible. And he planned to do just that, right after breakfast. Definitely breakfast.

His wife, Julie, had that breakfast all ready for him as he walked into the brilliant sunlit kitchen. He took the time to smell the bacon, and he saw the pancakes. Yep, it must be Saturday! He liked Saturdays. There were pancakes. Eli tested out his Big Happy Smile. Yep, it still worked!

"Good morning, sleepyhead."

"Good morning, dear."

"And what grand adventure do you have planned for today?"

"Something without monkeys."

"Yes, well, I kind of figured that."

"I think I may go fishing!"

Julie just smiled. Eli Lewis was quite the fisherman. Fly-fishing was his game. The sport of officers, as he put it. And when it came to such sport, Eli was serious about his fun. Never stand between him and a trout. However...

"Dear?"

"Yes?"

Julie pointed out the window at the seriously bright sun. "We're still in the desert. The fish are in the freezer."

Eli lost his smile and gave it a pout, until he looked down at his pancakes. "Yes, well, a man can dream."

"You dream all you want, dear. The fish can wait."

"They're going to have to."

Julie added the bacon to Eli's plate of pancakes, and that made it all better, as bacon so often does. She also had a suggestion.

"How about a nice drive out of the desert and up into the mountains?"

"The mountains are still in the desert."

"Don't argue with your wife, dear."

"Yes, dear."

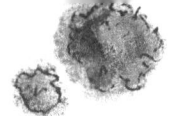

"That's better."

Eli went to work on his pancakes and bacon as Julie started to clean up the kitchen and ponder what to wear for a nice drive in the country. And in the mountains! She fluffed her hair and frowned. These drives were tough on it. They had a convertible, and with the top down, her hair got seriously tangled. Especially the way Eli drove. He was prompt. She was thinking about a pixie cut, but don't tell him that. She wanted it to be a surprise (and it would). Julie looked over at Eli and smiled. Yeah, that pixie cut would sure wake him up. But not today. Maybe she'd wear a hat today. That would help.

Eli wrapped up his breakfast and took his plate to the sink, rinsing it off and setting it aside. His work here was done. He looked up to see his wife giving him the twice over. This could not be good, but she was smiling. That was a smile, right?

"Nice shirt."

Eli was wearing a wild Hawaiian shirt. Another officer, another pilot on the base, had brought it back for him after a fast flight to Honolulu and back. It was just the thing for a Saturday. The anti-uniform. Eli liked it, but now he was getting the stink eye from his wife for it? He planned to defend.

"What? No?"

"They can hear it next door."

"Good. No reason to sleep in on a Saturday. What?"

Julie leaned in for a closer look and frowned. "Are those topless natives?"

"Not everyone can afford a shirt, dear."

"Not everyone can afford *that* shirt."

"It was a gift."

"And worth every penny."

Eli pointed back toward their bedroom. He could play this game. "I can go back and put on yesterday's uniform. The monkeys didn't spit on it much."

"Oh, no, no, you wear what you want."

"I will."

"Just a drive in the desert."

"No one will see the topless natives, dear."

"I will."

"Wear your sunglasses, dear."

"I will."

CHAPTER 2

Eli gave a big wave to the great outdoors, with a smile to match. "Then we're all set! Let's go for a drive!"

The knock at the front door was timed so perfectly that Eli immediately looked at Julie as though she had made it happen. How did she do that? She just smiled and shrugged. She had no idea either, but then, they both knew it wasn't their problem anyway. It was Saturday. Whoever was at the door had to be Ashley's problem. And then Julie made sure that it was.

"*Ashley, someone's at the door for you!*"

The answer came from upstairs.

"*I've got it!*"

They could both hear the fast footsteps down the stairs, and Eli grimaced, waiting for the fall that never came. She made it! Whew. They could hear the door open, but little else after that. Eli shrugged at Julie, and Julie shrugged right back. They'd find out what was going on soon enough when Ashley told them.

Ashley Lewis, their darling daughter, was a junior in high school and was one busy girl. She always had things to do, places to go and people to see. Well, mostly boys to see. Eli was starting to wonder about that. They lived out in the remote New Mexican desert. Where did all of these boys come from? Were they mail order? Eli was starting to suspect that and wondered about their monthly postage bill, when Ashley walked into the kitchen with the latest young man in tow. Almost literally. She had caught a small one this time. Eli wasn't sure he was legal.

"This is Jimmy!"

Julie Lewis smiled at the young boy, who smiled back, all nervous, and with good reason. He obviously hadn't planned to play "Meet the Parents" right off the bat like that, but hey, here he was, and there they were. Boom. All he could do was smile and be ready to duck. He did, and he was.

"And this is my dad."

"Hello, sir."

"Hello ... Jimmy?"

"Yes, sir. It's short for James."

"I see."

Jimmy himself was short for James, as he was noticeably shorter than Ashley. His wild shock of unruly blonde hair emphasized the contrast between the two kids, as Ashley's longer, straighter hair

15

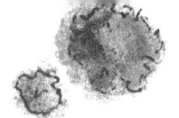

was almost, but not quite, black. Eli had to stifle a laugh. It was like looking at a pair of salt and pepper shakers. He wisely did not mention that. But he still chuckled.

Eli also thought that Jimmy looked somehow vaguely familiar, but he couldn't quite place him. Maybe Jimmy's father worked on the Western Witch Project? Even Eli knew he couldn't ask the kid that, but he might ask Ashley later. Maybe she knew. Why did that kid look so familiar? Too young to be a baseball player. Too short to be a movie star. Eli shrugged and tried to not stare. Then he had an idea and smiled. He hoped he looked happy.

"How would you two kids like to go for a ride up into the mountains with us today?"

Now, in all honesty, that was exactly what Eli Lewis said. Exactly what he asked his daughter and her little friend (to whom he had just said hello). And here's exactly what both kids heard:

"How about we both stare right at you for, like, six hours straight? Won't that be fun?"

The blonde kid paled. Eli thought he was going to faint. He took that as a no. Ashley was savvy. She saw the question coming and had the reply ready before it even got there.

"We should, and we would, but we told some kids we'd meet them downtown."

"Ah…"

"Yeah … sorry. Next time?"

Julie jumped in to save the day for all of them. "Well, you two kids have fun, and we'll be back before dinner. Make sure you are, too."

"Oh, we will!"

And with that, Mrs. Lewis put on her hat and tied it firmly in place as her husband decided to go with no hat at all. He wore enough hats all week long. No hat today. Julie grabbed her husband's baseball cap as they walked out the door. She knew he'd want that later, after the top of this head started to glow. It was, after all, the desert. The front door shut with no uncertain authority, and just like that, the two kids were left standing in the hall, almost in shock over the situation and their good fortune. Jimmy was only slightly confused.

"So we're going downtown?"

"Nope."

"But you said…"

"Yep."

CHAPTER 2

"So whadda we gonna do all day?"

The Lewises didn't live on the military base itself, but rather in a small community east of the base, but well west of the big city of Roswell, such as it was. They were, for the most part, surrounded by other military officers and their families in homes that all looked alike, but no one minded that. They were all used to it. It was sort of off-base military housing, which they liked. Eli put the top down on his car, Julie sat herself down and adjusted her hat, and just like that, they were off for a drive in the desert. The perfect Saturday adventure!

In a military community full of secrets, how Captain Lewis managed to buy a brand new car, and a brand new convertible at that, was something of a secret right there. Everything was still scarce after the war, and cars were not yet plentiful, but yet there it was: A brand new convertible. And there he was driving it. How did *that* happen? You can blame the monkeys.

While it was true that Captain Lewis had made a good name for himself as a bomber pilot during the war (there were medals), a lot of men did the same and there was no car in it for them. What made it happen for Eli was something no one could say out loud, but with certain papers signed, certain things happened. And the car was made available for purchase.

Apparently, Capt. Lewis was doing work that required that he be able to scan the sky en route to places unspoken, for reasons best left unsaid. He needed a mobile platform for observation. He needed a car. A fast car. A convertible car. Now, in truth, everyone thought he was watching for Commies, and no one said otherwise. Commies were the enemy now, and they were everywhere. Even in the sky, apparently. The fact that he might need a car to keep up with flying monkeys occurred to no one. The secret was still safe, and he got a spiffy car out of it. Julie didn't mind at all. Ashley minded even less. It was a very cool car. Eli smiled a lot when he drove the car and put the top down every chance he got.

Today's road trip took them to the southwest, out around the bottom of the military base and toward the high mountains to the west. They could see the mountains from the base, of course, but they knew that getting to them would take time. They were never as close as they looked. Mountains never were. Good thing they had a fast car. The world around them in the desert basin was barren

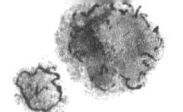

and beautiful and stark, stark white. The desert was a change of pace and place for both of them, and they found it to be an adventure worth sharing. The drives were fun. The kids didn't know what they were missing. Or maybe they did.

With the slam of the front door, the two kids had been left alone for the day in a big house with nothing to do. And that might have been a recipe for disaster had it not been for Jimmy's total violation of Rule Number One right off the bat, and no, not the rule you're thinking of. The other one: The Army Brat Rule.

"So what does your dad *do*?"

Every bell and whistle went off in Ashley's head, so loud she was sure Jimmy had to have heard them. He did not. He just stood there, waiting for an answer. *Really?* Was this guy that dumb? As it turned out, yeah, he was that dumb. He was a civvy, a civilian kid, and Ashley knew that, but still, there was a rule: DON'T ASK. Thankfully, Ashley had the right answer all ready for that stupid question, should anyone be dumb enough to ask:

"Oh, my dad's an officer. He doesn't have to do anything."

And with that, they both laughed, the question was dropped and they got on with their young lives. Of course, Jimmy was a goner now. That is, a one-date pony. And a short date, at that. That one stupid question was all it took for Ashley to know he was a no go. Brats don't ask. Brats know better. This kid didn't know any better, so he had to go. By lunch time, definitely. Ashley smiled, knowing that she had the afternoon to herself now, but she couldn't exactly just pick Jimmy up and throw him out the door (well, she *could*, but she didn't). Now this was suddenly going to be a mighty short date. Short guy, short date? Ashley smiled. She even knew just how to end it. Worked every time. Well, every time it had to.

"My dad's got a record player—come on!"

The big, dark wood floor console was a combination of a radio and a record player. It weighed about as much as both of them put together. Maybe a little more with all of those records. Ashley carefully lifted the heavy top on the record player side, locked it into place, and then opened the door to the record cabinet below that. She started to sort through the records. Looking for just the right one ... something annoying... Ah, there it is! The Date Killer!

"Your dad lets you play with this?"

"He does when he's not here."

CHAPTER 2

"Whoa."

"Let's try this one!"

With far more enthusiasm than the situation might warrant, Ashley made a big production out of putting the big black record in place and hitting all the right switches on the player. The turntable began to spin with a low hum, the record dropped into place with a thump, and the tone arm took on a life of its own, moving up and over and down and... And it worked! Music filled the room, and yet both kids just stood there, staring at the record player. And at the record. They watched it go around (and around). Jimmy started to feel a little woozy from that and had to look up and away, dizzy and confused. This date was as good as over, and the band played on.

"I don't get it."

Ashley smiled. "It's *jazz!*"

"There's no words."

"They're all in your head!"

"I got nuthin'..."

"Yep."

As the Lewises drove out of the White Sands basin and up into the mountains to the west, the raw desert gave way to vegetation, if only on a limited New Mexico scale. It wasn't as though they drove up and into a thick, deep, dark forest. Far from it. But with elevation came variation, and maybe a small tree here and there among the cacti. Julie did enjoy the drive and loved to watch for anything she hadn't seen before, be it animal, mineral or vegetable. Then a violent swerve of the car got her undivided attention. She was not amused by that at all. Almost lost her hat!

"WHAT WAS THAT?"

Eli looked over and smiled. "Snake in the road."

"HITTING IT WASN'T AN OPTION?"

"Nope."

"AND WHY NOT?"

"Professional courtesy."

"Well, just don't hit that car."

Eli took his foot off the gas and was already headed for the brake. He got serious. "Hadn't planned on it."

The car was old and worn and parked off to the right side of the road, but why? Eli passed it, but then pulled over and parked his

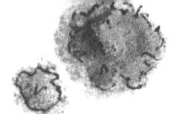

own car. He looked at the other car in the rearview mirror then shut his down. The day just got serious. No one was smiling.

"Break down?"

"Or look down?"

"We'd better go see."

There were several reasons for an old car to be parked on the side of the road right there, and most of them were mostly harmless. The climb up into the mountains could have taken its toll on the poor old thing. Or maybe this seemed like a good place to stop for a high-altitude picnic. Sure, why not? Or maybe someone wanted a better look down into the restricted military airbase below. It was that last possibility that had the Lewises on edge. They had seen this sort of thing before. They were about to see it again. It got grim as they got out. Julie looked over at Eli.

"You bring yours?"

"Nope."

"Hope it's just a picnic."

"Yep."

The "yours" she was referring to was Eli's military issued Colt M1911A1, a very serious officer's sidearm. He had, however, left it locked up at home for the day, thinking he needed a day without any seriousness in it at all. But now here they were, and all he could do was make the best of it without the heavy hand cannon for backup. They both walked past the old car, one on either side, and looked in as they passed. No one in it, but plenty of stuff in the back seat. Someone was traveling. Eli looked at the tag. Not a local. Not a good sign. He looked up and looked around. Now, where were was the owner? He pointed.

"Let's try that way."

"Why that way?"

"It looks to be the easiest path back to the east if that's the view they wanted."

"Fair enough. Looks dangerous. You go first."

Neither one tried to be quiet about it, but they did stop talking as they walked. The path wound up and around and over a low, rocky pass, and sure enough, there on the other side, with a great view of the glaring white basin to the east, were two young people just sitting and watching the world. Eli took some comfort in the fact that neither one had binoculars. But then, neither one looked completely

CHAPTER 2

harmless, either. The officer regretted leaving his gun at home, but he opened with a dangerous gambit anyway.

"*Privet!*"

Both kids jumped, as neither one had heard them coming. At second glance, the boy was a young man, perhaps in his mid-twenties. Not a kid. And the girl? Younger. Still a kid? Too young to be out in the desert with an older man? Tough call there. Eli elected to let that go for now and see what the young man said.

"Oh, hello. Didn't hear you."

Eli smiled. "Soft shoes."

No accent. The young man didn't have a foreign accent. So far, so good. Eli walked up closer, but not too close. Julie hung back, walking slower. She watched the girl. That was her job. Eli stopped right next to the guy. And was the girl laughing? He thought so but didn't dare stare. His worry was the male of the species. He didn't look at him either. Eli just looked out across the valley and squinted. He had to admit, it was a spectacular view. And a great view of the base. There was no doubt that was why they were there.

"Great view."

"Yes, sir."

Eli looked over at the young man and gave him a smile. One of his unnerving ones. And yeah, the girl was laughing. The young man was not.

"You come up here often?"

"First time."

"For the view?"

"Yeah..."

Now there was no doubt that the young man knew what he was dealing with, even if Eli was in his wild Hawaiian civvies. The military aviator sunglasses gave him away, along with his overall attitude and demeanor. Once an officer, always an officer. It was tough to turn off. Eli didn't even try. Eli looked out and down, all around the basin and then up at the sun.

"You know, this time of day, you get a much better view from that big ridge over there."

Eli pointed to a distant ridge on the far side of the basin, and he was right. From that ridge, they'd have the sun at their backs and a closer look at whatever happened below them. The young man leaned in and squinted.

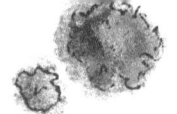

"The highest one in the middle there?"
"Yep. That's the one you want. Higher *and* closer."
"Is there a paved road?"
"Oh yeah, easy enough to get to from that other side. Loop around the base either way from here to get to there."
"A better view?"
"Much better."
"Thank you!"
"Any time."

Eli started to walk away and gave Julie the eye move to follow. She hadn't said a word but had heard it all. Almost out of sight, Eli turned back.

"Oh, and at least *try* to have a picnic."
"*Yeah...*"
The girl finally spoke. "I *told* you."
Eli ignored that. "*Proshchay.*"

Now Eli could clearly hear the girl laugh out loud. He smiled at her and then turned and walked away. Julie followed, and they both watched their step. It would do no good to fall now. Just walk. Just get away. Say nothing else. It wasn't until they were back in the car, on the road and up to speed, that Julie finally had to ask.

"Do you really think they were Russian?"
Eli could laugh now. "Nah, just a couple of kids."
"He was kind of old for a kid."
"Airplane junkie."
"And the girl?"
"I'm going with runaway."
"Should we tell somebody?"
"We got nothing. You get the license number?"
"Well, no. Did you?"
"Nope. This is my day off."
"But what if they're spies?"
"If they're spies, the other side has seriously lowered its admission standards."
"So, not spies?"
"He's a snooper. California plate on the car. He's a city boy. She's a desert girl. Probably from Arizona. Boot tan on the legs."
"You noticed her legs?"
"Don't change the subject. We're talking spies here."

"And what else did you spy on her?"

"She didn't mind being outside, was comfortable in the high desert, and she thinks the guy is an idiot, but it's his car and she needed the ride to get away."

"Whoa, Sherlock."

"Thank you."

At this point, Julie started to laugh. Eli didn't get it. "What's so funny?"

"So you sent the city idiot and the desert girl off to play on Rattlesnake Ridge!"

Now it was Eli's turn to look over and smile. "Yeah, I kinda did, didn't I?"

"How big was that snake you shot up there?"

"A little over seven feet."

Julie looked up at the brilliant sun. "Nice day to bask in the sun on a big rock."

"Yep."

CHAPTER 3

THE HANGER WHERE THE NEUTRAL BUOYANCY AIRCRAFT WERE kept was just the top floor of a building much larger than it looked. The chimpanzees lived on several floors *under* that building, and while the ground floor hanger had no windows at all, that same ground floor hanger looked to be nothing *but* windows from the outside. These were all "periscope windows" that channeled natural sunlight down to the subterranean complex beneath the hanger itself. Down to the chimps, who appreciated such things. It was clever, it worked, and no one could see inside.

The complex itself, the underground floors, offered living quarters for both the chimps and the handlers if the handlers needed to stay overnight (or overday, depending on their shift), medical facilities for the chimps, the training complex, including the flight simulators, the pre-flight prep area, and a sort of great big Monkey Jungle: A gymnasium-sized room that was an underground jungle. It was tough to keep the humans out of that one. It did look like fun. (And it was.) The underground complex was large enough that the chimps never got bored and the humans could get lost. There were phones in almost every area and along every hallway that you could pick up just to ask where you were. Your tax dollars at work.

In the middle of all of this serious work, there was also one large glass jar in the Flight Operations Room. This was where all the action was when the Western Witch was in flight, and the big jar served as fair warning. It was full of ten dollar bills, and the newbies learned The Rule right quick: You say, you pay. That is, any time you might be tempted to blurt out "Not my circus, not my monkeys!" you had to put a buck in the jar. That was The Rule, because yes, this WAS your circus, and these WERE your monkeys. Now put yer buck in The Banana Bottle, kid. Capt. Lewis still hadn't figured out what to do with all of that money, but no, they didn't have to buy their own bananas. They got shipped in fresh every week. Again, tax dollars at work.

It was early morning on a Flight Day, so every floor of the complex was humming. Everyone was there, and everyone had a job to do, even the monkeys. Especially the monkeys. They needed to be checked over medically, cleared for flight, fed, cleaned, dressed for flight and then calmed down for that flight. It was the usual monkey mayhem, but by the time they were set to board, those chimps had to be cool, calm and collected. That was the toughest part of the pre-flight right there: Calming the chimps down. They knew what day it was, and they were ready to *go*! It was fun, yes, but it did get wild at times, and those chimps could scream loud enough to be heard on the next floor. Feisty little hairballs, those monkeys. And dangerous animals at times like these. One flight prepper got bit.

"*SONOFAWITCH!*"

That, combined with the monkey's louder than normal scream, brought everyone to a halt in the flight prep room and brought Capt. Lewis right over. By the time he got there, the prepper was holding one hand with the other, but the captain could see the blood. Not good. The monkey got moved to another station. The new prepper kept his hands to himself.

"Are you okay, son?"

"Yes, sir."

"That would be a 'No, sir.' You're bleeding."

"Yes, sir."

"Let's get you to medical. What happened?"

"The zipper on her flight suit caught her hair."

"Yeah, that'll about do it."

Capt. Lewis motioned for a couple of others to help the prepper get to medical and get the attention he needed for that damaged hand. Then the captain motioned for someone to mop the blood off the floor before someone slipped and fell. (Safety first!) After that, it was all about the chimp. The captain walked over to where the animal was by then, but he didn't get too close. No smile at all now. This was suddenly annoyingly serious business.

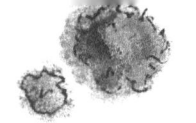

"Who's the flight team today?"

"Waldo and Kookie, sir."

Capt. Lewis looked around and only saw one chimp in the room. "And which one is this?"

"This is Kookie, sir. The female."

Capt. Lewis looked around again. Still only one chimp in sight. "So where's Waldo?"

"Not sure, sir. We think he's in the Monkey Jungle, but we can't find him."

"Any idea why Kookie bit?"

"Yes, sir, it was the zipper. Have a look right here."

The prepper pointed to a bare spot on the chimp that was sporting a small abrasion. Zipper burn. Ouch. The captain leaned in as close as he dared for a closer look, then he nodded and stepped back.

"Okay, we need to get these chimps some undergarments for these flight suits. Something comfy and tight to keep their hair out of the flight suit zippers."

"Like thermal union suits, sir?"

"Perfect. Can you make that happen?"

"Will do, sir."

"You're a good man. Take a buck out of the Banana Bottle."

"Yes, *sir*!"

And then, just like that, Capt. Lewis knew what the money in the Banana Bottle was for. It was the Reward Money. He smiled. Yeah, that works. Now, where *was* Waldo? The captain looked around just as a handler came in with the other half of the day's flight team. Waldo was in the house, and he was a mess. What was that? Capt. Lewis gave the handler a look. The handler just grinned.

"He was up in the tallest tree in the jungle, sir."

"So you threw mud at him to get him down?"

"No sir, I just waved this at him."

The handler showed the captain a jar of chocolate syrup. It, too, was a mess. And almost empty.

"The chimps like chocolate?"

"Crazy about it."

"Good to know."

"But they're very messy eaters."

CHAPTER 3

"Also good to know. Get him cleaned up and suited up. They've both got a plane to catch."

"Yes, sir."

The prep crew was a blur all around the captain, who carefully stood back and watched it all happen at a safe distance. He didn't want to get in the way, and truth be told, he was no fan of those monkeys, either. He'd much rather be fishing. And in his mind, he was. As all of this was going on well below ground, there was even more adventure to be had in the open desert high above.

Clayton Whittaker, the young man Capt. Lewis had caught eyeing, if not spying on, the base had taken the captain's advice to heart, bought a road map in town, and had found his way up onto what had to be the high ridge on the east side that had been pointed out to him as the better view: Rattlesnake Ridge. And it really was. Now they were closer to the base and much higher up, and what's not to like about *this* view, huh? Once he found a place to park reasonably off the narrow road, Clayton jumped out and ran for the view. He didn't want to miss a thing! Blanche took her time. The view would be there.

Blanche Miller was the country mouse to Clayton's city mouse, and that difference was a constant source of mild amusement for her. Yes, she understood that she would probably be just as helpless in any big city, but there was no big city out there. Just endless desert and heat and sun, and why was Clayton back in the car already? And so very wide-eyed, pale and panting?

"The stick moved!"

The country mouse didn't say a word. She simply smiled, collected her things, got out of the car, pointed in the direction Clayton had just run from, and as he nodded his head, she went for a casual (but careful) walk out that way. Nice warm day for a walk. A good day to bask if you're a snake. Yep. There he was. Right there on that big flat rock. Blanche took a minute to take in the view all around and had to admit that yes, this *was* the better view for what they wanted to see, but it was also a great place to be a snake. She watched the military base, and she watched the civilian snake, and when neither one moved very much at all, she found a nice long stick and made one of them go away. The base could stay where it was for now. Her work done, she meandered gently back to the car. There was no hurry. Clayton hadn't moved.

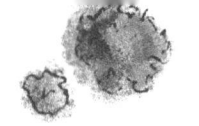

"You can come out and play now."

"The snake is gone?"

"And he apologized and offered me an apple."

"You ate snake food?"

Blanche gave up wondering how anyone could be that stupid (and did he work at not getting any of her jokes?) and instead wondered if Roswell had a bus station. She said nothing. She smiled and waved to Clayton to come out and play. He did, but oh-so-slowly and carefully. He tiptoed through the desert. It was weird to watch. As she walked behind him back out to the overlook, she would have given everything she owned for a single maraca to shake about then. She had never seen a grown man fly and pee at the same time. Might be fun. But not today. Mental notes were made. Maybe next time.

Back at the overlook, one big flat (warm!) rock, Clayton looked the whole thing over three times before he sat down once. On a towel. Blanche just sat down on the rock and never looked around at all. She knew where the stick was. Clayton was the nervous one, and his habit, when nervous, did intrigue his friend: He nibbled catnip. Straight out of the bag, just like that. Grab and gobble. Blanche had never seen that before and figured it had to be a city thing. In truth, it was even too weird for that. It was just a Clayton thing. He grew up in a house with too many cats, and weird ran in the family. He was a catnip junkie. And it did calm him down. Blanche smiled and added "ball of yarn" to her mental list. Then she laughed out loud. He had no idea why. She never said.

Far below their vantage point, the White Sands desert basin spread out, glaring bright white to the mountains to the west. In the middle of all that nothingness, the only something to see was the military base. Bland low buildings and long runways. Small vehicles (they were all small that far away) moved on narrow ribbons of dark roads around the base, as stick figures moved slowly from one building to another. Nothing happened very much, and very little happened at all.

Blanche had carefully, silently and slowly, inched her way back a little bit at a time as she sat there, just ever so slightly, to be sitting behind Clayton. Now he couldn't see her without turning around. She had good reason for this, and it had nothing to do with the base. The base might be a secret, but it was not venomous. Clayton could watch the base all he wanted. She planned to watch for the return

CHAPTER 3

of the legless venom tube. It was a really nice day, and there was no doubt the humans were taking up the locals' prime basking ledge. It was only a matter of time.

As they both watched the world below, it was Blanche that caught the trend. The traffic pattern. More vehicles were going to that building over there, far to the right and out near the runway, than to any other building on the base. It was a big building and had broad pavement leading to the runway. Had to be a hanger. Mighty lot going on there today. As Clayton kept his head on a swivel, trying to see it all and trying to see the snakes, Blanche simply settled in and focused on that one building. Something was going on there. She was sure of it. But what?

It didn't take long for her to figure out that they were on the wrong side of that building to see what was really happening down there. Too much was happening on the other side. On the west side. That had to be the big door side. Now they were on the wrong side. That's why that guy told Clayton to come over here. Blanche smiled as she looked all around. No more snakes yet. So far, so good. Clayton was still clueless and still looking all around. He hadn't seen the traffic going to that one building, let alone figured out they were on the back side of all the action. Blanche wondered what time the last bus pulled out of Roswell, and did they run on weekends?

Clayton risked hurting his neck, the way he jerked it around at every sound, thinking snakes actually made noise when they moved. It was all Blanche could do to not hiss and throw some heavy sand close behind Clayton, but she knew the truth: He had the keys to the car, and it was a long walk back into town. And she had no desire to go rummaging through a dead man's pockets. Still, it might be worth it just for the high-pitched scream. She had to weigh her options there as she watched all of the action down below. And there was plenty to see if you knew where to look.

All manner of machines were stopping by Hanger X, as she had dubbed it. From jeeps and sedans to three sizes of trucks: Small, medium, and large. Busy place, that Hanger X. There was definitely something going on in there, but was it coming out? If they sat there long enough, would they see an airplane roll out, fire up and take off? That might be fun to watch. She like airplanes. They were faster than buses. Trains were nice, too. And she was sure she had seen tracks running through town when they drove through. Big smile.

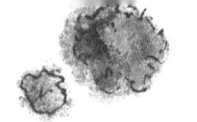

This day just got better. She had options. Options were good. She looked back over at Clayton, who still hadn't figured out where the action was down there on the base and couldn't sit still long enough to find out, even with the bit of catnip to calm him down.

It was flight day for the Western Witch Project, and that meant a busy day for all concerned. There were two big teams working on this: The flight crew and the chimp crew. The flight crew had it easy; all they had to do was fuel the aircraft, pump the hydrogen into the gasbag and then make sure everything worked without blowing it up. What could go wrong? They knew what could go wrong: The smallest spark at the wrongest time and the hanger would be gone, along with everything in it. Along with them. There was a mighty lot of brass in that hanger, and no, I don't mean officers. I mean real brass, not steel. No spark.

A smaller part of the flight crew was already in the underground control room, checking everything before the flight so there would be no mistakes during the flight and no bad words after the flight. All they wanted was what everyone wanted, just another boring day on the job. No surprises. The ground crew worked on the NBA in the hanger up on ground level, but still with the big hanger doors closed. No need to advertise. The aircraft would be rolled out, fired up, and off before too many people could see it too much. That was the plan. The ground crew moved as if in a dance. They had done this before, many times. They knew every step. Everyone knew their job, even the chimps, still hidden far below the hanger.

The chimps were happy to be doing this now. They, too, knew just what to do. They knew it was a flight day before anyone came to get them, but how did they know? This had been a long-standing mystery in the Western Witch Project over the last year or so. The chimps seemed to know it was a flight day before the handlers came for them to get them fed, cleaned and suited up. But how? The best theory they had: The chimps could smell the aviation fuel being pumped into the aircraft up above them long before the handlers came to get them. They sure couldn't smell the hydrogen. It went the other way: Up. But with the hanger doors still closed, the smell of that aviation fuel was strong in the hanger, and that had to be what filtered down through the underground building and told the chimps what day it was: Flight Day! Fuel = Flight. That had to be it. And they were ready to fly!

CHAPTER 3

Fed and cleaned (they were messy eaters), the chimps were zipped into their flight suits, with the handlers being extra careful to not snag hairs. The small union suits to be ordered had yet to arrive, so everyone was being extra cautious with the tight, pressurized suits. Monkeys bite hard. Once suited up, it was time to go up to ground, get seated in the craft and get that thing in the air. The chimps were happy to do that. It was Flight Day!

The two chimps were gently seated and strapped into the Neutral Buoyancy Aircraft inside the well-lit, but very closed, hanger. Their cockpit canopy was locked in place over them, and they heard the sound they had been waiting for: The big hanger doors began to slowly slide open, and the brilliant desert sun flooded in. The chimps screamed happy thoughts. The ground crew laughed. The motor tug hooked itself up to the NBA's front wheel, and the aircraft was towed out into the bright, glaring day. Props began to turn as the twin motors began to fire. Almost time to fly!

The strange craft was towed out to the end of the closest runaway and pointed into the wind. The motor tug unhooked and fled. The chimps were getting their instructions from their handlers through the radio now, and they knew just what to do. They, too, had done this many times before. With the engines warmed up, and idling up to preflight speed, the craft made an odd high-pitched scream. It was a warning: Don't look. Everyone on the base could hear those odd engines, and everyone knew what it meant. Be like Mr. Lot. Don't turn, don't look, don't see, don't know. And quietly, to themselves, "And please don't let it blow up here."

The radio silence came to an end as the underground control room and the base air traffic control tower both came alive and radioed up. The chimps in the NBA chattered back at them as though they knew what they were saying, and maybe they did. This was where it all came together and where everybody found out if they got it right. All it was going to take were three words from the hidden control room to the chimps, and if the chimps followed their training, the NBA would fly. No one dared to cut in now. There was a five-second radio silence, and then one voice said three words to the two chimps.

"*Fly*, my pretties."

It took both chimps to fly the NBA. Each had a different set of jobs to do, a different set of controls. One chimp pushed the engine throttles forward while the other watched and waited. The NBA lumbered, gathering speed as it rolled down the runway, faster and faster. A light came on in front of the second chimp, and the control stick that chimp held got pulled back, slowly but steadily, until it reached a preset stop. The aircraft rose up off the runway, and the aircraft *flew*. No one said a word in the control room or the tower. All breaths were held as the motors screamed and the craft gained altitude. The big thick silver disk, a giant bag of hydrogen being piloted by two well-trained monkeys, rose up above the military base and the empty desert. There was no hiding it now. Even Clayton finally saw it.

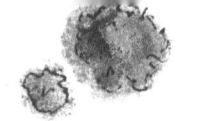

"**HOLY COW!**"

With the NBA pretty much right in front of his face, yeah, he had to finally see it. And of course he pointed. How could he not? He was Clayton. Blanche leaned over, reached out and yanked his arm back down. People might be watching them. She looked around. No one in sight, but who knew? She looked back down at the base. Mighty lot of buildings down there. Mighty lot of windows. And here's her hot date sitting in a pale desert in a big red plaid shirt. Stand out much?

Blanche was wearing all khakis and whites, the color of the desert, and cool to boot. She was comfy. This was her world. Clayton, on the other hand, looked like he stole his clothes from a lumberjack three sizes larger. She really did have to wonder where he got his clothes. Did he actually buy them like that? Had he lost a lot of weight recently? Or did he just steal a suitcase from the bus station and that's what he got? She never asked, and she tried not to laugh. At least he could dress himself. The only plus so far.

The weird airplane, whatever it was, climbed until it was far above even Clayton and Blanche, then turned west, away from them and toward the mountains in the far distance. They could hear the odd high-pitched motors. Clayton couldn't see the propellers, but he found his catnip. Between nibbles, he was amazed.

"It's got some kind of weird drive!"

Blanche was not impressed. "Yeah, those are two-stroke motors."

"Yeah, like spaceships!"

Big eye roll from the little lady. "Yeah, exactly like spaceships."

Blanche started to look all around. Where were the snakes when you really needed one?

"And we got to see it!"

CHAPTER 3

Blanche just smiled and wondered who got to see them. Clayton was a total standout in that desert. Somebody must be watching. And she was right, somebody was. Guards on the base did see them sitting up there, saw Clayton, but he was deemed "probably local," and the order was given to launch the NBA anyway. There was no time to drive up and check him out, and he was too far away to shoot. Small joke there (but it was mentioned).

As the NBA got smaller and smaller, Clayton got even more nervous. Apparently, the catnip really didn't help. Or maybe that was what made him so nervous. Blanche made a mental note to stop by the library one day and check that out, after she dumped this cat. For now, she had to play with him. Now, where's that ball of yarn?

Clayton finally looked away from the NBA and back at Blanche, who was still standing well behind him. On purpose.

"What *was* that?"

"A flying wing. Had you not seen one before?"

Clayton looked hard at Blanche. How did she know these things?

"Well, yeah, it was a flying wing ... but round..."

Blanche thought up a lie, and she thought it up quick. And it worked. "That way it can go in any direction it wants to without turning."

Clayton froze. The small wheels in his brain got stuck. "Well, yeah... That has to be it..."

Now, keep in your mind that Clayton just saw the NBA take off, climb, bank and turn like any other normal aircraft, only slower. Despite that, he was now convinced that it never turned at all, and just flew off in another direction. Sort of sideways. And just like that, Blanche had a great new hobby: She was going to see just how far she could lead Clayton down the very wrong paths, so to speak. This would help her pass the time and have some small fun, until she could check the bus schedules.

Far below them, and far below ground, Captain Eli Lewis was in the Western Witch control room and in command, watching over men manning desks and watching screens and dials, each of them with a job to do, and each of them doing that job. So far, it had been a perfect textbook flight: Take off, turn into the wind, do a big loop around the base and land. Done by lunch, home by dinner, and Bob's your uncle. Capt. Lewis never understood that phrase. His Uncle Bob was a bit of a lush. Funny, but useless. Maybe that was the joke? He wasn't sure. Back to work.

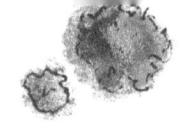

High up above the base, up on Rattlesnake ridge, Clayton and Blanche watched the silver NBA fight the headwind as it flew west toward the far mountains. It really stood out now against that deep, dark western sky, and it was Blanche who did the math. Deep, dark western sky, over there, to the west. Wind in our face, over here. There's a storm coming. She stopped watching the big silver gasbag as it turned to the north, and instead, she watched the dark clouds sailing up over those mountains over there, headed at great speed for these mountains over here. Headed toward them. They had time, no rush yet, but it was going to be a lousy afternoon. Maybe they'd have lunch at the bus station today.
    Her treat.

CHAPTER 4

IT WAS A TUESDAY IN JUNE. IT WAS SUPPOSED TO BE A LOVELY Tuesday in June, but now, suddenly, it wasn't. This was why they never flew on Mondays. They wanted to make sure the weather service had their main weekday A team, not their weekend B team, in place for a couple of days so they might get the weather forecast right. No surprises. And now? Surprise! Bad weather was approaching loudly, and bad words were spoken softly.

The dark storm clouds that Blanche first saw racing up over the high western mountains were now in full sight from the desert base far below. She could see the little uniforms on the base scurrying around now, moving much faster than they had been earlier when it was all bright sunshine and a happy day. This day was going to go bad fast. And here they were, here she was, still too high up and too far out. This was not safe. Blanche frowned and looked over at Clayton who, for once, looked worried as well. But not about the storm.

"I lost it."
"Lost what?"
"The flying saucer."
"You mean the *airplane*?"
"It just disappeared."

Blanche looked past Clayton to the storm she could see racing right at them. He seemed to not notice that storm at all. She tried pointing.

"We need to do the same."

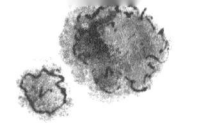

Blanche could see the massive bolts of lightning working their way down the far side of the desert basin at the leading edge of the storm and the far side of the base. It was a fantastic sight, but she had seen enough. They needed to get to lower ground and hide. *Now.* Clayton was still looking more toward the north for his flying saucer, oblivious to his own impending deep-fried doom just over his left shoulder. How could he not see that? She just shook her head. Were they all like this?

In the valley below, below the valley below, the radar technicians in the underground mission control room were all scrambling to verify what they could have seen for themselves if they only had a window. Yep, here comes a great big storm! Yep, right here, right now! They panicked, Capt. Lewis worried and Col. Baden fussed to himself in two languages. They needed to get that aircraft back, but first, they needed to find it. And how did this go so bad so fast?

By then, Blanche had gathered up what little they had brought to this foodless picnic and was about to grab Clayton by the hand and drag him back to the car. He was still too interested in that silly silver airplane and was ignoring the lighting that was closing in on them fast. It was over the base already. She tugged on the guy.

"We have to go NOW!"

"But the saucer..."

"It went back to Mars. We can follow it in the car. *COME ON.*"

By now, with the sun behind the dark clouds, the silvery craft was impossible to see. It was too high, too far away and flying in the dark. The chimps were not amused. They had front row seats to all of this, and they were screaming back at the thunder. Clayton still hadn't budged. Blanche gave up and made a run for it.

"I'll be in the car!"

Clayton never turned around to see her go. He just stood there, on a rock ledge on Rattlesnake Ridge, looking for his flying saucer that had obviously gone on to another planet entirely. The lightning was dancing across the wide basin, with the rain right behind it. Clayton never saw the lightning, ignored the thunder and was oblivious to the danger. Even the snakes were hiding now. Blanche was hunkered down on the front passenger seat of the old car, not daring to even look outside. If she had the keys, she'd be gone. She did not have the keys. She checked the glove box. No spare keys. Rats.

CHAPTER 4

The storm was a big one, a solid, powerful cold front coming in out of the northwest and not slowing down for anything as puny as mountains. The west side of the military base was under heavy rain by then. The west side was far less populated than the east side, but still, the entire base was shutting down as fast as it could. The crew in the air traffic control tower, the tallest building on the base, shut that down and ran for cover. No need to be up there! The guys underground had it made. If it didn't flood. Or if the power didn't go out. Or both.

Blanche Miller was down about as low as she could go in the car without sitting under the dashboard and on the floor. She thought about it. She could feel the car move, being buffeted by the gusts of wind as the storm started to climb the ridge. Even from her low vantage point, she could see the dust and sand and debris being blown up and around, past the car's windows. And it was cooler now. She could feel that, too, even from inside the car. And where was Clayton Whittaker? She had that one happy thought, an image of him being twirled up into the storm and gone, just like that, off to Oz. Poor Dorothy, she thought. The scarecrow's a better catch. She laughed a little, until the thunder took over again. Getting closer. Almost here.

Just about the time Blanche figured Clayton for a total goner (and was pondering how to hot wire the car once the storm passed), the driver's door flew open, the storm came roaring inside, and Clayton was right behind it. Along with at least a bucket of cold rain water. Thank you, Clayton. Blanche sat up if only to dry off. She was not amused. The door slammed shut, Clayton was there and he smelled no better wet. She knew that now. He was a wet, wind-blown mess. Yuck. She looked at him and said nothing. He, of all people, had the nerve to smile.

"It's raining!"

So many replies raced through her head she simply couldn't choose. Clayton was all wet, fidgety, nervous, and hopefully still had the keys to his own car. He was frowning now, going through his pockets with both hands. Hopefully looking for the keys. Then he smiled again. That was scary.

"Found 'em!"

He held up a ring of car keys with a dripping wet rabbit's foot. It was lucky for everyone but the rabbit. Blanche offered up a decidedly forced smile but still said nothing. They were not out of this yet.

Not by a long shot. Clayton put the key in the ignition and turned it. Nothing happened, of course. It never did. He pushed in the clutch, pulled the gear shift lever on the steering column back toward him and up and slipped the car into reverse as it started to roll backwards, back down the ridge the way they had come up from town earlier that day, in bright, warm sunshine now long gone. She missed sunshine and warm. With a rough bump of the clutch, the motor fired up, he turned on the headlights (safety first!) and they were good to go, *after* he got the car carefully turned around. No need to drive into town backward. People notice things like that. Then, and only then, did Blanche smile. It was as dark as night outside the car, the winds were pushing the car sideways and the rain was pounding down. The lightning flashes were blinding, and the thunder roared. On the plus side, and to his credit, Clayton finally stopped obsessing about the flying saucer. He was too busy trying to *not* drive off the mountain. Roswell or bust!

That was the scene on the mountain, up in the middle of the storm on Rattlesnake Ridge. It was all fear and panic, *Sturm und Drang* in any language. And oddly enough, the situation was even worse if you happened to be safe and sound and well below the ground. Ground control under the NBA hangar was in a total panic by then. They couldn't find Western Witch Flight 85. It was gone. Their radar screens only showed the storm, and that big storm filled those small screens. *Drang*.

Captain Lewis was pacing the room like a madman, looking at every screen, at every man, and waiting for an answer. Any answer. There was no answer. No one had any idea what happened to Flight 85 or where it might be by then. They could, however, tell you exactly where the storm was; it was right over their buried heads. That storm front filled the White Sands desert basin, and yet, more of it was still spilling up and over the western mountains as the leading edge was now far to the east. At least the lightning was slacking off. You know it's bad when you can hear the thunder and you're underground. It was that bad. The storm was that big. The chimps were that gone.

The lost NBA, tough for radar to pick up on a good day, was completely invisible in the heavy storm. It might have crashed for all they knew. How would they know? It's not like anyone was going to be out there looking. No one was going to see it. Not today. They

CHAPTER 4

knew the air traffic control tower had been abandoned as the storm moved in. No help there. Everything above ground, everything outside, was totally lost to the men sheltered safely underground. They were the last men on earth. At least until the storm let up.

Western Witch Training Flight 85 had been blown far off course by the approaching storm, was now invisible on radar and lost. And mad. Very, very mad. Chimpanzees don't get scared, they get mad. Then they get even. They were still flying, the NBA was still in the air, but they had no idea where they were or what to do, and screaming at the control panel didn't seem to be helping as much as they might have hoped. They tried screaming at it again, just to make sure. Nope. Still nothing.

Deep underground, Captain Lewis's focus had shifted from the where to the how. If no one knew *where* the NBA was, he wanted to know *how* this had happened at all. Specifically, he wanted to know how this strong weather front was not mentioned to anyone that morning as a very good reason to scrub this flight before they ever woke the monkeys up. This thing did not just pop up unannounced at 10 o'clock out of nowhere. Someone had to see this thing coming, and why weren't they told? Now the captain was mad. He knew what he wanted to know.

"Where's the weather wire?"

Everyone looked around, and one man held up a length of teletype paper. The weather wire. The captain took it and read it. He read it twice. Then he handed it back to the technician.

"That's yesterday's weather wire. It came in on the 13th. Today's the 14th. Where's today's?"

No one moved. The technician left holding the wire stood up and handed it back to the captain. He was scared, almost to the point of tears.

"Sir, that's what came off the wire this morning. I watched it print out."

Captain Lewis looked at it again. It was still dated the day before, and the forecast was good the day before. No mention of any front or storm or rain or wind. The officer did his very best to calm down and state the obvious.

"They sent us yesterday's forecast today."

No one said a word. No one dared. Not even Captain Lewis now. The captain looked to the back of the room, to the doorway where he knew Col. Baden would be. The colonel was still standing there, but he said nothing in any language. He gave no indication of any course of action. If he wanted to blow a buck, he knew exactly what he'd say, but no, not today. Not funny. (Well, maybe to him, just a little bit.) The horrible silence was broken by an excited voice in the middle of the room. Someone was still doing their job.

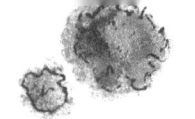

"I think I've found them!"

With that one happy sentence, the room went from deep, dark, silent despair to totally crazy, noisy pandemonium as everyone jumped to see what he saw.

"Yes!"

"There!"

"Right there!"

"They went right over us!

"And they're still going!"

"Still flying!"

"But the wrong way..."

"East..."

"Too far east."

Capt. Lewis was going nuts trying to see everything at once and figure out what was going on far above them.

"What's the weather on the surface?"

The base did have its own little weather station as a part of the airport, of course. Not much more than temperature and pressure, wind direction and speed, but at least it was *today's*.

"Sixty-five degrees up there, pressure's down to nine-eighty, strong winds still out of the west-northwest. Looks to be about fifty miles an hour steady, with gusts bumping the max to seventy. Whoop, make that seventy-five." Still a storm up there.

"Rain?"

"Light but yeah, it's still raining there. But not like it was."

"Visibility?"

"Bad but getting better. The cloud layer is rising as it thins."

Captain Lewis stared at the radar screen. He could see what he didn't want to see: He saw the blip that was the ship, and he saw the ground lines. The storm had pushed the NBA well off course. Too far off course. The odd aircraft, the secret aircraft with the top secret crew (the crew was a bigger secret than the craft), was now out over private ranch land east of the base and loose in the real world, and

CHAPTER 4

the weather was clearing. It would be seen soon. They couldn't stop the odd craft from going even farther out, farther off base, and the chimps couldn't fly it back against that strong storm wind. The captain walked to the back of the room. Baden was waiting. They had to talk. Pick a language.

"We're going to lose them."

"We already have."

"I don't want to do this."

"It's a part of the job."

"The bad part."

"Ja. Every job has one."

"Do it?"

"Ja. You have to."

They knew they didn't have time for a conversation any longer than that. Captain Lewis walked, marched, back to the front of the room so every man saw him, turned around and gave the order he never wanted to give:

"Scramble the ponies."

Everyone working on the Western Witch Project lived, off and on, with three big fears. There was always the fear of having to do it for real; that is, one day they would be strapping those chimps into an armed nuclear bomber and sending them off to war. They weren't ready yet to do that, and yet they were ready if they had to be. But not today.

And as it is with everything that flies, there's always the fear of the crash. The idea, the constant reality, that what goes up must come down. In that regard, these flights were no different from any other flight, no matter the craft and crew. No one wanted to see that happen, but everyone knew it could. And maybe today. It could still happen.

Then there was what just happened, what Captain Lewis had just initiated: The ponies had been scrambled. This flight was over, and it was not coming back. It was going down. No one said a word after that. All concerned just sat at their station and did their job. It would be over soon, and they would have the afternoon off. No comfort at all there.

Above the hidden underground crew, loud klaxon horns were going off all over the base, telling everybody this just got serious. In a hangar at the other end of the runway, two very human pilots were already suited up and ready to go. They jumped, grabbed their flight helmets and gloves and ran for their planes. Their planes had been fueled and checked that morning just as the NBA had been fueled and checked. Their ground crews had their planes running and warmed up by the time they climbed the ladders. Their hangar doors had been open all morning, ready to go. And now they had to go. They had a bad job to do.

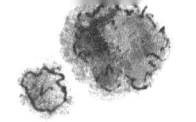

Air traffic control, now back up in their tower, had made sure those two planes had the base all to themselves, and all of the air around it. Nothing else dared to move until they were up and gone and done and back. Canopies were slid forward and locked in place, throttles went up and they rolled out for the runway. Nothing else dared to move. It only took a few minutes to go from nothing going on to everything happening at once as two P-51 Mustangs, the ponies, roared down the runway fast and leapt into the sky. They knew what they to do. They knew why they had been there, waiting as they did every time. But this was still the first time. All they needed was one last word. Capt. Lewis had to give it, and he did. No smile.

"Bring it down now."

"Yes, sir."

The two fighter pilots knew all about the Western Witch Project, of course. In a way, they were a part of it. It was their job to keep the secret a secret if it ever got loose. There had always been the possibility that one flight would go rogue, and the chimps would simply try to fly away for whatever reason. That had never happened, but it was always possible. This, today, was the same thing for a different reason: That storm front had rogued the plane. Now it was out over private land, out over the real world, and that had to be stopped before it was seen. The front was still pushing the plane east. It had to come down while it was still up. Before it got low enough for anyone to see. Before it landed.

So far, over the last couple of years after the war, this project had kept its secret. Oh sure, some people outside the project knew about it, but those that knew also knew to keep silent. Especially if they weren't supposed to know. Ashley Lewis was very good at that, and in a way, was a great agent to have out there, listening to what the other kids said. If there had been any mention of any monkeys, their parents would have heard about it fast. No kid dared to make a banana joke around Ashley.

CHAPTER 4

High up over the open ranch land between the military base and the town of Roswell, the immediate goal of two serious men riding two very fast ponies was to keep the secret project out of the public eye. Was it too late already? Maybe not. They had altitude. The NBA was still high in the sky, and it was still tough to see in those grey clouds. They were not yet too late. There it was. Right there. And they were closing fast. It was time. One last exchange.

"Target acquired. Confirmed action."

"Action confirmed. Bring it down."

"Yes, sir."

By now, the two fighter pilots had throttled back so they wouldn't simply fly right past the NBA. There was no way those two fighter planes could fly that slow and still fly at all. And no one knew what the chimps might do if they got buzzed by other planes. Especially two planes going that fast. So once in sight, once their target was acquired, the fighter pilots knew their job was as good as done. But it was still a bad job to do. Don't think, just act. They acted.

With their action confirmed, not another word was needed. The two pilots knew what to do, and they knew who was going to do it. From the start that morning, one of the planes had been in the lead all along: The first to fire up, the first out of the hangar and the first off the ground. The lead pony. The first shot. In the cockpit of that first pony, the red safety cap was taken off the firing button on the stick with the flip of a gloved thumb. The pilot frowned. He didn't like this at all, but this was his job. He leveled his plane and pushed the button. He saw the flash and heard the noise.

The fifty-caliber machine guns shook the plane, and with that single three-second burst of gunfire, the NBA was gone. The hydrogen in the big gasbag exploded into a massive fireball, and both pilots had to turn hard to avoid flying through it. The lead plane went hard to starboard as the trailing plane banked to port, just as they had planned all along. All of that for those three seconds. They were done. Their confirmation message was cryptic.

"Returning to base."

"Return confirmed."

The two fighter pilots never looked back. There was nothing to see. The hydrogen was gone in no time at all, and the flaming debris rained down on the desolate ranchland far below. The storm itself helped out by making sure nothing on the ground caught fire, and the wind did its part to spread the small bits and pieces far and wide. There wasn't much left by the time what little was left met the earth one last time. By the time those ponies had landed back at the base, it was all over. Nothing to see in the sky or on the ground. Done.

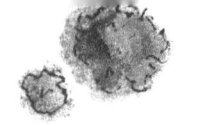

Yes, a small handful of people on the ground well out on that side of town *did* see that flash in the sky, but mostly, they figured it had to be weird lightning. No one heard the fighter planes, as they were high and fast, and the storm was still loud and close. They had made just that one fast pass, never flew over the town itself, and then they were gone. Unseen, the ponies went back to the barn, and the rain kept coming down. A lousy day all around. And did you see that wild ball lightning earlier? No?

There was a chance, a slim chance, that Clayton might have seen that fireball in his rearview mirror had he looked back at just the right time as he drove slowly to lower ground. And if he actually *had* a rearview mirror. (He did not.) As it was, careful driver that he was, he never saw the explosion in the sky well behind him, and neither one of them heard the fighter planes over the noise of the car and lingering storm. Clayton got them safely back down off of Rattlesnake Ridge and into the soggy wet town of Roswell, and Blanche made good on her promise to herself. They *did* have lunch at the bus station, and it *was* her treat. Clayton liked that. Free food! The chatter all around them in the small diner was all about the weather, and no one in the bus station had seen the flash of the NBA in the sky well to the northwest of town earlier. There was some talk about tomorrow's weather, and wasn't yesterday nice? At a convenient point toward the end of the meal, Blanche excused herself, got up and went off in search of the ladies' room and a bus schedule. She found both, and both were to her liking. She checked the schedule over before she stuffed it in her purse. She had options, and an escape plan! She was all smiles when she sat back down.

Clayton was still all wet.

CHAPTER 5

THE FRONT THAT CAUSED ALL THE TROUBLE WAS WELL AHEAD of the ground crew as they sped out in jeeps and trucks to try to grab what they could off the ground before too many people saw too much. Before someone else found the chimpanzees. Sure, the NBA itself was supposed to be a secret, too, but the big secret was the flight crew in that craft. Finding them and hiding them was their number one priority. That was Job One.

They had seen, on radar, where the craft had been shot down. They knew which way the wind was blowing and how hard it was howling, so they had a pretty good idea of where to go looking. It was all open ranch land and well outside of town, north of Roswell. They drove fast enough to get tickets they would have never stopped for, had they been offered. They were not. A tight military convoy in one big hurry? Yeah, let 'em go. They went.

By late afternoon, the late day sun was starting to show through the lingering high clouds to the west, casting a wonderful golden light across the desert, not that anyone noticed. But it was nice. The temperatures behind that front were down a little, so it wasn't the crazy summer heat they might have had to work in. That was good, too, but again, no one noticed. They were all watching the spotter plane, a small single engine craft, as it flew low and slow out over that wide open area, looking for what they were looking for: Motors and bodies. They found the motors first, still smoldering. That helped.

They had almost no competition at all that first day. Anyone who had seen the hydrogen flash in the sky, in the storm, had no idea what they were looking at, so there was no big rush, at first, for any souvenirs. The Army had the desert to itself, at least for that first day. They made the most of it and searched fast for what they wanted to find. The motors were an easy find, like little campfires out on the range. Col. Baden and his driver, Captain Lewis himself, got to the first one along with part of the salvage team with a truck. The crew got as close as they dared to the flaming motor. They shoveled sand on the thing to put it out as a larger truck pulled up and reality called collect. Someone had to ask:

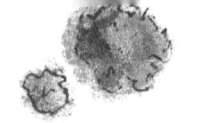

"How much does this thing *weigh*?"

It was a valid question. The motors that seemed so small and light on the aircraft itself now looked big and heavy on the ground. The odd black propellers were all broken off, but still, that small motor was larger than anyone expected when you stood that close. Baden was doing the math in his head as he watched the crew ponder the motor. He nodded as he thought. It helped. Then he spoke.

"Perhaps four hundred pounds as it is now. Perhaps a little less."

The guys on the ground looked at the low motor in the sand and the high tailgate on the truck. Four hundred pounds? They looked around. They're gonna need more guys. More soldiers were waved over, and with a little bit of planning, the six biggest men in uniform hefted the engine and hoisted it into the back of the truck. It wasn't pretty, but they got it done. By then, the spotter plane had found the other motor and gave a little wing wag, but it was no big deal. They knew what they were doing now. And they knew they could do this. Motors? Check. What else ya got? They knew what they wanted, the bodies. They had to find those bodies.

While the blast and crash itself went almost unseen out over the open desert in the storm, the convoy of Army trucks, and all of those guys in uniform out there searching for *something*, yeah, that did attract some attention. At first, it was just the ranch owners and ranch hands that saw them out there and saw them looking and finding, but it didn't take long before the word got out: Something was going on out there. Something came down. Then the curious began to arrive as well. Just a few at first, and they hardly knew where to go or what they were looking for. Or why. But they came anyway. They always do.

Given the nature of the blast, the altitude of the event and the prevailing wind in the storm, the debris was scattered out across miles of open ranch land. There were little bits and pieces everywhere, but truth be told, the Army wasn't interested in the little bits and pieces. As a matter of fact, the motors, even as odd as they were, were not a serious priority. The bodies of the chimpanzees were their number one critical mission, and if they found the seats and controls, those had to be snatched and hidden as well. Anything that might lead anyone to believe that this had been a manned, or chimped, mission. That was the secret that had to be kept at all costs. That's what they were really out there looking for. Everything else was incidental. The locals could have it, unless they got to it first.

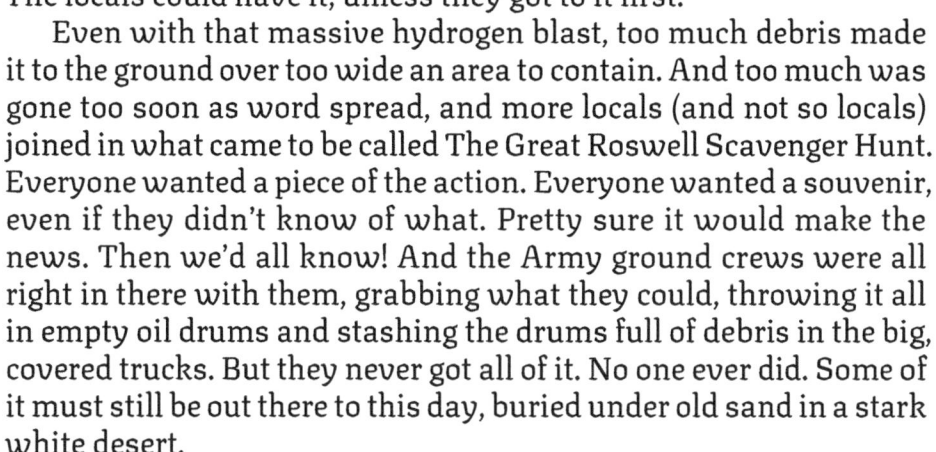

Even with that massive hydrogen blast, too much debris made it to the ground over too wide an area to contain. And too much was gone too soon as word spread, and more locals (and not so locals) joined in what came to be called The Great Roswell Scavenger Hunt. Everyone wanted a piece of the action. Everyone wanted a souvenir, even if they didn't know of what. Pretty sure it would make the news. Then we'd all know! And the Army ground crews were all right in there with them, grabbing what they could, throwing it all in empty oil drums and stashing the drums full of debris in the big, covered trucks. But they never got all of it. No one ever did. Some of it must still be out there to this day, buried under old sand in a stark white desert.

Every soldier out there had the same marching order: Find the bodies. Find the chimps. Cover them and hide them and keep everyone else away from them. This was the most important thing, but here's the funny thing, not every soldier knew what he was looking for. They were simply told to "find the crew first" and to hide the crew they found. Most of them had no idea they were looking for a couple of burnt monkeys. And no one who knew about the monkeys could even begin to guess at what might be left of them. Or if they would find them at all. But everyone in uniform was looking for monkeys, whether they knew it or not. And they were not finding.

It didn't take long for the hunt to become a race. No, the desert wasn't crowded with competition, but the debris field was spread thin and far, and no one was finding much of anything, let alone what they were looking for. Now there were four-man teams in uniform, all walking fast or running, all trying find the bodies before anyone else found the bodies. With every passing minute, the panic got pushed up a notch. They had no idea how far they would have to go or what they might find next.

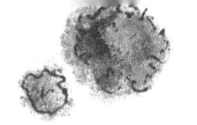

It didn't take long for the Army guys to simply stop gathering up the non-organic debris. Burnt bits and pieces of what had to have been an odd old airplane had no interest at all now. They ran right past that junk. The blast, the hydrogen, had blasted and burnt most of it far beyond any possible recognition, and the fact that it wasn't a normal airplane to begin with made any sort of identification even harder. No one even tried. The few locals, the few ranchers, that happened to be out and about that evening did pick up a smoldering piece or two, only because they were still hot, and that seemed odd. Invariably, as they did, they looked to the sky. Did this come from there? Maybe. Who wants to know?

Captain Lewis was driving his own assigned jeep, and he was not amused by any of this. With Col. Baden in the passenger seat, he was trying to take it easy and not actually bump his superior officer out of the vehicle, but it wasn't easy. It was rough terrain, and they were in a hurry. Baden was watching the small spotter plane overhead, and Lewis was watching for cacti. Neither one had time to blink. The captain saw all of the debris on the ground and knew "weather balloon" was going to be a tough sell if people saw how much debris there really was. And there was no way they were going to get all of that picked up any time soon. If ever. He was pondering the idea of running road graders across the desert to bury it when Baden shot an arm out to point off to the left. Nearly hitting him.

"*Gehen Sie schnell!*"

Captain Lewis risked a look to the left and up and saw the spotter plane doing tight circles over something. Only one thing it could be. Eli got grim.

"Hang on, Gorton!"

"Ja!"

The jeep got dropped down a gear and the gas pedal met the floorboard. Dodging cacti became a hazardous game. The colonel tried to laugh, but he was bounding too hard and too high, and all he could do was hang on. There were no deserts in Germany, and he never got to meet Rommel. Almost there! There! Yes! Right there!

By the time they slid to a grinding stop, the ground crew already on the scene had the body covered in several army blankets, and they were waving a big truck over. Captain Lewis got a salute from everyone as Col. Baden simply walked the other way to calm his nerves after that wild ride.

"Just the one?"

"So far, sir, yes."

Lewis looked at the shape of the blanket. It was larger than any chimp, and he knew why. "Still strapped in?"

"Mostly, sir, yes."

"Intact?"

"As near as we can tell, yes."

Captain Lewis stood up in silence and looked all around. There was nothing else to be seen, and now, there was no plane in sight. A truck pulled up, and the ground crew looked to the captain. He simply waved his arm. Yeah, load the nasty thing. Get it out of here. They moved in unison without another word. It wasn't that heavy. In seconds, it was stashed and hidden. A larger, heavier tarp was pulled over it, and some useless crash debris was piled in front of that. Nothing to see here. The truck pulled away, all gears and noise. As the truck left and it got quiet again, Col. Baden arrived on the scene.

"Just the one?"

"Yes. For now."

Both men looked around. Nothing. Not even the plane.

"How far apart could they be?"

"You'd be surprised."

"Not anymore."

"Which way? Back upstream or downwind?"

Col. Baden looked back the way they had come. He did not want to do that again. He looked ahead, where they had not yet been. Why not? He nodded that way and both men went back to their jeep. It was getting late. The idea of searching the desert in the dark did not appeal, but maybe that was the answer: Just follow the coyotes to the food. They sat down in the jeep and looked at each other. No questions, no answers. Just one humble request.

"*Langsam.* Slow, please."

"Ja."

Baden smiled at the captain's oddly accented German, but at least they did go slow. They had elected to continue down range, thinking that the second chimp had to be farther along. They could not have possibly missed it in the search back the other way. Could they? No.

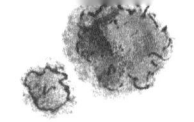

Well, maybe not. At least, they certainly hoped not. All they needed, after all of this, was for the ground crew to miss the second chimp and some civvy to find it. How do you explain a burnt monkey in a weather balloon? Captain Lewis was pondering that grim dance of words as he drove carefully and slowly across the desert, back to watching for cacti as Col. Baden was looking for that spotter plane. It had to be up there somewhere. Unless it gave up and went back to base. There wasn't much light left. The captain turned on the jeep's headlights. It was that late.

No one smiled. There was nothing to smile about. The only saving grace in this whole mess was the fact that the Western Witch Project was so top secret, they would not have to answer any questions about the event. Well, not many, anyway. And Captain Lewis knew *exactly* why it happened. It was that late weather report. Yesterday's weather report today. And was it still today? Eli had to think about that. It had been a long day. He just shook his head, and Baden noticed.

"*Was?*"

"It's been a long day."

"Ja."

It was just then that Capt. Lewis caught too much commotion off to the right as Col. Baden was looking to the left. Someone was over there, waving their arms and literally jumping up and down. Someone in a uniform. And now they're yelling? Subtle. Real subtle. The captain got a firm grip on the wheel and gave the colonel a little warning.

"Hang on."

The jeep spun around to the right so fast it was only Baden's weight that kept all four wheels in the sand. It dug in, and they almost got stuck, but no, they kept going. Good jeep. The guy waving was down to waving just one arm now, knowing that they had seen him, but now he wasn't so easy to see, what with that lone tree right there. He kept pointing up to it. And was he actually smiling? He was. This had better be good news. It was. Capt. Lewis turned the engine off but kept the headlights on.

"Sir, there's one up there."

"One what?"

Now the young man in uniform looked around, to see if anybody was listening. Better late than never. He lowered his voice.

CHAPTER 5

"One of the crew members, sir."

Capt. Lewis walked very carefully over to the tree and looked up. There *was* something up there, but he didn't have a flashlight. Baden joined him under that tree, but there wasn't much to see. They could hear a larger truck approaching. Sounded like one of theirs, but was it? It was. Good. Brighter lights. Eli walked back and turned off the lights on his jeep. No need to try to push start *that* in the sand. By the time he got back to the tree, there was a crew. And there was light.

By the light of a truck as big as the tree, they could see that yes, that *was* a body in the tree. It was burnt badly and twisted, but it did appear to be all there. Capt. Lewis had to smile at that small victory. There would be no need to go looking for just parts of monkeys. And they had them both now. Or would, soon. This one was up high enough to be just out of reach until a taller soldier reached up and was just able to grab a cuff. He was careful to not touch the exposed burnt body. That looked nasty, even in the dark. With a fair amount of energetic tugging and pulling, the soldier got the body out of the tree with no grace whatsoever. It landed with a loud thump in a mangled heap at the base of the tree. Everyone stepped back, and no one said a word. It smelled really bad. No one would be going for barbeque tonight. Capt. Lewis and Col. Baden took a quick bent-over look at what they had there. As if they didn't know. Then it was time to go.

"Wrap it up and ship it home. Base hospital."

"Yes, sir."

Blankets appeared out of the dark, and the body was covered, tucked, rolled, then carefully hauled around to the back of the truck. It was heavier than it looked. It got hoisted into the back of the truck with no dignity whatsoever, but the job got done and the chimp got hid. Good job, and done. The captain looked at his watch. Home by midnight, maybe. Now what?

"Sir, what about the rest of the debris?"

Capt. Lewis looked around as though he could see anything at all in the gathering gloom.

"Did you find the seat this one was in?"

"Yes, sir. That's what led us over here."

Lewis took another look around. Still nothing to see.

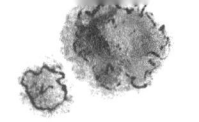

"Then let's wrap this up for the night and do another general broad sweep tomorrow for any big pieces you might find. Just get that body to the base hospital right now."

"Yes, sir."

The soldier ran, the big truck fired up, and after it lumbered off into the night, Capt. Lewis and Col. Baden took their own sweet time driving back out to the closest road and only getting lost once trying to get back to the base and back to their own cars so they could go home. Little was said along the way. Now, with both chimps safely tucked away, it was just a weather balloon. Unless someone saw the chimps, nothing else they might find mattered. And there was still plenty to find.

There was still a lot of crash debris out there in the desert, strewn all across the open ranch land to the northwest of Roswell. As they drove back to the base, Capt. Lewis was trying to think of what the biggest piece might be, and how could he explain it if he had to? They had both chimps, and they had both seats. The controls, by now, should be burnt, bent and mangled to the point that they could be anything. The bananas that were on board, if they made it that far, might be an odd thing to find in the desert and tough to explain, but he could claim ignorance if asked. Those had to be a local thing. And then he almost cost himself a buck and laughed out loud at that. Baden looked over.

"So *now* it's funny?"

"Well, these *are* our monkeys, and this *is* our circus."

"Ja. And we are the clowns."

"Ja."

The rest of the drive was quiet, and they got back to the base and their own cars with no further drama or comedy. *Gute nacht*s were exchanged, and the colonel drove off in search of dinner. The captain took that moment, alone, to look up at the night sky and all of the stars. The storm was gone, and the stars were out. A mighty lot of them. Having no idea who, or what, might be looking back, he gave all he had left to whoever might be listening.

"Oh, stop laughing."

The storm that had driven Clayton and Blanche off of Rattlesnake Ridge earlier that day had kept them in their rented rooms for the rest of the day on the other side of Roswell. Well away from all of the action across that open ranch land on the northwest side of town.

CHAPTER 5

Clayton had managed to change into dry clothes, and they did go out for a quick bite to eat before it got dark, but not far and nothing was said, that they heard, about any sort of odd crash earlier that day. It was still too early for rumors, but not by much. They fell asleep listening to the radio that night. The next day got crazy quick.

"Mighty lot of stuff out there."

That was the first they heard of it. Something they overheard someone say the next day when they went out to breakfast. They were sitting at the counter, and the voice was somewhere behind them. No idea who. Both Clayton and Blanche had to work hard to resist the urge to spin around to hear the rest of the conversation, but they heard it just fine from where they were.

"Another weather balloon?"
"Oh, that's what they'll say."
"But no?"
"Not with that much trash in the sand."
"One of their oddball airplanes?"
"Yep. Gotta be."
"Where?"
"Out on Foster's spread, north side of town."
"Lot of room out there."
"Lot of stuff."
"Think we'll hear anything about it?"
"No more than you just did."
"Yep."

They heard it all, and by then, Clayton was thinking about catnip and gasping for air. Blanche rolled her eyes and looked around. *Any eligible cowboys in here? No? Fine. I'll go with what I've got.* Now Clayton was wolfing down his breakfast, and she knew where this was headed, where they were headed: Back out into the desert for a little scavenger hunt. At least he paid for breakfast. She left the tip. Every time. She made him wait long enough for her to go back to her room for her hat and a few things. You know, just in case. After that, it was all about going, well, where exactly?

They had no idea where the "Foster spread" might be, and all they had was "north side of town." So Clayton drove north out of town, taking ever smaller roads because it seemed like a good idea at the time. And it was. Blanche saw them first and pointed.

"There. Over there."

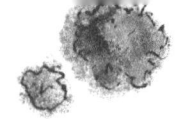

"What? Where?"
"That. There. Army trucks."
"Yeah, so?"
"We're nowhere near the base, Sherlock. And those guys are looking for something. Savvy?"

Actually, no, he did not savvy. Clayton couldn't savvy his way out of a wet paper bag, but he did pull over, if only long enough to not savvy and drive.

"No, not here."
"But they're right there."
"That's *why* not here. They're headed that way, north, so drive up a ways, and we can beat them to the good stuff they haven't found yet."
"Yes!"
"You're welcome."

Clayton floored it, such as it was, and the car wandered off at its own slow speed anyway. It was not a fast car. Two gentle rises in the road later, he found a place to park, pulled over and asked first. It was the polite thing to do.

"How about here?"
"As good as any."

And with that, he shut down the car, pocketed the keys, and they got out to survey the scene. That didn't take long. There wasn't much to see. This was not, as Blanche observed silently to herself, where the deer and the antelope play. This was more like where they come to die. There was nothing but nothing as far as the eye could see. A cactus here, a small tree there, and a lot of sand and scrub. *Welcome to Snake City*, she thought. This should be fun.

"Let's go for a walk."
"After you."

They didn't have to go very far off the paved road and out into the vast nothingness before they found something. Clayton was finding all sorts of small burnt bits and pieces, and as they looked around, they could see the impact marks the pieces left as they fell. Yeah, this was that stuff. Clayton was going nuts trying to pick it all up and save it. He was running back and forth to the car and filling the trunk. Blanche smiled. At least the desert would be clean. She looked as she walked, but she saw that not everything had made an impact. Not everything was from the crash. Some stuff was just stuff. The desert had been there a long time, collecting things since

CHAPTER 5

day one. She looked over at Clayton. He wanted it all. Of course he did. Another eye roll. She was getting good at that.

Blanche Miller was learning to be a bit more selective in her search. There would be no more Claytons, thank you very much. And she didn't need every little bit of desert trash, either. Ah, but what she did find intrigued her very much: Flight controls, burnt hand grips. Whatever it was, whatever crashed, it was manned. That was interesting. She carefully buried the grips in her hand bag (she brought the big one today). Did Clayton see her do that? He did not. Of course not. Small smile. *So what else we got out here?*

Clayton was busy filling the trunk of the car with all manner of trash. Now, yes, some of it really *was* from the crash, but he had no idea that maybe some of it wasn't, so he took that, too. Blanche looked at the trunk and wondered what he thought he was going to *do* with that. Build his own UFO? That might be worth waiting for, but only if he planned to fly it. Blanche took a moment to get her hat out of the car while she was there. Clayton showed no sign of letting up.

It was going to be a long day.

CHAPTER 6

WITH AN INFORMAL TEAM MOTTO OF *"VERSAGEN NICHT!"* (do not fail!), they had to admit that they did *versagen*, at least a little bit, that day. To help even out the score, there was some small comfort taken in the reality that while they had lost the craft, they found the bodies. Now all they had to do was get rid of them. To that end, not everyone had run out into the desert to search for chimps.

One of the team from the Western Witch Project was sent straight to the base hospital, to pave the way for the secret disposal of two bodies. (There would be no mention of exactly *what* those bodies were.) Even before the ground crew got to the crash site, the hospital was being prepped for the delivery and disposal. With the entire base being restricted to begin with, the idea of a secret situation to be dealt with was not uncommon, even in the base hospital. *Especially* at the base hospital.

The team member spoke with the hospital administrator, and after looking at the hospital floor plan, they had a pretty good idea of how to get the bodies into the morgue with the least number of eyes around. The administrator knew to not ask questions and could only assume that the bodies they'd be dealing with were not American service personnel, but perhaps of a foreign nature and covert intent. *And you want me to make them go away? Yeah, we can do that.* They had a plan. Now all they needed were the bodies.

The bodies arrived separately, in two large trucks, about an hour apart. In the great hurry that they were in, each truck simply drove up as close at it could to the door it was led to by the team member already there, and the still-wrapped bodies were hauled out of the back, around the truck and through the door. Just like that. Limited exposure, but some exposure, nonetheless. Anybody see that? No one could say. They were all too busy trying to get the job done. It was getting dark. That helped. The bodies went straight to the hospital's morgue, and there was now an armed guard at *that* door.

The two trucks went from there to a secure hangar on the other side of the base, where the collected crash debris was all piled over in the corner, away from prying eyes. It would be dealt with later. Tomorrow. Maybe the day after that. Most of it would simply be thrown away. It wasn't as though they didn't know why it crashed. Anything that had anything to do with the chimps, the small seats and controls, were set aside to be disassembled, crushed and buried on-site. They saved the motors. Baden insisted.

The base coroner wanted to know if the team wanted to know how the chimps died. In all honesty, they did not. It hardly mattered if they were killed by the blast or the crash or simply died of boredom on the way down. The coroner took a look anyway. It was his profession, his fascination. As it turned out, one of them had been shot by the pony. That .50 caliber round made it all the way through the craft, and the chimp. The other died in the crash, having survived the blast. And it was the coroner's curiosity that sparked the madness that followed. He didn't bother to cover the morgue's hallway windows. And people saw what they saw as they walked by.

Not everyone in the base hospital was military staff. Not everyone who had access to that building had the security clearance they maybe should have had that week in that building. In that hallway. Past those windows. The coroner and his staff had laid out two burnt chimpanzees, still in their small, silvery, pressurized flight suits, on the autopsy tables, and anyone walking down that hall on the other side of those windows saw the scene: Two small, long armed, hairless, greyish dead bodies in metallic suits... In space suits... Whoa, aliens!

And so it began, and that's how it began, but not right away. Even the civilians in the military hospital knew to say nothing about what they saw when they were there. Without clearance, you never knew what you might see that you shouldn't have seen, and everyone who saw those dead grey aliens were all pretty sure that they weren't supposed to see them. So while they were all at work, no matter what their job, they kept their heads down and their mouths shut. Don't even smile, someone might ask why. It was all serious secret business. Until they got home.

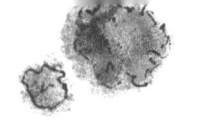

But they saw what they saw, even if they did get it wrong. Very few people in the base ever knew about the Western Witch Project. Certain doctors and upper administration knew, as they did have to deal with the chimp bite, and who were all of these other guys working there on the base that they never saw so much? Most were told that it was a classified project and that was all they were told. Everyone knew not to ask. Except for the ones that didn't. And they saw aliens! Foo fighters!

By the summer of 1947, the phrase "foo fighter" had found its way into common military usage to describe the odd unidentified aircraft that had been seen in both theaters of operation during World War Two. The idea that they were space aliens toying with Allied fighter pilots became the common unauthorized explanation for what they saw, even if so very few people ever actually saw them. By 1947, everybody *knew* about them, and these had to be them! We finally shot one down! Just look! Right there! Aliens! The burnt bodies of two dead chimpanzees were only on those slabs for a day or two, but that was all it took. The seeds were sown. Kudzu wishes it should grow so fast.

The coroner and his staff had no idea what they had just done. All they did was examine the bodies and write up the reports. Causes of death? One died of a large-caliber bullet wound, the other from crash impact trauma. Both bodies were burnt, but that was not the cause of death for either one. Now, what do we do with them?

The crash was forced on the flight on Tuesday, and by Tuesday night both of the chimps' burnt bodies were in the base hospital morgue. The coroner and his staff looked them over on Wednesday and Thursday ("Yep, they're dead!"), and by Friday morning, they were back to being Capt. Lewis's problem. And what *did* he want done with them? He'd be right over. It was a nice day. He drove his own car over to the hospital, top down.

By the time he got there, the monkeys were back in their cold lockers in the morgue, minus their flight suits and boots. Those had been bagged and were handed over to Capt. Lewis when he got to the hospital.

CHAPTER 6

"Does the hospital have an on-site incinerator?"
"Yes, sir."

He handed the bag back with a nod. They understood. But there was still the matter of the two bodies no one was supposed to see that people did see. At that point, Capt. Lewis had no idea how many people had actually seen those bodies in the morgue as the staff had examined them. That would all come to light later. For now, it was all about hiding the evidence. Both of them.

"Do you want the bodies, sir?"

Lewis didn't answer right away. He had to think about it. Did he want them? He silently shook his head. No, he did not. But someone was going to have to deal with them. Someone was going to have to make sure they went away in such a way that they could not possibly come back to haunt or annoy or inform. And that someone was him. But no, he did not want them. They'd make lousy bookends, but great doorstops. He was still thinking about his options when a morgue staff member offered a suggestion.

"Incinerator?"
"Complete to ash?"

Eyes were met, looks exchanged and heads were sadly shaken.
"No guarantee there."

"Can they be *cremated* to ash without anyone seeing what they are?"

More looks were exchanged, but no smiles were offered. Tough question.

"We don't do that here on-site."
"A private company in town?"
"Yes, sir."
"With security clearance?"
"No, sir."
"Hmmmm..."
"Yes, sir."
"We can bag them in one body bag like one human body."

There was, at that point, just the merest hint of a whiff of optimism in the air. But no smiles yet.

"We can tie 'em together with rope that will burn up with them. It will look and feel like one body."

"Now it's just one big guy in a body bag."

59

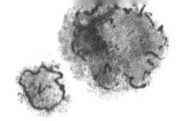

"That might work, but what keeps them from wanting to look in the bag first?"

There was an awkward silence until someone in the back spoke up.

"They can't look in the bag. He was a devout Flanbanian."

Capt. Lewis was frantic to find the source of that voice.

"Excuse me?"

"It's the body of Corporal Hanbak Bruunne. He came here after the war from Eastern Europe. He's Flanbanian. They have very strict customs. No one sees the body after death."

The captain had to smile at least a little bit at that one. "And they'll do it like that, cremate it, bag and all?"

"They will if we tell them they have to."

"Can we get an armed guard to stay with it the whole time, to make sure?"

Looks were exchanged and nods were offered.

"Yeah, we can do that."

Now the captain smiled big, but it wasn't over yet.

"Sir?"

"Yes?"

"What do you want done with the ashes?"

Eli Lewis never blinked or hesitated. "They *were* my crew, a part of my team. I'll take the ashes."

"Yes, sir."

"Make it happen."

"Yes, sir."

Back outside the base hospital, and on the way to his car, Capt. Lewis tried not to smile, but he did look all around. Nice and quiet there on the base that day. Just the way he liked it: No drama. He looked up at the sky. It was a prefect warm summer day. Light blue sky, light white clouds, a light breeze. Too bad this couldn't have been Tuesday. Oh, well. The big car (with the top still down) fired right up, he ground a gear to find reverse, and then it was back to the office, but maybe the long way around. It was a nice day. Maybe stop at the PX for a Coke and a Hershey's bar. A quiet little celebration.

As he drove, he thought about the situation: Sure, they had lost a flight for the first time in two years, since the start of the Western Witch Program (not counting that first little blooper which they would not count), but as of right then and there, Capt. Lewis felt he had a good handle on the situation. They had found the bodies, and now no one else would find the bodies. He spoke out loud as he drove across the base alone, practicing his public voice delivery:

"Weather balloon. It was a weather balloon."

He smiled as he drove and as he watched a plane take off under human control. Very smooth. Nice to see. The captain did wonder how long it might be before they would be able to put another NBA in the air, but for now, it was all about the duck and cover. All about that weather balloon they had just lost. *Sorry about the debris, folks, but it's all perfectly harmless. Just a weather balloon. You can keep it. You're welcome.* He found a parking space at the PX.

The Post Exchange, on a Friday, was teeming with officer's wives, none of them his. Captain Lewis smiled and nodded to the ones he thought he knew and spoke to the ones he did know. He made his way to the small café in the building, checked his watch and decided it was close enough to be time for lunch. He added a sandwich to his Hershey's bar and Coke and found a seat toward the back, where he could relax and take it all in. He took his officer's cap off and sat it down on the table. Big smile. It was a good day so far, but that was as far as it got. He had company waiting for him back at his office. He left his hat on and leaned over to the clerk sitting at the desk outside his door.

"How long has he been here?"

"Half an hour, at least."

"Lovely. No more than fifteen. You know the sign."

"Yes, sir."

Every office, military or not, has a system to dispose of the unwanted. The chimps get cremated, reporters get hustled. In fifteen minutes, maybe less, Capt. Lewis would take off his cap, run a hand through his hair and put the cap back in place. Adjust it just right. There ya go. That was the sign. At that, the clerk outside his office would call another clerk in another room, and *that* clerk would call Capt. Lewis with an absolute emergency that he had to attend to right away, sir. The interview would be over, and the reporter would be walked out the door. *Thank you, come again.* The door's always open, except for when it's locked. But first, the waltz.

"Hello, Bob."

"Hello, Eli."

"How's life in town?"

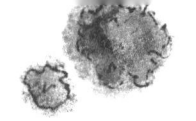

"Oh, the usual. It's all traffic and tourists in the summer, but they do bring cash."

"Thoughtful of them."

"I understand you had a bad start to the week."

"Yeah, we got a weather balloon caught in that storm."

"A weather balloon?"

"Yep."

"In that storm?"

"Yep."

"Eli, why would you send a weather balloon up in a storm like that?"

Eli gave Bob a grim smile and for just this once, and quite possibly the last time ever, the captain did not lie to the reporter. He opened his top desk drawer, pulled out the infamous wrong day weather report and handed it to the reporter, who looked it over and smiled.

"Yes, Monday was nice."

"That's what came in off the wire *Tuesday* morning. No mention of any front or storm."

The reporter took a closer look at the piece of paper. Then he pointed to it. "But..."

"Yep. Wrong day."

"You gonna send them the bill for the balloon?"

"I should, shouldn't I?"

"Can I talk about this?"

Eli hesitated before he answered. "You can talk about the crashed weather balloon, and maybe question why it was sent up in such bad weather, but let's not mention this piece of paper until we get a why back from the who."

"Fair enough."

The captain took off his cap and ran a hand through his hair, smiling all the time at the reporter. There was a good chance he was fooling no one, but then, if he was, the reporter was kind enough to play along and not laugh. There was time for one last scene in the play.

"And in our defense, the weather *was* nice Tuesday morning."

"Oh, I'll give you that, that storm rolled in fast."

"Caught us completely off guard."

"I would imagine so."

CHAPTER 6

The phone on the desk rang right on cue. The captain knew he owed somebody a buck from the Banana Bottle. He made a point of losing his smile before he picked up the phone. The reporter only heard one side of the conversation. The side he was supposed to hear.

"Captain Lewis here."

"Yes."

"Yes."

"I see."

"Shut everything down, and I'll be right there."

To make it look good, he waited that extra moment before hanging up. Then he looked back up, still no smile. He gave it a sigh for effect.

"Trouble in Paradise?"

"Cattle stampede."

The reporter stood up first. He knew a clear signal when he got one. Smiles and nods were exchanged, and hands were shook. The reporter started for the door. He knew the way out. Capt. Lewis followed him.

"I'll give it a mention in Sunday's paper, but nothing about that odd weather wire."

"Bury it?"

"B Section."

"Thanks."

They had been walking through the office, talking, and now they were at the door. The reporter did look around before he spoke again. This was not his first rodeo, and he knew where he was. He almost whispered his last question.

"So you're manning the weather balloons now?"

And just like that, Capt. Lewis's happy little world came crashing down around his ears. The reporter held up a "say no more" halting hand, smiled, turned and was gone, leaving the officer standing there with the screams of a thousand monkeys in his ears as the building spun around. He managed to make it back to his desk, sat down and called Col. Baden.

"Ja?"

"Someone saw the monkeys."

A series of short unpleasant German words were uttered on the other end of the line, and in the silence that followed, Capt. Lewis explained that he had just spoken to a reporter about the weather balloon that had crashed last Tuesday, and the reporter let it be known that he knew that there were bodies in that crash. Baden had to ask the obvious next question.

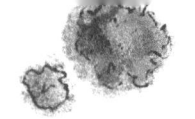

"Did he know they were monkeys?"

"He didn't say."

"Hmmm."

Capt. Lewis elaborated. "He's a local reporter. I've worked with him before. He can report this our way and not say a word."

"If he can do that, he's a good reporter."

"The best."

"So we do what we have to do."

"And what do we have to do?"

Capt. Lewis thought about that, and he knew that Col. Baden was right. The reporter had been kind enough to give them an escape hatch in that trap of his. All they needed was a manned weather balloon. Or at least something that looked like one. Eli thought about it.

The telephone was put back down, and Capt. Lewis had a new project: He was going to have to get his team to set aside the Western Witch Project long enough to create a manned weather balloon. He was pretty sure it didn't have to actually work, but it did have to look as though it might. A plausible diversion. A physical lie. Then he looked at his watch. But not today.

It was still a nice day outside, and the drive home with the top down did help his mood. By the time Eli got home, he was smiling and almost laughing. A manned weather balloon? Yeah, they could do that. Might even work. Any volunteers? Julie saw her husband's smile and offered one of her own.

"A good day, dear?"

"No, we're sunk like the Titanic, but at least we won't run out of ice."

"Dinner's on the table, dear."

"*Mmmmmm!*"

"And Ashley has company."

"Hmmm."

The captain, with a quick change of clothes (out of the uniform and into the civvies), became Eli, or Mr. Lewis if you were the new kid at the table. Dad if you were the girl. He looked himself over in the mirror, straightened the shirt, put on a big smile and strode on stage. It was time for the Friday night show, and he had the first line.

"Hello, Jimmy!"

"This is Robert, Dad."

Eli didn't miss a beat. Still smiling, he put out his hand, and it got shook. Good shake. This one can stay.

"Hello, sir."

"Hello, Robert."

Julie had already sat down at the table, leaving Eli the only one still standing up.

"Sit down, dear. Dinner's getting cold."

"On my way!"

Eli took his seat. There was a moment of silence as they all took in the feast before them, and then it was mob rule as everything went everywhere all at the same time. Robert, to his credit, smiled, laughed and kept up with everything, using both hands to pass and grab. As it turned out, he had one brother and two sisters at home, so dinner at his house was even wilder and louder. This would be a night off for him. And he might actually get some food.

"So how was your day at work, dear?"

Eli froze mid-mashed-potatoes, big bowl in one hand, big spoon in the other. Julie winked. The game was on. Eli found his smile and got himself some mashed potatoes.

"Oh, you know, same old, same old."

"Sorry to hear about your weather balloon, sir."

And this is where Eli nearly choked to death on those mashed potatoes, and nearly sprayed the kid with that mouthful of them. Julie was shaking she was laughing so hard, and Ashley just went on like she never heard a thing. Not even an eye roll there. Julie, when she finally could, reached out and put a comforting hand on Robert's arm.

"Robert's father works at the Daily Record, dear."

Eli frantically did the math in his head and added it up. "Bob?"

"Yes, sir. He says you're the best officer on the whole base."

Eli gave a frantic wide-eyed look at his wife. "And you were going to tell me this when?"

"Oh, dear, I thought you *knew* you were the best officer on the whole base."

Now Ashley was laughing out loud.

"What's so funny, daughter I plan to send off to college not soon enough?"

"Nothing, Dad, I always knew you were the best!"

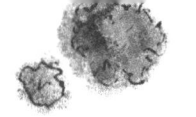

Eli turned his attention to Robert, who had sat calmly, mildly smiling through all of this. It was just another night at the grand pandemonium dinner table for him. And were there more pork chops?

"And did your father say anything else, Robert?"

"Well sir, he does have a theory about the crash."

If Eli went pale, and he did, everyone was too polite to mention it. All of a sudden, hiding in the underground monkey jungle for the rest of the year and eating bananas seemed like the very best plan of action until all of this blew over. But he was stuck at his own dinner table at the moment. And of course he had to ask. He could see that Robert was just bubbling over with the answer to his next question.

"And what might that theory be, son?"

"The weather balloon was a government purchase, so it was the lowest of three bids. There had to have been a flaw in its construction, as it was a *weather* balloon, but it couldn't take the weather. My dad blames the company for the loss."

Eli didn't move. He took that information in, and that information took over. It was good information to have. Very good, indeed.

"So your father thinks I should go after the company that built the balloon for the loss of their lousy product?"

"Yes, sir."

With that, Eli stood up, dug out his wallet and handed the kid a dollar bill. Robert took it in shock. *That* was a first. Big smile.

"Dessert is on me after dinner. I'll drive. Top down."

"Yes, SIR!"

After that, it was all food and chaos, and Robert knew how to help with the dishes and drying. At one point, Eli leaned over to his daughter, having the good sense to whisper his next line.

"This one's a keeper, dear."

"For at least a week, I promise."

"That's my girl!"

The officer was a gentleman and as good as his word. After everything got washed, dried and put away, they all piled into the car after the top was put down and drove off to the ice cream shop as the sun made a beeline for the western mountains. Eli, having been so recently caught off guard by the weather, did take that moment before he sat down in his car to take a good long look at those western mountains, to see what might be coming over them. *Nothing? Good. Let's go.*

CHAPTER 6

It was a perfect evening for ice cream, all golden light and warm. The ice cream shop was Friday night crowded, but Eli found a spot to park, and they all sat in the car with their cones. (Carefully, as to not spill a drop on the seats!) Robert thanked his host for such unwarranted hospitality, and as it turned out, he did *not* have to pay for the ice cream, so he got to keep the buck. Best date ever, as far as he was concerned.

And now Captain Lewis was contemplating how he might blame the exceptionally fictitious Acme Weather Balloon Company for the failure of that lost weather balloon. Perhaps a flock of desert ground cuckoos were driven into it by the storm sharp beaks first, and it simply was not up to the task. The balloon's skin was too thin, too cheap. Yes, that would do it. He was sure of it. It had to. Somewhere in the crowded ice cream shop parking lot, a car horn sounded.

Beep-beep!

CHAPTER 7

THERE WAS NO CASUAL DRIVE UP INTO THE MOUNTAINS FOR Eli that weekend. After the bad week at work, he didn't want to venture out of the house at all. All he wanted to do was scrunch down in his big chair in the living room and hide. He was not a public person. Not now. He knew this might go badly now, this crash that wasn't a weather balloon. A manned weather balloon? Would anyone really believe that? Would he really be able to sell that? He sat down lower in his comfy chair. *Call me when it's Monday and I have to go back to work. And hide there.*

Captain Lewis's job had always been about doing more than he could say that he did. As a bomber pilot in Europe during the war, he dreaded time off. A weekend pass in town meant he had to watch every word he said about anything he did. Never give 'em anything to go on. Never give 'em anything. Like so many other pilots at that time, he went off base dressed down, so he maybe didn't look like an officer. So he didn't look important. *Who? Me? I don't do nuthin'. I push a broom.* Mighty lot of broom pushers in that last war. Just ask 'em.

And now here he was, just two years later, less war and even more secrets. He knew he never could talk about the Western Witch Project when it was going well, and now that it wasn't? Now he could say even less. No wonder he didn't want to go outside, but it was a nice day. Julie tried to help. Tried to get him motivated and moving.

"Why don't you mow the yard, dear?"

"I mowed the yard last week."

"Yes, well, with all of that rain…"
"I see…"
"Just the backyard. No one will see you. I promise."
"And if they do?"
"Frying pan to the back of the head."
"My head or theirs?"
"Let's let that be the surprise."

Eli thought about that and figured it was a win either way, and a fifty-fifty proposition at worst. It was time to mow the yard! He did struggle to get out of his chair (he was in deep), but he did manage, got to his feet and went in search of his lawn mower. It was right where he left it last week. And he had to admit that, yes, it was a nice day outside. He rolled the silly mower thing around the house and into the backyard. Nice and private back there. She was right about that. He began to push, and it began to mow. It was that simple.

Even unmotorized as it was, Eli's reel mower did make a sort of low, happy spinning noise as it cut the grass, and the noise blocked out enough of the real world all around him to give Eli a chance to simply walk, push and think. He was multi-tasking! And thinking way too much about way too much. Mostly about monkeys and weather balloons. In that order.

He knew the crash was his fault. He had ordered it. He had caused it. That no one thought to check the date on the incoming weather wire was not as incriminating. A simple oversight. That one was the weather bureau's fault. Ah, but what about those burnt bodies? How did they get seen so soon? Eli kept pushing the lawn mower. It was amazing how much he could get done out there if he didn't think about what he was doing. He was going to need a bigger yard. Maybe he'd do the front.

The staff assumption was that the chimps' bodies were seen out there in the open desert where they fell. One was even up in a tree! How could you miss a thing like that? And both had been out there for few hours before the crash team found them. So yeah, that had to be it. That had to be where they were seen. That was not where they were seen.

The first chimp found was still strapped into his seat, so that was just another big chunk of burned junk in the sand. Had anyone seen it, they might not have realized what they were looking at. That it was any kind of seat at all, let alone a small flight seat with a chimpanzee still strapped to it. As for the other one up in the tree, that was miles away, and miles farther away from anyone that might have wandered by that day. Mighty lot of open space out there. That's why they were there. So no, the chimps were *not* seen in the desert, but they were seen in the hospital, in the morgue, on those slabs. And no one had thought twice about that.

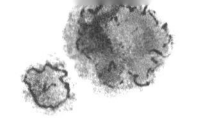

It was funny, but now not funny, that everyone saw those windows between the morgue and the hallway, but no one thought about them as the chimps were being checked out. The windows were there to allow observation without proximity. Not everyone wanted to stand right next to dead bodies, so they could look through the window. And yes, a few people did that day. You almost had to look, whether you wanted to or not. Morbid curiosity, as they say.

And what those few people who walked by saw through the morgue window were short, long-armed, humanoid bodies. Clearly not human, but something like human. And those small silvery suits? Space suits. Space men. Aliens. No question about that. Had to be. Say nothing, just keep walking. Mention it over dinner at home later. And so the word got spread and the yard got mowed.

Julie Lewis refueled the lawn mower by feeding Eli lunch, and with just the two of them in the house, he knew he could talk. He knew he could trust his daughter, but she was seldom alone on weekends, so this was their chance to chat, just the two of them.

"You got that backyard done in record time, dear."

"Thinking too much and pushing too hard."

"You're going to feel that later."

Eli scrunched his shoulders. He knew she was right already. "I can feel it now."

"Let the front yard go, then. I'm sure the neighbors won't mind."

"We'll see. I've got the mower all warmed up."

"Very funny."

"I thought so."

"And you just keep right on thinking, dear."

At that point the front door opened, and they both looked up as Ashley came in with what even Eli knew was a new boy. Red hair! This kid had red hair! He appreciated that, and by now, Ashley knew just what to do first.

"Dad, this is Ralphie. His dad manages the bus station downtown. He's been to Chicago!"

CHAPTER 7

Eli offered up a warm smile and a hand. It got shook.
"Nice to meet you, sir."
"Same here, son."
And with that, the entire conversation came to a total screeching halt all around. No one knew what to say next, and everyone just looked at everyone. Even with the smiles, it got weird quickly. Ashley did the only thing she could.
"Well, we gotta go!"
Eli didn't mind but had to ask. "Not to Chicago, I hope?"
"Dad?"
"I hear Las Vegas is nice this time of year."
"DAD!"
Ashley grabbed the boy by the hand. He didn't seem to mind.
"Bye!"
Julie offered up a, "Be back by dinner," but by then, it was offered up to the back side of a suddenly closed front door. She looked over at Eli, who was still all smiles for no reason at all.
"Well, he seemed nice."
"Whoever he was."
"Ralph E."
"Hmmm."
Both parents stared at the back side of the front door long enough to forget why they were looking at it to begin with. They now had an easy afternoon at home. And it was a nice day.

Taking advantage of that nice day, Clayton Whittaker had convinced Blanche Miller that they needed to go back out into the open desert and start the search for debris all over again, just to see what everyone might have missed the first, second and third times around. Blanche didn't mind. It was either that or hang around in town, and that was just awkward with Idiot Stick. He was not a people person. He *thought* he was, and that made it all even worse. She was tired of cringing. *Let's get out of town. Let's get him out of town.* So off they went.

By then, everyone who was interested had a fairly good idea of where the debris had landed, and the direction of the spread. Clayton's uncommonly wise thought for the day was to go back and start at the beginning of the spread. Look around up that way for the early stuff, the first stuff down, and see what might still be found. It worried Blanche that that made sense to her, but she went along with it anyway. She brought her big hat and plenty of water. Desert girl!

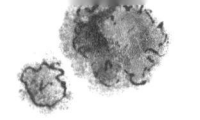

The debris field was huge. It fanned out for miles in length and may have been over a mile wide downwind. The strong wind that day had blown even the heaviest pieces far afield, and that constant wind kept the sand from burying all of it. There was still much to be seen and much to find. Clayton was in scavenger heaven. Blanche got him to park at the top of a hill. She insisted, and he didn't mind. Great view! She didn't do it for the view.

Clayton, for all of his weirdness and paranoia, never locked his car. Blanche wasn't entirely sure if it even *did* lock. She had never seen him even try. Did that take a different key he didn't have? She had no idea, and she did mean to ask him about that someday. But not today. Today was all about a nice walk across the wide-open world. And about the snakes. She mentioned the snakes. It was a nice day for snakes, too. And yes, she did that on purpose. The young lady smiled a sly young lady smile. Clayton simply freaked out.

With the mention of those long reptiles, the debris was forgotten, and Clayton was watching all around his feet as they walked. Blanche lamented that most cacti do not have low limbs to catch heads, but there were still a couple of close calls. The mental image of Clayton getting stuck to a cactus head-first was all it took for Blanche to laugh out loud and then have to explain why. She made up a joke he would never get, and she was covered. He never got any joke.

Now she, too, watched for snakes as she walked, but she had played this game many times before back at home, so it was no big deal. She could do this. She stepped heavy. That served as a thumper, to warn the snakes that might not feel her softer footfalls in the sand. She also knew to not look up too much. No such thing as a venomous bird. But that's not to say she didn't appreciate the view. The desert was, to her, the best view there was. Born and raised a desert girl, she was in her element. Clayton, on the other hand, was simply lost. Literally. She stopped and looked all around. No Clayton. He really *was* lost. How did that happen? This struck her as tremendously funny, and she couldn't help but laugh. This was *so* worth the long walk back into town!

Clayton wasn't really all *that* lost, he had merely followed his feet, watched his feet, watched for snakes, and had veered off to the left as he walked, ever farther from Blanche. And since downhill was easier than uphill, he had unwittingly walked down into a shallow ravine, deep enough to be hidden from her view. And as he looked around, he was sure *he* wasn't lost, but now where was Blanche? She must have gotten lost. *Oh, look! Debris!* He reached down into the sand and came back with something. No idea what, but it was a keeper! The next of many.

As Clayton kept looking down for snakes and at his feet, Blanche was looking all over, taking in the big picture and the glorious desert. It was different here than where she was from farther west, but it was still the desert, and it was still where she belonged. She had her big hat pulled down tight, and she was making good time to, well, wherever she was going. And she was following tracks. She hadn't really thought about it at first, it was just something she did. She followed the tracks. Then she stopped and took a closer look at those tracks. Tire tracks. Truck tracks, judging by the size of them. Army truck tracks by the looks of the tread pattern. And she followed those Army truck tracks all the way to that tree. Too late for the party by the looks of it.

Blanche looked back, looked all around for Clayton. No Clayton, and no idea where he might be. She looked back at the scene around the tree and smiled. It was going to be a good day after all. Carefully and lightly, she stepped around the tree, ever closer, and always watching her feet and the ground around her. For snakes? No, for footprints and tracks. She found two out of three. (No snakes yet.) But she did find other things in those lower branches. Odd things.

With great care and deliberation, Blanche pulled things out of the tree that did not belong there: Torn pieces of odd silvery fabric and clumps of what had to be burnt fur. Not hair. Not human. Close to human, but not quite. She stopped long enough to dig through her handbag for a small paper bag (she had everything in there) and made sure all that she found got placed in that little paper bag. This would be a part of *her* collection. As she looked up, higher into the tree, she saw the prize: A larger piece of the metallic fabric. It was stuck to a branch and fluttering in the light breeze. It called to her. *Come get me! Get me! Time to climb!* And climb she did, after she looked all around. *No one there? No one to see? Good. Up we go!*

She was wearing a skirt long enough and full enough to let her climb up into the tree without a show you shouldn't see. This was not the first time she had ever done this, climbed a tree in a skirt, but she had to admit, if only to herself, that it *had* been a while. Still, she knew what to do; she knew how to climb a tree. And that chunk of fabric calling to her wasn't all that far up. She had this. And in a short time, she did. The tricky part was getting back down. That took longer.

Once back to earth, and once her skirt and hair were straightened, Miss Blanche Miller took a good close look at her new prize: A piece of torn silver fabric, charred on one side, larger than her hand but not by much. What did she have here? Then she had to laugh. She knew *exactly* what she had here. It told her. She had the label.

"COOPER-DOUGLAS FLIGHT SUIT, PRESSURIZED, USA."

Now, she was pretty sure that "USA" was not actually an alien-inhabited planet far outside of our own known solar system, so she figured there was a good chance this whole thing was what it was, a military thing. There wasn't enough of the suit left in the tree to get an idea of the size of the inhabitant, so she was still figuring it was a human crew that crashed. And with the label in English, it was probably one of ours. She made very sure that piece of fabric got tucked, unfolded, into her secret paper bag. Another look around. No Clayton. No anyone. No problem. And no aliens, either.

With her prize safely stashed and her feet back on the ground, Blanche took another slow walk around the tree, looking at all of the tracks and prints. All human, all military. Those tire tracks, those boot prints, they all made sense now. The military base lost an airplane the other day in that storm, and one of the crew members landed up in the tree. Alive or dead, she had no idea, but the piece of fabric was in bad, burnt shape, so she had to go with dead. Too bad, so sad, but it was *not* a flying saucer full of aliens. That much she knew for sure now. And she also knew she'd be keeping that piece of information (and that piece of fabric) to herself. She saw no need to bother Clayton with the annoying truth. Wherever he was. And where was he, anyway? And who's doing all of that yelling?

Once she stepped away from the tree and toward the source of all the noise, the only noise out there, she did see arms waving just beyond the rise. Arms in a plaid shirt? It had to be Clayton. It was time for the damsel to rescue the knight, as is so often the case. She smiled, made sure her bag of goodies was safely tucked away and trudged out toward the source of the noise. But not too fast. There was still the chance of snake in the forecast. She picked up a stick along the way. A nice long one. She snapped off all of the small side twigs as she walked. There. A perfectly good snake stick. Now, what have we here? Comedy gold, apparently. Big smile.

With a good view of the noisy scene from the top of the rise, Blanche took it all in and laughed out loud. How could she not? There was Clayton Whittaker, quite literally hopping from one foot to the other as he waved his arms frantically and was screaming like a little girl. No wait, she thought, she never screamed like that when she was a kid. This guy sounded like a hamster on helium. It was hilarious, and she needed a good laugh. Yeah, this was it. She took her time about that whole rescue thing.

Once she got that out of her system, she walked softly and silently toward Clayton, but kept her eyes on the snake. It was big, and the tail made noise. Sounded just like a maraca. Blanche smiled at that but knew not to laugh now. Slowly, carefully, she got closer to the snake and ignored the lunatic just beyond the snake. She looked at her stick. *Sure hope it's long enough. Longer would be nice. That's a big snake. Oh, well. Here we go.*

In one smooth, fast, I've-done-this-before move, Blanche dug the stick into the sand to one side of the snake and instantly did a violent pitch fork move, tossing the snake well up into the air and over to the side, off the path and into the scrub. Then she offered her friend but one word of sound advice.

"*RUN!*"

They both did just that, and by the time the snake figured out he had been hoisted and flung, Blanche and Clayton were back up over the ridge and much closer to the tree. Blanche made sure she stopped where they could look back on the scene they had just fled. No snake now. She planned to downplay the tree. Clayton was breathing hard. He seldom ran, ever.

"You saved my life!"

"And I taught a snake how to fly."

"Thank you! Wow!"

"You're welcome, just don't make a habit of it."

"There was no way around it."

"Did you try explaining your UFO theory to it?"

Clayton stopped and looked at her. He didn't get where this was headed at all. "Why would I do that?"

"Pretty sure it would have wandered off on its own if you had."

"Very funny."

"I thought so."

As Clayton and Blanche wisely decided to call it a day after the snakes started flying but before Clayton could focus on the tree that Blanche didn't want him to see, life at the Lewises' had gone from calm and comfy to just plain annoying. All because of that modern inconvenience, the telephone. It just wouldn't stop. All because of one small story buried in the B section of the local paper about a crashed weather balloon. And because they really were listed in the phone book.

Eli had taken the first two calls, and was even polite to the first one, answering that reporter's questions as best he could, but mostly telling him that he couldn't. That reporter got it, understood the military secrecy thing, but the next one did not. Eli hung up on that one, and refused to even answer the phone the next time it rang. So began his new game: How many times would the telephone ring before the caller gave up? The average was ten, but Julie was not amused with that new, and decidedly useless, information.

"What if it's Ashley, dear?"

"And where is Ashley?"

"Downtown with friends, I believe."

"Hmmm."

The phone started to ring again, and they both just sat there and looked at it. On the sixth ring, Julie couldn't take it anymore and picked it up. Now it was Eli's turn to roll his eyes. His daughter had taught him well.

"Hello?"

"No, he's not. May I help you?"

"I'm his wife, Mrs. Lewis."

"Julie."

There was a longer pause here as the voice on the other end of the line had a longer question to ask. Julie did that lip-flapping thing with her free hand as Eli watched. Now it was amusing, and he smiled. And would she want to come to work with him and answer his phone there? She put her hand down and lost her smile. Uh-oh.

CHAPTER 7

"Well, Mr. Manning, I really only know what you already know. Yes, they seemed to have temporarily misplaced a weather balloon the other day. Yes, it once was lost, but now is found. Amazing, really."

Eli chuckled at that but got a fierce hush thing from his wife. Whoops! He covered his mouth and watched in awe. She had this. She was good at this. She was leading the caller in circles like a pony at a birthday party. It was a joy to behold.

"Oh, no, sir, I don't believe the weather balloon pilots are free to do interviews, but you'd have to ask them that."

"No, you can't talk to them."

"Yes, that does make it tough to ask, doesn't it?"

"You should call my husband at work for more information."

"His number? Oh, I can't give that out. You'll have to ask him about that when you call."

"Yes, well, goodbye!"

And with that, she hung up, folded her arms and looked at her husband.

"And that's how it's done, son."

Eli could only stand and applaud his incredible wife. And then he had to ask, "How did you learn to do that?"

"Dear, we have a teenage daughter. What do you think the boys get when they call here?"

"Brilliant!"

"Thank you, dear."

And then the phone started to ring again. Both of them looked at it, neither one went for it. It stopped after ten rings. Both of them counted. By the tenth ring, Eli had the cord that ran from the phone in his hand and was following it back to the wall. In the silence that followed the tenth ring, he held up the cord in his hand, still attached at both ends. He was not amused.

"Hard wired at both ends. We can't unplug it."

Julie was still standing right by the phone, and she smiled and gave him a nod. "But of course we can."

With one small move, the phone's handset was picked up and placed next to it. Eli could hear the dial tone. Julie walked back into the kitchen, returned with a hand towel and wrapped the handset in that. It got quiet. Problem solved. She gave her husband a look.

"Anything else?"

Eli pointed at the wrapped phone. "You do that a lot, do you?"

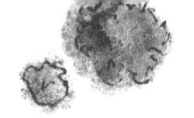

"Only when I want a nice afternoon nap."
"But what if I try to call you?"
"And where would you be?"
"At work, I believe."
"Hmmm."

CHAPTER 8

CAPTAIN LEWIS'S MONDAY BEGAN AS SO MANY MONDAYS DO for so many of us With a meeting. This had been a constant tradition with the Western Witch Project, even when things were going well, a meeting first thing Monday morning to start the week. Now, mind you, the going-well meetings were shorter and a lot more fun, but still, here it was Monday morning, and there they were in a meeting. Just like always. For these meetings, Col. Baden was in charge, being the highest ranking officer in the building. He was not smiling. There was no reason to.

"So where do we stand right now?"

He was looking at Capt. Lewis.

"We seem to have found almost all of the crew-related crash debris *and* the crew. They will be cremated this week, and the ashes will be returned to us."

"Almost all?"

The captain grimaced. "Some smaller control handles are still missing. One panel of gauges."

"Anything that can get us in trouble?"

"We've got both small seats."

"Good."

"We might still go with weather balloon as the official explanation."

"Might?"

"There's been a glitch."

"What is the glitch?"

"We might have a small problem."

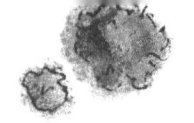

"In this, there are no small problems. What is the problem?"

Capt. Lewis recounted his short meeting with the local newspaper reporter and that reporter's parting words about the weather balloon being manned. Baden was clearly not amused by that.

"How did he know?"

"The bodies fell on public land; they were out there for anyone to see."

"Ja... Did he have photos?"

"If he did, he didn't say."

Baden said nothing right away.

"What did he say?"

Capt. Lewis had to think about it. *What were his exact words? Not sure. He paraphrased.*

"Something about us manning the weather balloons now. It was not a question."

Slowly, slyly, Colonel Baden's frown became a smile. It was not a happy smile, but it was a smile, nonetheless. Had the men in that room been standing, they would have all taken a step back. It was that kind of smile. A serious German smile.

"So that is what we do now."

Baden's wicked smile went suddenly casual. It was no more inviting, but maybe slightly less dangerous.

"We at least try."

Now there was a bit of movement and murmur in the room and the team thought about that. Could they man a weather balloon? It was a fine topic for a panel discussion, until Baden set them straight on the subject.

"We don't actually have to *do* it, we merely have to *look* as though we do."

Some smiles all around.

"Can we do that?"

Captain Lewis looked around the room at his team. They were all smiles now and some thumbs up. The captain looked back at the colonel and nodded.

"Yes, sir. My staff assures me that we can do that."

"Then do it."

"Yes, sir."

"Launch with dummies first."

From the back of the room: "You'd kind of have to be."

"I heard that."

The meeting descended into verbal chaos, as Baden left them to their own plans and devices. No one else dared to leave or wanted to. It was all too much fun now! It was one serious thing to have to design and build a thing that worked, but now, to build a thing that didn't *have* to work? That would be a lark. A happy prank! And they needed this after everything.

It would be easy enough, they knew, to get a real weather balloon or two just to work on and modify, to play with. They had plenty of spare parts for the Neutral Buoyancy Aircraft and their simulators, until Capt. Lewis pointed out the forgotten obvious.

"Gentlemen, this won't be for the chimps. This has to be for a full-size human crew of two. No small seats, no small controls. The whole point here is to hide the chimps."

After a short bout of "Oh, yeah" from all around the room, the verbal plans were kicked up to full-size and the party was still going strong. Now pencils were out, and things were being sketched, and Capt. Lewis liked where this was going. He particularly liked the sketch of the crew sitting side by side.

"Whose idea was this?"

One man raised a low hand. "Mine, sir."

"I like that."

"It would be easier to balance the crew pod that way, and by looking both ways, they get to see everything all around them."

"Nothing sneaks up on them."

"No, sir."

"Like a storm."

"Yes, sir,"

"Take a buck from the Banana Bottle, son."

"Yes, sir!"

There was no doubt in Captain Lewis's mind that this team could build a mock-up of exactly what they needed, and there was a very good chance that they might actually fly the crazy thing. With just dummies, of course. But full-size dummies, to be sure. There were no immediate volunteers in that room, but they were going to need *someone*. Someone to fake it, to pretend to have flown in it, at least.

The Mustang pilots? Captain Lewis had to think long and hard about that. He needed men who knew how to fly, yes, but those guys were maybe over the top about it. They were fighter pilots. Yeah, they were a perfect fit for the job, all slim and trim and deadly serious, but they weren't the sort of guys to just sit there and do nothing, which was all they'd have to do if this were done for real. And did those fighter pilots even *have* a sense of humor? They were gonna need one for this. The captain thought long and hard about that option. Who else did he have? Who else could pretend, but with the real-world knowledge to make it look real? The only other crew that came to mind were the chimps, and he was pretty sure *that* was right out.

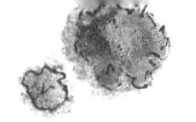

By the time the meeting finally broke up and the team wandered off in search of more coffee, there were fistfuls of drawings going out with every man, and Capt. Lewis knew they could pull this off. Then he had to laugh. It would be funny if it worked so well that it became the new norm and manned weather balloons happened. The captain silently shook his head. Yeah, it was time for more coffee.

By late that Monday afternoon, a portion of the NBA hangar was cleared away and made ready for the materials coming in for the MWB (Manned Weather Balloon). Calls had been made, and two weather balloons were already on their way. They needed two seats but few controls. There wasn't much "control" involved in a weather balloon. It went up and you hung on. Getting it back down was the challenge. The team was treating this as a very real project, and they decided they were *not* going to build a fake manned weather balloon. They knew they could build a very real one. Whether it flew with a crew or not was up to someone else later.

Capt. Lewis, watching all of this wild activity, was feeling much better about the grand lie. It might not be a lie for very much longer. They may have a couple of very real manned weather balloons by the end of the month. But would they actually launch them? Baden was inclined to say yes to that, but Lewis wasn't so sure. There had always been that one question no one had ever answered about these things: Where do these weather balloons *go* when you let them go? No one seemed to know. Maybe they were all still up there somewhere. Who knew?

By the end of that week, the week after the forced crash, it all seemed to be going so very well. The bodies of the two chimps had been successfully cremated, and no one that shouldn't have seen them ever saw them. The ashes were returned to the captain on that Thursday, and for now, they found a quiet home in the bottom of his locked file cabinet in his locked office in a secure building on a restricted military base. Capt. Lewis had thought about spreading those ashes in the underground monkey jungle area, but then there was no telling what the other chimps would make of *that*, so, for the time being, they were safe right where they were. One less problem. *What else ya got?*

By the end of that same week, two shiny new weather balloons had been delivered to the NBA hangar and were now laid out in long, flat (uninflated) lines back over on one side. The team had to admit that the balloons were much larger than they had anticipated, but they could still work with that. Now they were calculating balloon lift capabilities and weighing the seats they had on hand. And did we have any lighter seats available? Someone held up a folding chair. *Very funny. Now put it down.*

Capt. Lewis and Col. Baden were smiling more now as they stopped by the hangar from time to time to check on the progress and offer encouragement. It seemed, more and more, that they might really launch one of these things, just to say that they did. Very publicly, for all to see. And could we get one of the mannequins to wave an arm as it rose? The design team had to think about that. A definite maybe there. They would work on that.

By Friday afternoon, Captain Lewis was all smiles and all ready for what might have otherwise been a very unpleasant event, the first official media meeting about The Crash. (Capital letters now.) With the dead chimps about as gone as they could possibly be, and the live ones all secure below ground, the captain had been rehearsing his straight-faced delivery of the phrase "manned weather balloon." The fact that he almost had two of them back in the hangar by then really did help. It wasn't that much of a lie.

The media event was not held in the NBA hangar or anywhere near the captain's office. The base had a public building right up by the front gate for this sort of thing, so no one had to drive around on a base no one should drive around on. The captain was feeling festive and drove his own car to this one, leaving the jeep at the office. He met Bob there, the reporter he knew, on the way in and complimented him on his son. That helped. *We're all just good friends here, right?*

There were no more than ten or so reporters in the room, but then, it wasn't that big of a room. There were extra seats. Good. It hadn't gotten too crazy yet. Maybe this will just blow over now. It took Captain Lewis a moment to figure out where the front of the room was supposed to be, as the chairs were facing all directions. He simply walked to the wall opposite the door, and that was the front of the room today.

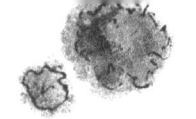

"**Gentlemen.**"

Chairs got turned around, and the room got quiet. Capt. Lewis smiled. The game was on.

"As you all know, we suffered a setback here last week with the loss of a new type of weather balloon."

In the pause he offered, a hand shot up.

"Yes?"

"There were two men in that balloon?"

"Yes, this is something new for us, but no, they were not actually *in* the balloon."

This got a mild chuckle from the group, as no, they would not have been in the gas filled balloon itself. Score one for the captain. Another hand over there.

"Was this the first manned weather balloon flight?"

Captain Lewis gave that reporter his warmest smile. It, too, was a lie.

"As far as you know."

"Will there be more after this accident?"

"It's too early to say, but we generally don't give up that easily."

"Will we be allowed to watch a future flight?"

The captain pictured that mannequin with the arm waving. "I would think so, but it's too early to say when."

"Can we meet the crew?"

That stopped everyone right there. Great question. Now they were all looking at the good captain, waiting for the answer they all wanted to hear. And the captain let them wait.

"Gentlemen, you know this is a restricted base, and so much of what we do here is not done in the public eye. This project, while not strictly a military one, is still not a public one. It's obviously going to take us some time to get comfortable with it before you get to see much more if it."

"So that would be a 'no'?"

"Yes."

"So it's a 'yes'?"

"No, it's still a 'no.'"

"But you said 'yes.'"

"That was a 'yes' to the 'no,' and I would also say 'yes' to two aspirin about now."

The room erupted into laughter as Capt. Lewis smiled, and that reporter had no idea what had just happened. He saw this as good a time as any to wrap this puppy up.

"Gentlemen, I think we're about done here. I will let you know if there's anything else we can say on this matter, but for now, you have all of the information we can release at this time."

Captain Lewis looked over at Bob, the reporter he knew, and both smiled. He got a nod from Bob. That was much appreciated. He also knew to get out before anyone tried for a last question. Around the room and out the door and down the hall and gone. He had parked out back, and the reporters would not be allowed to follow him through that building. They had to go out the front door. And please do. Now. They did.

By and large, the media men went away happy that day. The whole "manned weather balloon" thing had been officially confirmed, even if they did not get to meet a pilot or crew member. Maybe they would later. A definite maybe there, right? Or maybe not, the more they thought about it. And what just happened there?

Capt. Lewis stopped long enough in the back of the building, away from prying eyes, for a quiet cup of coffee before he drove back to his own office on the other side of the base. He wanted to give all of those reporters a chance to leave without him being seen. That seemed fair enough. And as he sipped and stalled for time, he thought about those Mustang fighter pilots. He was going to need to meet them. And could they act?

Well outside the base, and over on the far side of town, Clayton Whittaker was in seventh heaven. Maybe eighth. He had taken the time that day to empty out his poor, long-suffering old car, and he had carefully hauled all of his precious "UFO" parts and pieces up into his rented room. They were everywhere, all over the bed, the floor, the dresser, the chair, everywhere. He had amazed himself with all that he had found, just as Blanche had amazed herself by still being there. She, however, was resigned (content) to stand out in the hall, as there was no room left in the room. Fine by her.

Now, yes, Blanche had also found a few interesting things on her own out there in that open desert over that previous wild week, but also, she had the smarts to keep her prizes safely packed away. In her locked suitcase. The unmentioned were in with her unmentionables. So there. And she did smile at that, but not at Clayton. Well, maybe a little at Clayton, but for all the wrong reasons.

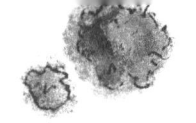

As she looked over his vast and varied collection of such a great many things, it struck her that it was all still desert dirty. He hadn't bothered to clean up or dust off a single thing that he had picked up out there. She knew the car was a mess from all of that, and now his rented room looked like a sandbox threw up, in a junkyard. Clayton didn't quite see it that way, of course.

To Clayton the Clueless, which was about the nicest thing she might silently call him, this was all priceless proof of extraterrestrials on Earth! They were here! They lived among us! Blanche resisted the obvious punch line, "But they're lousy pilots." This whole adventure had been on Clayton's dime—the rooms, the food, the gas for the car, all of it. She had bought a few small things for herself, of course, but her fine strange friend picked up the tab for the bulk of the trip. It was like a mostly free vacation in New Mexico! But this new vacation was getting old. And so was Clayton. Blanche looked at his room full of dirty debris. Wow. What a mess.

And it was right about then, as she took it all in, that Blanche felt the warmth of a presence close by. Just over her left shoulder, in fact. She turned and smiled. It was the owner's wife, come to clean the rooms. *Hey, not a problem, here ya go.* Blanche stepped back and waved the nice lady into the not-so-nice room. *Knock yerself out.*

That went about as well as expected. The woman *did* take one step in, which was all the farther she could go, and all the farther she had to go. Bad words were spoken softly, and in a flash, the woman was gone. Knowing where this had to be going, Blanche took that opportunity to make one last sweep of her own clean room and gather her bag for the soon to be sudden flight. She saw the owner himself racing down the hall toward Clayton's room as she stepped back out of her own. She had time for a quick lean in and one cryptic comment to Clayton.

"I'll wait in the car."

"Huh?"

Blanche gave a wave over her shoulder to the owners as they reached Clayton's indoor sandbox, and she was gone before it started. She knew how it would go. How it had to go. She put her suitcase on the floorboard in front of her, under the front passenger's seat. Clayton was going to need the rest of the car for all of that junk of his if he got it all out. She even opened the trunk for him, knowing he might be a bit pressed for time when he got there. He was.

"Holy cow, they threw us out!"

"Can't imagine why."

"They said I wasn't allowed to bring all that stuff in!"

"Go figure."

"Yeah!"

"Be right back."

"Take yer time."

It took three trips, and then a fourth, just to make sure. By then the trunk was full, the backseat was a mess, and could she hold this?

"No."

Whatever that nasty piece was, Clayton put it on the floor on his side, back by the seat away from his feet. Blanche watched him do that and figured the first time he hit the brakes it was going to get real interesting. She might learn some news words before the crash, but she doubted it. Clayton let the car roll backwards, bump started it in reverse, and they were off. They had to be off. Because they sure couldn't stay there. But where? She had to ask.

"Any ideas?"

"Camp out in the desert?'

"Tent? Cots? Sleeping bags? *Snake repellent?*"

"Oh, yeah."

"Just drive."

As Clayton drove and Blanche just sat there, smiling and wondering how it all might end, and when, life under the NBA hangar on the air base was going, well, weird. Somehow, the chimps knew something was up. Or down, as the case may be. They seemed to understand that two of their kind were gone, and that was a problem for them. They missed their friends, and where were they? The fact that their handlers were being extra careful with them only seemed to make matters worse, as the monkeys wanted answers. WHERE WERE THEIR FRIENDS? It was tough to explain.

With no actual NBA flights scheduled until they got that whole "manned weather balloon" thing out of the way, the chimps were given more "flight time" on the underground NBA simulators, but they were not amused by the fake flights, and most of those ended in chimp fights. It was not pretty, and it was dangerous to intercede. Monkeys fight dirty, often literally. Don't go in there. Why? Just don't. More time in the jungle room went better, but not by much.

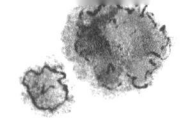

As big as a high school gymnasium, minus the basketball court, the jungle room was the one place where the chimps could be alone and hide, and that's exactly what they did. They hid. And they hid very, very well. It didn't take long for their handlers to lose track of what chimp was where, and which ones were *supposed* to be in that big room. But no one could say for sure. There was a list being kept of which chimp was supposed to be where, in there or elsewhere, but then again, no one had seen them all in one place for quite some time. So, well, keep an eye out.

The team had to give up on the flight simulators. The chimps were crashing and trashing them, and bananas were the nicest thing they threw. Everyone knew that now, and "duck and cover" took on a whole new, and far more serious, meaning. The chimps were mad. And their aim was getting better. A bad combination.

By then, Capt. Lewis was getting daily updates on the problems and the lack of progress. If anything, the situation was going the other way, getting worse, and they were losing what they had with the chimps they still had. The captain made sure the colonel was in the loop on all of this, and as they watched their project struggle, only one answer came to mind: They needed more chimps. Keep these, of course, but add more to replace the loss. Maybe that was what was needed, to bring the group back up to size. The handlers concurred, Col. Baden agreed and wheels, figuratively speaking, were set in motion.

It wasn't going to be quick or easy, as the whole project (and every monkey) was classified top secret, but yes, there were funds available. Of course there were. Approval was given, verbally. Nothing in writing. Never in writing. Phone calls were made from phones off the base and unlisted to people who knew just enough about what was going on and yes, they had a few extra chimps. The San Diego Zoo was a joy to work with. They knew how to keep a secret. *How many ya need? We're running a special on chimpanzees this month!* Capt. Lewis bought two and got one for free. Such a deal. Now all he had to do was get them there. Back to New Mexico, without anyone seeing them. Just like the last time.

CHAPTER 8

They knew, by then, to not fly the chimps in from the coast. It was something over 600 miles, and chimpanzees do not fly well until they have been trained and conditioned to do so. Gently. A 600-mile ride in the back of an Army truck would go even worse, but how about a train ride? Yes, a train ride was the way to go. And it was easy enough to keep the secret like that. All they had to do was use a military train car with the windows blacked out, and the railroad was happy to oblige. For a price, of course. Always a price.

The train car and its military crew, the guards and the handlers, were hauled out to San Diego, the chimps were acquired and secured, and then, carefully, that train car was attached to an eastbound freight and brought back to New Mexico with no one seeing a single chimp anywhere along the way. *Just another secret military railroad car passing by. Nothing to see here, folks. Move along.* Of course, it didn't hurt to keep the chimps lightly sedated for the trip. That cut down on the bites and the flinging.

Win-win.

CHAPTER 9

ONCE THE SEDATIVES KICKED IN, THE TRAIN RIDE WENT WELL for almost all concerned. The rolling joke was "Sedatives all around!" but no, they were not, if only to ensure that they did not run out of sedatives for the chimps en route. That would have been a very bad thing, indeed. The chimps got nervous with the first hard jolt as the train started out from San Diego and the couplings all connected, *bambambambam*, one car right after the other. That first series of hard jolts as the train starts rolling is always the worst, and the chimps had not traveled by train before. They all screamed. Fifteen minutes later, the sedatives kicked in and they were all silly; happy and grinning like drunk baboons, but don't tell them that.

With the three new chimps living large up on Cloud Nine, the military guards and handlers could relax somewhat, and since it was a freight train, there were no worries, as they were moving, of any other people, civilians, stumbling into the car looking for the bar. It was only at the infrequent stops in the big freight yards that the armed guards got busy guarding, as there was no telling where they were and who might be there, looking for a free ride to anywhere else. In theory, they had everything they needed right in that locked car: Food, drink and sedatives. All they had to do was sit back, relax and wait for someone to tell them that they were finally there. Whenever that might be. Any minute now ... or maybe later. It was tough for them to enjoy the ride with all of the windows blacked out. Not much to see, and not much different from them being underground, really. Life was funny that way, but only the chimps were laughing.

CHAPTER 9

Slowly but surely, the freight train made its way east. It made good time in the open country, but it was slow going in the few cities they went through. There was a small celebration when they found out that they had finally crossed into New Mexico, and it wasn't long after that that a knock on the door at a stop told them they were home. Well, close to home. But was it close enough? The military railcar had been uncoupled and left all alone on a siding in Roswell. Now all they had to do was get three chimpanzees out of that car and onto the military base without anyone seeing them. Including most of the people on the base. There was some talk of slapping them in blonde wigs and dresses and calling them "Shirley Temple," but that wisely got shot down. Still funny, though.

The easiest way was simple; they sedated the chimps, wrapped them up and put them in a dark-windowed sedan for a quick ride to the base while they were still knocked out. After that, they let them "thaw out" in the jungle room. It had been a long train ride. They all needed to thaw out, even the guards and handlers. It was going to take some time to get these new chimpanzees acclimated to their new underground home and everything that went with it. This was not the zoo. Not by a long shot.

And so it was that for the price of two (and a train ride) the Western Witch Project got three new chimpanzees. Well, three slightly-used chimpanzees, at least. They were not young, but hardly old. Could they be trained to fly? That was not the first question or, indeed, the team's number one priority. Job One was to integrate these new animals into the existing group. And hopefully, the addition of these three would help calm the group as a whole. That was the real goal. And like so very many things that go wrong, it seemed like a good idea at the time.

As it turned out, and as the handlers found out, there was a very good (bad) reason that they got that third chimp for free. He was a rogue, a trouble maker. A danger. He did not work and play well with others. Not with other humans, and certainly not with the other chimps. On the plus side, this jerk monkey did make it easy for the other two new ones to fit in with the old established group, as now they all had a common enemy, but what about that third chimp? That third chimp was a serious and dangerous problem. Capt. Lewis was not the least bit amused and gave the order to keep that chimp sedated, but he knew it was only a short term solution.

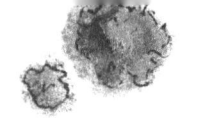

Could they send the chimp back to San Diego? Not easily. Someone might notice and ask where it had been and why it was there. The easiest solution fell to him, and he put that off for as long as he could.

The training of the two chimps that were trainable got underway, gently, even as they were being accepted into the larger group, and that group itself was finally settling back down to a dull roar. Apparently, this was exactly what the group needed: The right number. The number they knew. Looking back over the previous two years, yes, there had always been a certain specific number of chimpanzees in that underground complex. Take two out and the rest of them noticed. Put two back in, even a different two, and all was well again. And with the real NBA flights on hold, there was no rush to bring the new chimps up to flight-ready speed. The team was far more rushed to get their fake MWB diversion off the ground. Literally. But carefully. They didn't want the MWBs to be a secret, but the secret was that they didn't have one yet.

While a large part of the team was still dedicated to keeping the chimps healthy, happy and trained, there was a small subset under that hangar that was rushing to build two manned weather balloons and to get them out in the public eye, the media's eye, as soon as possible to keep up the illusion that that's what had crashed in the storm. This was as close as it was going to get to a fun job, and these guys were pushing to make the lie real. Somehow, somewhere along the way, the idea that it was supposed to be just an illusion got lost, and these guys were building the real thing. It became a matter of pride. They would do this. *Versagen Nicht*! They would not fail.

As public as the whole manned weather balloon thing was going to have to be to get the lie across to both the media and the public, the Western Witch Project itself was still classified very top secret and kept well hidden. Sure, the military staff on the base knew there was a big hangar over there full of odd aircraft, and they saw them take off and land from time to time, but the big secret, the chimpanzees, was still kept well out of sight and out of mind. If you didn't know, you never saw them. And even if you did, you never said. No banana jokes. Ever.

Not everyone on the base knew about those Neutral Buoyancy Aircraft, and fewer still knew who was flying them, and especially not *why* they were being trained to fly them. That was the biggest secret of all, the one that had to be kept at all costs. For the price of

CHAPTER 9

two weather balloons and a few old seats? Not a problem. They could handle that. And if it worked, it was a bargain. It sure beat having to tell the truth. "Why yes, we're actually teaching monkeys to fly nuclear bombers. Problem?" Good idea, bad press. They all knew which way that would go if they got there. The goal was to never get there. This was as close as they had ever been. The weather balloons were there to save the day.

With the little bit of media notice and press that they did get right after the crash, the team knew to hide even lower. They all worked to offer less of a public presence around the NBA hangar. Work times were shifted so there was never a crowd arriving or leaving all at once, no big shift change, like some odd secret factory. Now cars were being parked all over, and staff was walking to the building, everyone coming from a different direction and no one looking up. Never look to see who might be looking. Unless you want them to see. Nothing to see here.

At some point, yes, they knew that they *did* want the public to see, to see the manned weather balloons, and to make sure everyone knew *that* was what they had been working on all along. Of course they were, did you not know? Well, now you do. MWBs, or Manned Weather Balloons. There ya go. Bye, now! And why are you still here?

There was, of course, an underlying issue in all of this: The Russians. Those dirty commies. They were now the enemy and the eyes that never blinked.

Sure, yeah, we were all great pals back in the war, but that was two years ago. And now? Now we gotta watch out. Russians spies were everywhere. Or, at least, you assumed that they were. That's why Eli spoke Russian to Clayton the first time they met, to see if he jumped. (He did not.) And if he had? It would not have gone well for him. The Russians were the enemy now. The Russians were why they were teaching the monkeys to fly.

In odd moments, and deep underground with no one around, Capt. Lewis did ask questions of Col. Baden. The colonel had been much closer to the Russians at the end of the war and knew even then to run west when he could. Quietly, and hopefully without the colonel noticing, the captain was also trying to figure out if he had ever actually bombed the colonel back during the war. It was entirely possible, but the answer was elusive. They also spoke of their current work, and the new question arose: What would the Russians do?

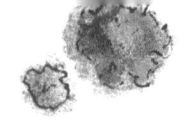

At that point in time, by the summer of 1947, they knew what few knew: It was a wicked fast race. The Russians had the information by then, the designs for nuclear weapons, and it was only a matter of time before they had The Bomb. A couple of years at the most. Ah, but how would the Russians deliver such a device? With bombs big enough to take out their slower planes, how would *they* get around that? What would the Russians do? Baden got serious, frowned, and nailed it.

"They would just do it."

"Excuse me?"

"They would load the bomb onto a plane, wish them luck and send them off to die."

"And not tell them?"

"No, they would not tell them."

"But..."

Baden raised an imaginary glass. "Vodka bravery. *Napítok!*"

"They'd kill the bomber crew, just like that?"

"No big deal if you are Russian."

Capt. Lewis settled back in his chair as the reality of the thing sunk in. "Just as the chimps are no big deal to us."

Baden shrugged. "Da."

Both men said nothing for a while until Baden spoke again.

"War is war. It is the worst game on earth."

"And now we can't quit the game."

"No one walks away from this table."

Capt. Lewis refilled their coffee cups. Baden refused at first, but then, yes, please. A tea drinker until he arrived in America right after the war, he wished very much to be an All-American, and coffee was The All-American Drink. Gorton Baden found that yes, he liked coffee very much. It was much stronger than tea, and stronger was good! And would he like another cup? Ja! *Bitte!* He held that cup with both hands. There'd be no spilling a drop.

Running on caffeine and sugar (and a little bit of cream in the colonel's cup), the two men sat there and solved all of the world's problems in about three cups flat. Their attention, for the sake of levity, turned to their current non-problem, the idea of manned weather balloons, and both men smiled at the mere thought of the thing. It was good to have a lighter burden. A small break from the big secret. The colonel, running on too much caffeine by then, had an idea.

"What about a mixed crew?"

"That might be possible."

"Both monkeys and men."

The captain's eyes went wide. "Oh, wait, no. That's not what I thought you meant."

The colonel had to think about that for a moment. "Ah, yes, sorry. I was not thinking. But what do you think?"

"The chimps are our big secret."

"Yes, exactly. This would give us a reason to have them."

"And then no need to keep them a secret?"

"Exactly."

"But they still fly the NBAs?"

"They would have to. The seats are too small for the rest of us."

Capt. Lewis gave the idea some serious thought, but smiled less as he did. "When the chimps get mad, they get dangerous. Strapped in that close to a human, the chimp could kill the human."

"So we arm the human."

"Bullets flying around in a pressurized cabin at altitude are never a good idea."

"You are right. It was the coffee talking."

The captain looked at the colonel's cup. It was almost empty.

"Would you like some more?"

"Did you hear me say 'no'?"

"*Nein.*"

"*Ja.*"

There was, after that next cup of coffee, some discussion about having humans fly the NBAs, but as Capt. Lewis pointed out, the NBAs were still a big part of the secret, and then had to explain the pun to the German, who still didn't get it. Plus, full-size humans would never fit in the chimp-sized cockpits, and no, they would not be hiring dwarves just for that. They would stick with the plan they had: Manned weather balloons. With just real men. The German had to admit that he liked that plan. It worked. "See?" he said. "I made a joke. A pun." The captain didn't get it. More coffee.

Without really seeing that they were doing it, both men began to speak of the manned weather balloon ruse as if it were real and would work, and what were they going to do with it? The captain was all for collecting high-altitude real-time data, as they could with a manned balloon, but there were two questions still drifting high above them.

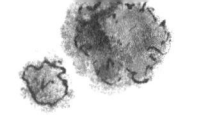

"How high and where to?"

Neither man had worked directly with real weather balloons, so they had no way to know for sure, but Baden gave it a good guess.

"On top of the air."

"So they will need oxygen."

"Oh, ja!"

"And how do we get them back?"

"We do not."

"But the crew."

"They bail out."

"Above the air?"

"Oh... *Ja*... Problem..."

Now the fake ruse became a series of very real problems. (And yes, a fake ruse is something real.) How do they get the balloon back, or at least the crew back, safely? Going on the idea that they might actually launch these things, what happens to these things when you do? Where do they go? Baden stared intensely at the floor before he spoke again.

"Maybe Afrika?"

That sounded as likely as anywhere else, as Capt. Lewis had never seen or heard of one coming down in the U.S. He had to wonder what the more remote Africans thought of that. Cloth from the sky! But what about the crew?

"We need to be able to vent the gas to get them back down."

"And parachutes."

"Yes. Maybe to bail out for a lower altitude?"

"Ja!"

Little by little, cup by cup, they were making it work and making it real. And even if they never launched the first balloon, now Capt. Lewis knew that he could face the media and answer any question about manned weather balloons as if they *were* real and *did* fly. He was going to know all about them before they ever did it. If they ever did it. Maybe now they'd have to do it. Just to say they did. The fewer lies the better, right?

"More coffee?"

"Nein."

CHAPTER 9

"*Nein?*"

By then, both men were suffering from a serious case of the coffee jitters; it was time to get up, get out and *do* something. Without a word being spoken, both men made a beeline for the surface, for the great outdoors, with the one obvious stop along the way. You can only rent coffee. In the last shade before the bright desert sun, there were some small words spoken between them and a parting of the ways as Col. Baden elected to walk in the sunshine. The desert was still a wonderful novelty to him, and he wanted to bask in that great warmth and bright light. Capt. Lewis understood that, but still elected to maybe not trot right out there just yet. He had places to go and things to see right there in the hangar.

Baden knew where he was going. This was no casual walk. He was headed for the OK Corral—the hangar where the ponies were kept. (That's what they called it over there.) If they were going to need humans to go up in those weather balloons, or even just pretend that they did, the Mustang fighter pilots were their best choice for that. And, as a qualified aircraft designer, he didn't mind spending the time to take another close look at those P-51s. They were, to him and a great many others, absolute works of art and perfection. Well worth the walk in the heat.

Even without the NBAs being scheduled to fly anytime soon, the hangar doors at the OK Corral were wide open, and the ponies were ready to run. The pilots were in the ready room, and the ground crew was simply on standby, waiting for those loud klaxon horns that told them to fire 'em up. They could be airborne in just a few minutes, ready to intercept anything headed their way. That was why they were there. As the colonel walked in, the crew recognized that walk just by the silhouette at the door, and they all snapped to attention. They saluted, he saluted, and then he waved them down. At ease. It's just me.

"Come for another look, sir?"

"Ja, they are beauties."

"Yes, sir, they sure are. Would you like to sit in one?"

The ladder was already in place for the pilot, but no. The colonel wisely declined.

"If I get in, I might not get out."

"Yes, sir."

"There are pilots here today?"

"Yes, sir, in the ready room."

The crewman pointed to a door, and the colonel took a moment to look at the door. Yes, that door there. Maybe it was time to talk.

"Ah, yes. Thank you."

"Yes, sir."

That was as good a time as any, Baden thought, to broach the subject of silly manned weather balloons with these serious fighter pilots. Would they be at all interested in at least pretending to sit in seats under a weather balloon? Or might that be insulting to their profession? The colonel designed aircraft, but he did not fly them. Certainly not fighter planes. He did, for a time as a young man before the war, fly small civilian planes, but wisely did not pursue that line of work during the war. He was content to sit at a desk. The overall risk seemed less if you didn't mind the bombs. The colonel walked through the door and the pilots stood at attention. So far, so good. There were smiles before words.

As Col. Baden sat down with the fighter pilots and had even more coffee with "The Pony Express" (they had to explain that one to him), Capt. Lewis had elected to stay right where he was and explore the situation at ground level in the NBA hangar. It had gotten surprisingly busy in there, even without the scheduled flights. As the captain walked around the huge hangar, he could see the empty space, still empty, where the one shot down belonged. No one was ready to fill that space just yet. Neither was he.

As for the other odd aircraft, the other NBAs that were still there, not a one of them looked as though it was anything that night actually fly. In every case, the lift gas had been pumped out of the bag, and that big silver cloth bag was folded, over and over, on top of the airframe that hung beneath it in flight. Even the odd black propellers had been pulled off of the engines, so there was no way to tell what these things might actually be. "Airplane" did not come to mind, and that was the whole point. Never look like what you are if what you are is a secret. The ground crew was doing minor routine maintenance on the machines, making sure that they *were* ready to fly, when and if. The captain stopped to chat with the crew. Everyone knew everyone. No secrets here.

"Will we fly again, sir?"

"Yes, but don't ask when."

"When? Oh, sorry..."

"As soon as people stop looking."
"The chimps are getting anxious."
"So am I."

Capt. Lewis kept walking as they were talking, with the idea that maybe these guys would shut up. Eventually he outpaced them, and they had work to do. As he walked alone, it got quiet, and then he was over on the other side of the hanger, looking at stretched out weather balloons and the piles of *things*. It was a whole different crew working over here. These were the underground guys, up on top to make this happen. Or not happen, depending. Smiles.

"Hello, sir."
"How's it going here?"
"We think we've got this. We think it will work."
"The fly or the lie?"
"We won't have to lie if we get it to fly."
"And you really think we can do that?"
"Yes, sir, I really do."

Captain Lewis took a closer look at the bits and pieces he could see there now. And were those lightweight flight seats? He pointed at two chairs bolted together facing opposite ways, just like the drawing he had seen. The guy standing there watching him smiled.

"Passenger seats out of spotter planes. They were the lightest we could find on base."
"Will they hold two fighter pilots?"
"If they don't mind sitting close."

The chairs were bolted to a floor frame, but there was no floor. Or anything else around the two flimsy chairs, for that matter. That concerned the captain. His smile went away.

"What are we doing for a cabin?"
"We're looking into small shipping containers, but they're all steel. We'd like to find aluminum."
"All about the weight?"
"Yes, sir. These balloons don't have near the lift of the NBAs, even if we used hydrogen, which we can't use in these. Too dangerous."
"So do you think this will actually work?"

The team member stopped smiling and stood up straight and tall. He was rather proud of this mess of parts.

"Yes, sir, I do."
"Then you keep at it, and you make it work.

"Yes, sir."

"Good man. Carry on."

"*Versagen Nicht.*"

"Yep."

Capt. Lewis walked out a little taller than he had walked in. When all of this had started, he figured he'd be lying to the press about those fake manned weather balloons. Now it looked as though he could offer them rides in the things. All the way to Africa. He smiled at the mere thought of it. Great way to get rid of them. And how many would he need? Then he thought maybe he'd just walk over to the PX for a Coke.

But not a coffee.

CHAPTER 10

CLAYTON LUCKED OUT. IT WAS STILL THE SUMMER OF 1947. There was no easy way for the landlord who had just thrown him out to warn every other landlord in town about this crazy UFO guy and his "collection." Oh, the landlord called a couple of his friends around town that he knew rented rooms, and he warned them about the blithering nutcase with all the junk, but there were more rooms for rent than he had friends in town. The odds were not in his favor, and Clayton never bothered with doing the math anyway. He was more of a live-in-the-moment kind of guy. And at that moment, he and Blanche were back out in the desert looking for more stuff. Of course they were. Where else would they go?

With the idea that they had no place to sleep that night quietly slipped onto the mental back burner of a stove that wasn't on, Clayton drove back out to the crash scene, to the area where they felt the debris had *started* to land. The first things to hit the ground. Somehow, Clayton thought that this was the place to be, the place to find the more important bits and pieces of that UFO. He was still convinced that was what it was, just as Blanche was ever more sure that it was not. They themselves were from two very different worlds. No, not literally. Geesh.

Clayton Whittaker was, for the lack of a better label, a pre-nerd. He kept his shirts buttoned up and his pants belted high. White socks every day. But no broken-framed glasses, oddly enough. He wore no glasses at all, not even sunglasses in the desert, and he was younger than he looked. Young enough to have escaped the various hazards of the last big war, but barely. He would have had to go to war in late 1945, but by then, the whole thing was over and the draft board was confused, so go home, Clayton. We'll call you if we need you. They never called. They did not need him. Big shock there.

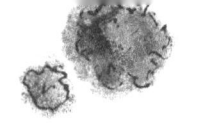

Home for Clayton was beautiful downtown Irvine, California, but that only added to his overall youthful confusion, as you might imagine. He grew up too far from the film industry to be a movie star, and too far from the beach to be a surfer. He was too early for computers and too late to be a cowboy. It was a confusing time for a young man on the lam. He worked at the grocery store after high school, saved his money, bought an old car and fled town after lunch. (Stopped to buy more catnip on his way out of town.) Figured he'd just go east until the next ocean stopped him. Got as far as Roswell, but he found a friend along the way.

Blanche Miller ran away from home but had turned eighteen by the time they got to Roswell. Just. Clayton totally lucked out there, but he never knew it. He never asked. And why did she run away from home on her eighteenth birthday? It was nothing more than the boredom of living in a small desert town. It was the thought of a wild and random adventure. A road trip. And Clayton did look mostly harmless when he stopped in Winslow for gas and a Coke. He bought one for her, he smiled (he did have a nice smile) and the deal was sealed. They ran away to nowhere together, and this was as far as they got. By then she was thinking she had maybe lucked out there, too. She still wasn't that far from home. She could get back. She kept looking back west. Yep, not that far at all. She had never even heard of UFOs before she met this guy, and by now, she had heard enough. West is that way, right?

Clayton parked the car on a hill, as he so often did, Blanche gave him a smile and he jumped and ran. Not because of the smile. This had become his obsession, this crash and the idea that what had crashed was a flying saucer from another planet. Blanche wasn't quite sure what to blame for this. Hollywood or the catnip? Had Clayton maybe been dropped as a baby? Fallen off of his bicycle a little harder than most? She had no idea, but then, here she was, watching an almost grown man go running off into the desert to collect junk for his trunk. She just shook her head and got out of the car slowly. She had all day, and they truly had nowhere to go. She put on her hat and wondered where they might end up that evening. Where

CHAPTER 10

she might end up that evening. It was hot out there, and Clayton was already long gone. Not a problem.

While there was no doubt that Clayton already had enough trash in his car to build his own flying saucer, he was still on the lookout for *That Piece*. The one chunk of junk that would prove, beyond a shadow of a doubt, that it had been a UFO from the planet Xyphon X-1. (He had just made that up the day before, but it sounded great, and he kept it.) Something with cryptic alien runes would be perfect. He was on the hunt, and he had the plan, to go back to where the stuff hit first. Start at the top. And that's where they were, upstream from where most of the debris had fallen, and where the craft, whatever it was, had at least begun to fall, if not actually hit. The debris had to be fresher there. If there was anything there. What was there? Anything? Maybe a little, but you had to look lots. And mind the snakes. Always mind the snakes.

Without really thinking about it, Blanche had seen which way Clayton had gone when he got out of the car, and she, too, went that way, if only to make it easy for her to rescue him later. She knew it would come to that. It seemed as though it always did. And did she need a big snake stick yet? Maybe not yet, but she did start to look for one, out of habit if nothing else. No stick. There was plenty of stuff, but no stick. Oh well. So she looked at the stuff that was there. Burnt stuff and other stuff, desert stuff. She could tell the difference, but Clayton, city boy that he was, could not. He just picked up everything that he found that wasn't a cactus or coyote. She was a bit more selective about what she picked up. Clayton being the exception to that rule, obviously.

They were walking in easy sight of each other but walking some small distance apart. Things found were held up as descriptions were yelled back and forth. Clayton was finding nothing but incredible UFO parts and pieces, of course, and he knew exactly what each one was. Of course he did. Blanche held up flowers and knew them all by name. As if Clayton would know the right name if she yelled it. So she started making up other names just to see if he knew. Nope, he didn't know. What fun! But then, as they walked farther upstream from the downwind debris, Blanche started to find truly interesting things. Brass things. Of the .50 caliber variety. Those she did *not* wave at her crazy friend. Those she hid.

The first one she wrote off as a fluke, but she kept it anyway. It was cool. The second one made it real, and she automatically looked up into the bright, and very empty, blue sky overhead. And when she looked back down there was a third one over there. They all got silently saved, and there were more. They were all fresh, clean, shiny brass and not a one of them was burnt. They hadn't been out in the desert for very long. Just got there, by the looks of them. Clayton was still waving stupid stuff and yelling. She looked up, smiled and waved back, but made sure she did not wave a brass casing. All were hidden. All were kept. He'd never know. He could keep his silly UFO, she had a serious mystery going on here. Or maybe not. Maybe now she knew.

By the time they decided to turn around and head back to the car, she knew what she knew. Someone shot down something. Did the Army Air Force shoot down a UFO out over the desert? No, it did not, and she had the proof with that clothing label she found in the tree the other day. Did they shoot down one of their own? That was what it was starting to look like, but there was no telling what the Russians were wearing those days. She thought she knew for sure it was not an alien flying saucer from whatever planet Clayton had just made up. She'd bet the spent brass she found out there in the sand on that one.

Now as they walked back toward the car, Blanche made a point of walking over closer to Clayton and getting him to walk farther over *that* way, away from where she had found all of the brass. No need for him to find one, even if he'd never make the connection, just to be on the safe side. That side over there. Go that way. He did. He was easily misled. She liked that about him.

As they got closer to the car, there were more people out there in the middle of that nowhere desert. Was it the weekend? And who were all of these people? And why were they all walking toward them smiling? Because they all knew a nut when they saw one, and maybe this would be fun. They were all carrying things. Burnt things and other things. Clayton was happy. This was his element, and he was in it.

The locals could see that Clayton was a nut, but a harmless nut, and if they gave him stuff, he was a happy nut. This was an easy way to clean up the desert and get rid of the junk none of them wanted anyway, and they sure didn't need to have their horses trip over any of that crap out there. *So here, kid, what part is this?* Clayton always knew. Smiles all around.

By then, both Clayton and Blanche felt they knew what had happened out there, in the stormy skies over that open desert not so very long ago. While not calling it an interplanetary invasion, Clayton was completely convinced that an alien UFO had crashed in the desert, in that storm, and the bodies had been picked up by the Army and hidden on the base. And the Army had their own flying saucers, of course. He had seen one go flying away that day. Big round silver thing. Couldn't miss it. He hoped to rebuild the crashed UFO with the parts he had been collecting, and if anyone had any more, he would be interested in seeing what they had. Blanche's eyes were starting to hurt from all of the rolling.

Blanche, as she listened to all that Clayton had to say to anyone that would listen, was pretty sure she knew better. She, too, had found a few things out in that desert, but far fewer than Clayton. Small things. Important things. Serious things. Just two things alone made all of the difference; the clothing label told her the aliens were not all *that* alien, and the brass casing told a very bad tale, indeed. Somehow, for some reason, the Army had to shoot down one of their own. Had they been infiltrated by the Russians? Had the crew turned? Something had gone horribly wrong up there in that storm, and they had to be brought down. And she had the proofs. Quite a few of them, actually. Would she ever know more? Know the whole story? She doubted it, and Clayton's version had to be more fun. No wonder he was so popular. She smiled as she watched him deal with the locals.

It didn't take very long after the crash for Clayton Whittaker to be "that saucer guy" in Roswell, especially if you were the type that ate out a lot, as Clayton and Blanche always did. You saw him, he saw you, and more often than not, he was talking about flying saucers, whether you were or not. It was his number one (and only) topic of conversation. Wanna talk about something else? Try talking to the girl next to him. She's got a wider range. But the saucer guy? Yeah, there ya go, saucers.

It became his mission and his obsession. He didn't care about anything else, news, weather or sports. Didn't listen to the radio (his car had one, but did it even work?), and Blanche had never seen him even pick up a newspaper. Pretty sure he could read. Maybe…

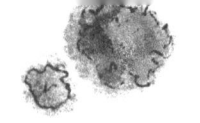

Oh, wait. Now she was curious about that. *Could* he read? She might have to test him on the subject. But not today. Or maybe later. Blanche smiled. She had a new goal. This could be fun. She started to watch him very closely. To see if he read *anything*. Ever. It was not looking good...

Mostly what Clayton did was talk. Make things up and talk. He had become, in his own mind at least, the local self-proclaimed expert on the UFO, on the flying saucer that had crashed outside of town the other day. He could tell you all about it, and you didn't even have to ask. Just pretend to listen. You had no choice in the matter. There was no off switch. Most folks were at least polite about it at first, and yes, they might listen for a while, but there never seemed to be a big finish, or even a stopping point, so after a while, people just sort of drifted away. Or ran when they saw him coming. They did that a lot, too.

Blanche simply held back a step or two and followed along behind to take it all in and watch people's reaction to a genuine nutjob. You don't often get a real live nutjob in a small town like Roswell, but thanks to the crash, they now had at least one. And he was a live one. Blanche watched, waiting to see if he ever stopped to read anything. *Anything*. A menu. A street sign. A candy bar wrapper. Nothing. He read nothing. His eyes never seemed to recognize the existence of lettering. This got to be a fascinating thing for her to focus on. It was either that or hop the next bus west. She thought about that, too.

After a few hours out in the hot sun and the great white desert, the car was full, and they were empty. It was time for a late lunch or an early dinner, depending on how the car felt about starting. Clayton carefully packed his latest prize pieces on the floor behind the front seat. Blanche had her fine collection of .50 caliber brass shells safely tucked in her big handbag, and she kept both hands on that bag. Clayton had never expressed an interest in the bag, and she didn't want him to start now. She wanted very much for the car to start now, but she knew that wasn't going to happen, either.

Clayton's old car had a bad starter. Or maybe it had no starter at all, Blanche never knew for sure. That's why he always tried to park it on a hill, and he could start it rolling forward or backward. He was good at that, but the hill was the thrill. No hill, no thrill. And then she had to push. Yes, really, *she* had to push start the car. To his credit,

CHAPTER 10

Clayton had explained the situation to Blanche right from the start, when he met her in the gas station back in Arizona, and she asked if it wasn't kind of dangerous to gas the car with the engine running. He pointed out that the tank was in the back and the engine was in the front, so no worries, but yeah, a bad starter. She shrugged and got in anyway. How bad could it be? She was learning. He gave her That Look.

"Can you?"

"Guess I have to."

"Guess you do."

Blanche put her secret stash handbag on the floor on her side up front, hiked up her skirt and kicked her feet a little deeper into her boots. Yeah, she could do this. She looked at the road. Looked about level, but was it? Clayton could feel which way the car wanted to roll, even if she couldn't see it.

"Which way?"

"Forward!"

"You got it!"

Clayton was convinced that Blanche could not possibly drive a stick shift car. His was three-on-the-tree, and yeah, it's not the easiest machine to drive smoothly. He did okay, but he was sure she just could not possibly handle such manual machine complexity. She let him think that and pushed the old car down the road out of sheer mad anger every time. She was getting good at that. She could feel him shift the car into second through her hands on the car body and knew to stop pushing then and let it roll on ahead of her. He'd let out the clutch, the car would bounce, cough, start and go. He'd get it stopped down the road, she'd climb in and they were off. Sure, it was getting harder to push with all that junk on board, but maybe she could get him to put more air in the tires. That would help.

With the car running and stopped, Blanche hoofed it up the road and jumped in. Handbag still there? Yep. She looked over at Clayton, who simply stared back. No "thank you"? No "thank you." Doofus, duly noted.

"You owe me lunch."

"Back in Roswell?"

"No, in St. Louis. I know a place there."

"It's gonna take quite a while to get to St. Lou—"

"Roswell, Clayton. Just drive back into Roswell."

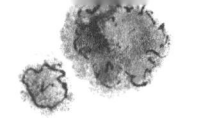

"But you said…"
"It was a joke. My fault. Won't happen again."
"Oh."

With her little background investigation still on her mind, Blanche had a plan: Stop somewhere new. Make him read a menu he didn't have memorized. That might be fun. As they rolled down Main Street, she offered up no after no for all the places they had been before, before she saw the one they had never been to at all, Mama Tucker's. Right there! She pointed and he looked.

"Let's eat there!"
"There?"
"Yes, there!"
"Okay…"

We have to give Clayton a little credit here, as he did find a slight incline and made sure he parked the car to make it easy to roll start after lunch. That helped a little. It also helped that Blanche could see the bus station from there. That helped her a lot. Big smile. Yeah, let's eat. He was buying, but she brought in her purse full of brass anyway, still not sure if the car locked.

Mama Tucker's was busy with a late lunch crowd, so Clayton and Blanche went for a couple of spinning stools at the counter. The menu was posted in big letters across the top of the opposite wall, and Blanche watched Clayton very carefully. He never even glanced at the folded menus on the counter, but he squinted at the wall. So maybe he needs glasses? Maybe so. Then came the jolt—he was driving. He needed glasses and he was doing all of the driving. Oh, boy. Life just got interesting as the waitress showed up in front of Blanche first.

"What'll it be?"
"The soup and sandwich special, please."
"You got it. To drink?"
"Got Coke?"
"Yep."

The waitress looked at Mister Squinty. She tried squinting back at him, but he didn't notice.

"And what'll it be for you, Dead Eye?"
"Can I get a ham and Swiss on rye?"
"Sure, but it'll be beef, that okay?"
"That's okay."

CHAPTER 10

"And cheddar, no Swiss."
"Okay."
"On white bread?"
"Sure."
"You got it."
"Mayo?"
"Don't press yer luck."

The waitress took off for kitchens unknown as Clayton was thrilled to tell Blanche about everything he found that day that she saw him find. All she had to do was sit, smile and know that he would never ask what she might have found. Not that she would tell him. She looked down at her handbag, safe at her feet. Still there. Still safe. Like a pecan in the bakery, Clayton was on a roll.

"I wonder how much of it I could actually build."
"Of what crashed?"
"Of the flying saucer, yeah. Do you think I have enough to build one?"
"Oh, at least one."

Clayton's eyes went wide. "Wait, how many were there? Do you think two UFOs hit together and that's what caused the crash?"

Blanche couldn't resist. She knew it was wrong to lead him on like that, but the girl couldn't help herself. It was just so much fun! She tried to not smile and was quite serious. And was that the ladies' room right back there? It was.

"Maybe they weren't used to flying in the air."
"Of course! They were used to flying in space! The air caused them to crash!"

Arnie Benton had heard the whole conversation from his stool at the counter and had to scoot closer to hear more. Of course he did. Arnie Benton was a reporter for the El Paso Times, and he was supposed to go back to El Paso that afternoon, since this whole crashed weather balloon story thing was kind of a waste, until just right then and there. So maybe it wasn't a manned weather balloon? Maybe it was something else? Arnie was leapfrogging the lunch counter stools until he was right next to Clayton, who had been looking the other way, at Blanche, the whole time. She saw him coming, but Clayton didn't. That's why Clayton jumped when Arnie finally spoke.

"So you think it was a flying saucer that crashed out there?
"*WAH!*"

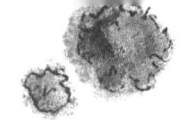

"Oh. Sorry. Arnie Benton, El Paso Times. And you are?"

"Clayton Whittaker, Irvine, California."

Clayton never raised a hand, so Arnie put his back down. Clayton also failed to mention the nice young lady sitting right next to him. Blanche didn't mind. As a matter of fact, she liked it that way and looked the other way. Arnie had his notepad out by then and pencil at the ready. And Clayton was ready.

"It was a flying saucer, you say?"

"Oh, yeah, it had to be. I've got about half of it in my car if you want to take a look."

"I might just do that later, but tell me more now."

All Blanche could do was give it one great, big eye roll, slip off the high lunch counter stool and make her way to the ladies' room. Maybe her soup and sandwich special would be waiting for her when she got back. If she wasn't so very hungry, it would have been a beeline for the bus station about then, but no, food first. Well, after this quick pit stop. She knew she wasn't going to miss a thing out there. Not for a good long while. Poor Arnie. He had no idea. Or maybe he did.

Arnie was thrilled to meet a genuine UFO nutcase. He had heard about them, of course, but had never actually met one. He was all smiles and was planning to milk this cow for every last drop. And he did have a camera in his car. This was going to be great. He could make a story out of this! With photos! That whole weather balloon thing was nothing. Nothing to it. The usual government cover-up, but if this was what they were covering up, he was all over it!

"So where do you think they are from, these flying saucers?"

"I'm thinking they had to have come from Xyphon X-1. It's the only planet advanced enough, you know."

Arnie nodded his head, as serious as he could be, as Blanche walked up behind Clayton at that moment, heard what he said and had to turn right back around to not get caught laughing so very hard. At least she knew where the ladies' room was. By the time she got back the *second time*, her food was there, and she gracefully moved her lunch a couple of places away so as not to be seen as a part of that scene. She was sure her name would not get mentioned. It had better not.

Maybe she'd just wait in the bus station.

For the bus.

CHAPTER 11

COL. BADEN HAD QUIETLY ARRANGED A FOLLOW-UP PUBLIC press conference without telling Capt. Lewis until that morning. Late that morning. As in right before lunch, which was before the conference that afternoon. And as funny as that wasn't, no one laughed. There also wasn't much Capt. Lewis could do about it, either. Baden was his superior officer, and dealing with both the public and the press was part of the captain's job in the Western Witch Project, even if that project was never, ever named in front of the public or the press. Hiding it was a big part of the job.

"You have a meeting at one today."

"With whom?"

"With whomever shows up."

"Oh."

"You're welcome."

Capt. Lewis could only smile at his shrewd commanding officer and silently thank him in a great many other ways and in two different languages. The captain also considered learning French just to annoy the colonel. That might be fun. In the meantime, and to his credit, the colonel did manage to give the captain very little time to worry over that sudden public meeting. About an hour, tops. Just enough time for lunch. With a quick bite to eat, the good captain elected to leave his personal car right where it was and drive his assigned jeep across the base to the public meeting. It was much less conspicuous, and he wanted that about now. Get in, get out and get gone. He got all of that, but he almost didn't get there in time. Had to find a parking space first.

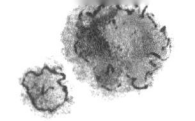

The meeting room at the one public building at the front of the base was surprisingly crowded by the time he walked in. So much so that the captain started to worry about exactly what Col. Baden had said when he had announced this meeting. Why were all of these people here? What were they expecting him to say? He had no idea. There was no doubt he was getting a bad feeling about all of this and, as he looked around, he did not see the colonel in the crowd, either. Or at the back door, as he usually was. Mighty lot of people in that room. They can't all be reporters. *Ah, well,* he thought. *Here we go.* The captain tried to smile but wasn't so sure he got it right.

"Good afternoon."

There were polite murmurs from the crowd, and the first hand up in the air was a guy front and center. The raised hand was holding a pencil, the other hand a reporter's pad. No doubt about this guy, and he did look vaguely familiar. A reporter, but not a local. Maybe El Paso? Yeah, had to be. No name came to mind. Capt. Lewis adjusted his smile to see if he could get it to fit and pointed at the guy.

"Yes?"

"Will we be hearing more about the UFO that crashed off base today?"

"The UFO?"

As soon as he said it out loud, he knew he said it wrong. He should have said, "*What* UFO?" Too late to take it back. The captain was already down by one, and the game had just begun. Arnie Benton, the reporter from El Paso, smiled and went in for the extra point. Big Texas smile. Almost a disturbing grin.

"Yes, we all understand the base has the crew from the craft, we were just all wondering when we might see more of the flying saucer itself. Maybe get some photos?"

Capt. Lewis felt the room spin, just a little. They were two questions in, and it was already out of control. All he thought he was going to do today was talk about the manned weather balloons and about how those flights might resume soon and maybe mention the crew without naming them, and now this? A UFO? Where did *that* come from? And who *was* this guy?

"Excuse me, but you are…?"

"Arnie Benton, El Paso Times."

"Ah, yes, of course. That's in Texas, right?"

That got a small laugh, and even Arnie had to smile. Score one for the captain, but he was still down on the board. And now it was the captain's turn to go for the extra point.

"Mister Benton, if we *had* a UFO, which we don't, it might be unlikely that we would say that we did, don't you think?"

"But it crashed. Pieces were everywhere."

"We're talking about the debris on the Foster Ranch, yes?"

Arnie didn't know. He looked around the room and saw the local people looking right at him and nodding their heads, yes.

"Yes, sir, I believe we are."

Now the captain offered up a fine, sly smile. The score is even, and he's going in for one more. Better take notes, kids, this is how it's done. The captain looked out over the crowd and waved a hand, pointing at everyone and no one.

"Before I go any further, I have to ask, are there any Russians in the room? Any Communists at all? Anyone? Anyone? Yes? No?"

Again, the captain got a solid laugh with that and the upper hand, and even Arnie had to kind of duck down and let the man run the show. It was his show now. It always was. No smile from the captain now. This just got serious. As opposed to real.

"I can tell you that we are working a new type of high-altitude observation platform. We're calling it a manned weather balloon, but it might be something more than that."

A voice in the crowd, not Arnie: "Will it be armed?"

"Not for now, no. We're still very much in the testing phase."

"How high is high-altitude?"

The captain smiled. This was going well now. About time.

"Higher than the building we're standing in right now."

"But..."

The captain lowered his head and gave the questioner a Very Stern Look. He shut up.

"*Oh.*"

"Yes. Well, we are not yet to the point that we can say much about it, other than to say that we can't say. When we can say, we will."

"So it was a manned weather balloon that crashed?"

Capt. Lewis did hesitate for that one split-second. He still did not like this weather balloon idea, and hated the idea of having to confirm it, but he was stuck with it for now. But not for long. For all of about three seconds, as it turned out. Then a new voice, a louder, shriller voice spoke up. It was Clayton, wide-eyed, with his arm up.

"It was a crashed UFO, and I can prove it!"

Frantic to find the source of that statement, Capt. Lewis saw Clayton Whittaker in the crowd, all mad smiles, looking all around the room and pointing at him. Great. Just great. The captain recognized the kid, and yep, there was Blanche right next to him, and both of them were standing near that reporter. How cozy. The captain kept his smile as the room went silent, and then he looked over at the reporter.

"Arnie, maybe you should be interviewing this guy!"

"Already have."

"And?"

"He's got quite a collection."

Clayton barged in again, and again too loud. Blanche had already stepped away.

"Enough to build a flying saucer!"

And the captain for the win: "Well then, son, I think you should."

There was more small laughter around the room, but Clayton was too wildly focused to hear it. This was his big chance. Blanche heard it all, from an increasing distance.

"Well then, I think I will!"

"Well then, I think we're done here. Thank you all for coming over today."

Now everyone else in the room, Arnie included, was completely unsure about what had just happened. That crash, was it a weather balloon or a UFO? And was that kid really going to build one? Was this all some kind of joke? Were UFOs real? Was that crash even real? No one knew whether to laugh or not. And was this over already? Should they go now? Capt. Lewis gave it a try. May as well lead by example and leave. All he had to do was get through the crowd.

The captain could see Clayton and that reporter in a heated discussion in the middle of the room, so he went for the wall. The far wall. Yeah, he could slip around that way, along the wall and out the door. Everyone else was looking somewhere else and no one was looking at him. Well, almost no one. Blanche wasn't blinking an eye. She was looking right at him. Involuntarily, as he looked at Blanche, he fingered his wedding ring. Yep, still there. Still married. And does that girl *ever* blink? He tried smiling. She smiled back. Hers was the better smile by far. There was no doubt where this was going. She was coming right at him. No way out. And he was *that* close to the door. Almost gone, but not quite.

As they met, both smiled, but neither one said a word. She put her hand out as if to shake his. Gentleman that he was, he put his hand out to shake hers, but that wasn't what she had in mind. He felt the cold brass he now held in that hand, and he knew exactly what it was without having to look down. She kept her smile, but then she looked down and walked away without saying a word, leaving Capt. Lewis standing there, all alone in that crowded room, holding a spent .50 caliber brass shell from a P-51 Mustang. He wasn't smiling any more. He was in shock. And she was gone. He slipped the shell into his pants pocket and made his way out of the room. Finally.

Just as the press and the public turned right and went out the front door, Capt. Lewis turned left and went for a cup of coffee. He knew where he could go that they could not, and he needed that cup of coffee bad. Doors were opened for the man in uniform. Here, have a hot cup. Staff understood.

"Bad meeting?"
"Strange meeting."
"Strange good or strange bad?"
"Not sure yet."
"So it's not bad yet?"
"No, not yet."
"That's good."

Capt. Lewis tried to see through the door, to see what Blanche was doing. It wasn't working. No X-ray vision, but he had coffee, and that made him smile. It was good coffee. Strong. He needed that right about then.

"I guess..."

She knew, and he knew she knew, but how did she know? She must have found that brass out on the Foster Ranch. It wasn't a desert relic. It looked brand new. She must have done the math. Then Capt. Lewis did the math. She's the dangerous one. Not Clayton, not Benton, and not the locals. That girl knew more about what was going on than most of the staff on base. He was sure of it now. A Russian spy? No, she was something worse, a clever girl.

Capt. Lewis looked around. He was going to need more coffee. Ah, there it is.

As Capt. Lewis sipped strong coffee behind locked doors, the small crowd that had stopped by for the public press conference had all made their way back outside to their cars. Clayton and Arnie were in deep discussion now as they stood at the back of Clayton's desert-dusty car, talking about how to build a flying saucer. Only one of them was serious. The other was a reporter from El Paso. Blanche stayed back, but others, local people who had followed Clayton out just to hear what he had to say, all joined in.

"How did you know it was a UFO?"

"What else could it be?"

"Well, the officer said it was a manned weather balloon."

"Have you *seen* the men?"

"Well, no..."

"You wanna know why?"

"Why?"

"Because there *weren't* any men."

"So it was unmanned?"

"IT WAS AN ALIEN SPACESHIP!"

"So ... where are the aliens?"

And this is where someone else spoke up quietly.

"In the base hospital. Dead."

That stopped the party for a minute, but then someone got it going again.

"Let's see what you got in yer trunk, son."

Clayton popped the latch and raised the heavy steel trunk lid. He propped it up with a stick. The back of the car was crammed full of all sorts of odd bits of pieces of *something*, there was no doubt about that. But what?

"That's a flying saucer?"

"*Was.*"

"You think you can build something out of that?"

"I can sure try."

"I wanna see it when yer done."

"Me, too!"

"OKAY!"

By then, Clayton really was excited about building a UFO from that pile of burnt, broken trash in the back of his car, Arnie was

CHAPTER 11

wondering just exactly how much truth he was looking at in the back of that same car, and Blanche was wondering if the village of Irvine missed its idiot. Capt. Lewis, now standing outside a short distance away and taking it all in, was wondering why they didn't all just please leave. Blanche looked up, saw him and smiled. He offered a silent thank you with a gentleman's polite nod. She did have a nice smile.

One by one, the civilians all found their cars and drove away, each of them pondering the idea that maybe there *was* something to that UFO thing. Something *did* crash, and the kid was really sure about what he saw, and then there were those dead aliens in the hospital, and sure, yeah, UFOs. Why not? Capt. Lewis just shook his head and went for his jeep. Maybe he could hide out in the underground monkey jungle for the rest of the afternoon. Pretty sure the monkeys wouldn't mind. Maybe he'd offer them coffee. That might be fun.

By the time Clayton sat down behind the wheel of his old car, it was down to just him, Arnie and Blanche in the parking lot. Blanche very quickly explained the situation to Arnie and, gentleman that he was, he told her to step back. He had this. The parking lot was pool-table flat, so it hardly mattered which way they went with it. Clayton aimed for the front gate. That was nice of him. And Blanche did help, ignoring Arnie's protests. It was so much easier with two! Wow! She could get used to that. Bump, roar, thank you, gone! Blanche jumped in the front seat as Arnie went for his own car, all smiles for everything he had seen and learned that day. All about UFOs.

But did he believe a word of it? He was, after all, a reporter, and reporters were not supposed to believe anything without the facts to back it up. So what's the fact, Jack? He listed the facts silently in his head as he drove slowly off the base. The guard at the gate waved. Nice of him.

Fact: Something odd crashed on the Foster Ranch. There was too much debris for it to be a weather balloon, manned or not, and not enough crap scattered around out there for it to be an airplane, and most of it was badly burnt. That was a fact.

Also fact: There were bodies taken to the base hospital. Not human bodies, from the sound of it. From the descriptions offered, they were shorter, human-like forms with longer arms, larger eyes and almost no noses. Grey. Hairless. (Burnt.) Obviously alien. Arnie was tempted to joke about Mexican midgets escaped from the

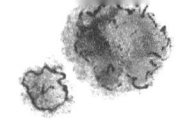

Tijuana Traveling Circus (hey, they'd be alien!), but no. He did not. This was something else entirely. Something serious. But what? Arnie kept driving. And Arnie kept thinking. Always thinking.

As it turned out, everyone came away from that quick little meeting thinking about something. Arnie was pondering the possible reality of aliens and spaceships, Clayton was pondering building a spaceship from the junk in his trunk, Blanche was pondering nice reporters from Texas, and Capt. Lewis was pondering young women handing him brass shell casings from a Mustang's machine guns. So, as it turned out, that quick little meeting had given them *all* something to think about. But now what would they do about it all?

Capt. Lewis parked his jeep in his spot by the NBA hangar and was headed back to his office by way of the coffee pot when he meet Col. Baden at that popular junction. Coffee all around! And all smiles, but both grim and happy. Baden asked about the meeting.

"So the meeting, it went well, ja?"

Capt. Lewis tried to smile but gave up as he poured a cup. Baden noticed that.

"It went off the rails."

"What is rails?"

"It was a train wreck."

"What train?"

Now the captain smiled, if only for the unintended confusion. The colonel spoke English. The captain spoke American. They were, in the words of Mark Twain, two men divided by a common language. The captain sipped his too-hot coffee, immediately regretted *that* and tried again.

"Now everyone thinks it was a UFO."

The German was confused. "UFO?"

"A flying saucer full of little aliens from another planet."

There was a long moment of silence as Col. Baden processed this new information, and then, slowly at first, a smile formed on the German's lips. A fine, wide, sly German smile of the sort you never want to see on anyone, and especially not on a German. He tried not to laugh.

"And was it not?"

"Well, no, of course not. It was a ... um ... *oh*."

CHAPTER 11

By then, Gorton Baden had set his coffee cup down, he was laughing so hard and loud. Everyone looked up and noticed and wondered what the captain had done that got that response. And how badly might this end for the captain? Not well was everyone's guess, but for once, they were all wrong on that count. The colonel finally braced himself on the closest table and was able to speak again, but still grinning from ear to ear. Still very happy. And the captain was still very confused.

"Ah, but don't you see, Captain? That has to be *exactly* what it was!"

"So now we pretend it was an alien spaceship?"

Baden waved a hand, still smiling as he faked a frown. "Oh, no, no, no, we can't tell them anything like that."

"But then..."

"But we can *tell them* that we can't tell them that."

Again, there was silence as Capt. Lewis began to process this new approach and understand just what Col. Baden had seen in all of this that he was just now seeing, but not yet liking. Soon, though. Very soon.

"So... We use the idea that we can't tell them that it was a UFO as an acknowledged denial?"

"JA! Reverse deniability! Do you not see?"

It was a twisty crooked road, but as Lewis came around the last bend, yes, he *could* see it now. The UFO they didn't have could replace the manned weather balloon they had to have, making it easier for all concerned and allowing him to lead everyone down a path of a wonderful real fantasy at no cost whatsoever to the United States Government. The Christmas Party Budget just got doubled. Slowly, carefully, it was his turn to smile as well. More so by the moment. *More coffee, Colonel?* Ja. Cups were refilled and it was time to plot and plan. And laugh. Now they could laugh.

"To my office, please."

"Yes, sir."

The two men, steaming cups in hand, went to the colonel's office and closed the door. Not that they had anything to hide from the staff. The staff in that building all knew the truth; they all knew *exactly* what had crashed. And they would be brought up to speed on this as well, just as soon as there was any speed to it at all. It was gaining all the time.

"So tell me all about the strange meeting, please."

Capt. Lewis started off mentioning the busy reporter from El Paso, but then he focused on the crazy guy, Clayton, and his loud UFO theory. Col. Baden smiled at that, as it gave them the easy out that they so desperately needed. They could hide the chimps and the NBA behind a UFO that didn't exist, and they wouldn't have to build a thing! When the captain mentioned Clayton threatening to build a UFO out of the crash debris he had in his car, Baden frowned. Lewis wasn't sure why that would be a problem.

"What if he does?"

"Does what, build a UFO?"

"Build an NBA from the crash debris."

"Gorton, that kid has no idea what he is building, and he's building from tangled, burnt crash debris with no plans whatsoever. Not even a photo of what it was."

"Yes, but how much debris does he have?"

"A whole carload."

"That is bad."

"He's not German."

"That is good."

"Should we confiscate the debris?"

"*Nein*, no, it might be amusing to see what the kid builds."

"And if he builds a UFO?"

"Then he supports our lie."

"The lie we can't tell?"

"Ja."

"So what's the worst that can happen with this?"

"Are there bodies?"

"Not anymore."

"Do we have the seats from the NBA?"

"Yes."

The colonel smiled, shrugged and sipped his coffee.

"Then there is nothing bad that can happen if he builds a UFO. Let him. But don't encourage him."

Col. Baden explained that the UFO was a much better lie than the whole manned weather balloon thing would ever be, as it made it sound more plausible that they *couldn't* say anything about it, it being a big government secret and all. So no comment. You understand. We simply say that we cannot say. We don't know who might be listening. The colonel winked. Capt. Lewis was catching on fast and liking it more.

"So all I have to do is say 'no' like I mean 'yes.'"

"JA! Can you do that?"

The captain dropped his smile and looked the colonel right in the eye.

"Absolutely not."

"*Was?* I... Oh... *Very good!*"

By now the captain was laughing and the colonel got the joke. Could the captain say "no" and mean "yes?" Of course he could. He was a married man. It was all part of the skill set. Capt. Lewis went over it all again, just to make sure he did understand the plan.

"So all I have to do is deny that we have a UFO."

"But make it sound as though we do by saying that we don't."

"How tough can that be?"

"For you, a piece of pie."

"Cake."

"Ja, cake."

"But we *don't* have a UFO."

"Ah, but they don't know that."

"So we lie like we do, when we don't?"

"Ah, but if we don't, it's not a lie."

"Now I'm confused again."

"And now all you have to do is confuse everyone else, just like you."

"Can I do that?"

"You're the perfect man for the job."

"Thank you?"

The colonel smiled, but the captain was still confused as he thought about this odd new reality. He wasn't sure if he was going to be lying about telling the truth or telling the truth about the lie. Either way, he was pretty sure this was going to be the easiest lie ever. No need for fake (or real) manned weather balloons, no need to coach fighter pilots in both acting and lying, or worse yet, really sending them up in a manned weather balloon. No need for anything, really, or anything real. Just tell the truth like you are lying. Just lie like you're lying. How tough could that be? Capt. Lewis was thinking that he was going to have to practice that. Pretty sure Julie could coach him on how to look even guiltier than usual.

It was all part of the skill set.

CHAPTER 12

THE MORE CAPTAIN ELI LEWIS THOUGHT ABOUT IT, THE MORE he liked this new, weird, Lie-About-the-UFO-It-Wasn't game. To lie about the truth. Except that, well, was it really a lie to say that he couldn't talk about it (because it wasn't true)? He never said there was nothing to talk about, only that he couldn't. It was more like the truth about the lie than anything else. It still confused him if he thought about it too much, so he didn't. He knew what he could say and what he could not say. All he had to do was tell the truth and make it sound like a lie. He also knew he would never need to mention anything about the entire Western Witch Project (the real truth), as the manned weather balloons were his fallback baseline in all of this. And those big chair bags were comin' right along! They might even fly soon!

Even with the whole crazy UFO thing gaining steam and more false credence every day, the team was still working on cobbling up those two very real manned weather balloons, and even he had to admit they were looking pretty good! He wasn't about to send anyone up in one, mind you, but it was nice to know that they were there if he needed to show someone *something*. And he still liked the idea of a couple of well-dressed mannequins, just to make it look good. And could they do that? His team assured him that they could. He had a good team.

In the meantime, he was pretty sure there had to be a UFO around there somewhere. Everybody said so, and they couldn't all be wrong, now could they? He kept looking. There was some small talk around

CHAPTER 12

the hangar about building one just to show it off, but he said no. Or at least not yet. It was supposed to be a lie, so they might not need it for real. Yet. And Capt. Lewis knew it was much better to let the public's wild imagination build that great, big, silver flying saucer in their minds. That way they'd never be disappointed in whatever the Army might have to offer.

"You know I can't say anything about any UFO."

"How about you tap once on the table for yes and twice for no?"

Capt. Lewis tapped twice on the table, and Arnie Benton laughed.

"Hey, it was worth a shot."

The captain just smiled.

Somehow, ace El Paso reporter Arnie Benton had been granted a one-on-one with Capt. Lewis to *not* talk about UFOs. Lewis blamed Baden, but Baden never quite got around to admitting it was entirely his fault. *Just meet with reporters*, he said. *You don't have to answer their questions. Give them a lot of coffee, get bigger mugs.* They got bigger mugs. It worked. It did speed things up, and meeting with Arnie Benton seemed like a safe bet. Capt. Lewis didn't mind this guy so much, and Arnie knew how to play the game. He knew it *was* a game. Some did not. But let's get this over with just the same.

"Arnie, do you know how much we do on this base that's public?"

"No, not really."

"We raise the flag every morning and we take it down every night."

"And everything else?"

"There is nothing else. That's all we do. And you can quote me on that."

The captain smiled. He loved this game, and Arnie enjoyed playing it.

"Mighty lot of land for one flagpole."

The captain got all squinty-eyed and looked around. "Oh, we've got two, but the other one's a secret. You can't print that."

"What *can* I print?"

"The flag's got 48 stars and 13 stripes. Over half of them are red."

"Sounds dangerous."

"It is if you mess with it."

"Hadn't planned on it."

That's when the captain turned the tables.

"How about I ask you the questions?"

"That might be interesting. Give it a try."

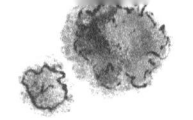

"Who's the goofy UFO kid?"

Arnie Benton was, at his core, a nice guy. It was a reasonable question, and the answer was not a secret. He flipped back a few pages in his notebook to make sure he got it right. The captain had earned that.

"The goofy UFO kid is one Clayton Whittaker from Irvine, California."

"Occupation?"

"Unknown, if any."

"Education?"

"He never said, and I never asked."

"But you're the reporter."

"He never gave me a chance. He never shuts up about UFOs."

"And who's the Bonnie to his Clyde?"

Arnie flipped forward a page or two. "Ah, here we go, Blanche Miller, 18 years old, from Arizona."

"Almost a local."

"So am I."

"So what is she doing with him?"

"Good question."

"I thought so."

"Not sure what she sees there. And neither is she."

"Hmmm."

"That's what I said."

"Do you think he's gonna build a flying saucer out of all that junk?"

"I think he's gonna try, and I sure hope he does. I could use the photo for the story."

"Do you really think there's a story here?"

Arnie looked around. He was in an office on a restricted military base talking to an officer who was nice enough to talk to him when he really didn't have to. He knew to play nice.

"Here? No. There's no story here. Just a flagpole. The story is Clayton now."

"Fair enough."

"You're welcome."

"More coffee?"

Capt. Lewis, as he got the reporter more coffee, said that he was pleased with how this interview had gone. The reporter got it, got what they both could say and could not say, and if there *was* a story in all of this, Lewis was pretty sure it was going to be said and printed clean, that is, no secrets spilled. And the captain let it be known that if it turned out that the big story was the weird kid, so much the better for all concerned. The officer walked the reporter to the door and made sure he was headed out the right way, as the wrong way might get him shot. No need for that. Yet. And as he watched the reporter leave, Capt. Lewis had to smile and marvel at how so very well it was all going now. Seemed a shame he had waited so long to take up lying. It made everything so much easier. Should have lied all along. Just think of the time saved!

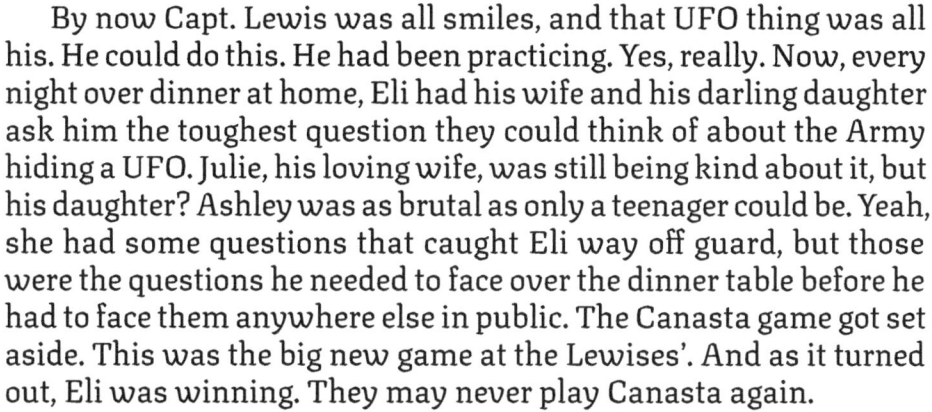

By now Capt. Lewis was all smiles, and that UFO thing was all his. He could do this. He had been practicing. Yes, really. Now, every night over dinner at home, Eli had his wife and his darling daughter ask him the toughest question they could think of about the Army hiding a UFO. Julie, his loving wife, was still being kind about it, but his daughter? Ashley was as brutal as only a teenager could be. Yeah, she had some questions that caught Eli way off guard, but those were the questions he needed to face over the dinner table before he had to face them anywhere else in public. The Canasta game got set aside. This was the big new game at the Lewises'. And as it turned out, Eli was winning. They may never play Canasta again.

The decision had been made and approved. Let the media and the public *think* the Army was hiding a crashed UFO and two dead aliens. Eli Lewis knew he could do that now. It sure beat telling the truth that he couldn't tell, and this was easy! Nothing to build, nothing to show! By then, the two chimps that were killed in the crash were the alien bodies being hidden at the hospital. Capt. Lewis: "I cannot comment on that, as there are parts of the hospital completely off limits to all personnel." And maybe there were, he didn't know. (Shrug.) In truth, the two dead chimps had been examined, cremated, and their ashes were still under lock and key in the back of the captain's office. Tell no one. And have you seen the flagpole?

The Army's game on the ground was going just as well. The ground crew that had rushed out into the desert that day after the crash had recovered all of the large pieces of the NBA that had come down, all of the pieces that could be identified for what they really were: The engines and props, the seat and controls, the landing gear. The bodies. A lot of the small pieces, burnt and bent, were left for the locals, and for Clayton. Mostly for Clayton. Captain Eli Lewis,

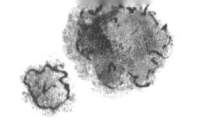

U.S. Army Air Force, was happy with this new angle of attack on the truth: Pretend to lie! It was almost fun!

Off the base and never all *that* far away, Clayton Whittaker was livid over the idea that the Army was hiding a flying saucer (and aliens!) on that big, restricted military base, and why wasn't that base open to the public? The taxpayers paid for it! Taxpayers owned it! It was his! Blanche had thought, for just a second, about asking Clayton if he had every really paid any taxes, but then thought better of it and let him roll. Her new calm was watching how other people dealt with the lunatic she was still sort of stuck with, but for how much longer? All good things must come to an end, but the crap just goes on and on. Blanche smiled. She knew the bus schedule. She could end this any time. Twice a day. But maybe not just yet. It was still sort of fun.

As annoying as her weird friend was, the whole scene, the entire series of odd events, was somehow fascinating. There was no doubt that something odd had happened out there on Foster's ranch, out in the open ranchland/desert in that broad, stark basin in that bad storm, but what? She knew for sure, something, some kind of unusual aircraft, came down in that wild storm that day, but maybe not entirely *because* of that wild storm. Maybe it was shot down, and maybe she had proof, but why did that have to happen? Why would the Army shoot down one of its own?

Blanche had thought about it a lot and was going with the idea of a rogue pilot. Maybe two. Had he (they?) stolen the plane? That made sense to her, but if they stole the plane, where did they get the flight suits? Could anybody buy one? No, they had to be regular pilots, but what went wrong? Were they *both* spies? That explained everything except one thing: If they were both a couple of Communist spies, how did the Army find out so late, after they took off and were flying away? Did they give them a "So long, comrade!" as they flew away? Yeah, that would about do it right there. Or maybe not. That was a long shot, no pun intended. Maybe there was way more to it all than just that. But she knew what she had. If only she knew what it meant.

In the purse she never let out of her sight (and slept with an arm through the strap), Blanche still had those shiny new .50 caliber brass shells, except for the one she gave to the nice captain. She also had that burnt flight suit label, that did seem to support her

CHAPTER 12

rogue pilot theory, and that burnt bit of hair that looked more like fur. That stuff was just nasty. She didn't look at it much but made sure she still had it. Maybe she needed to get that burnt hair tested, but where? How? For now it was safe in its own little brown paper bag, and that was safe in her purse. And she never let Clayton see what she had. Never mentioned it. He had no idea that she had any ideas. Or any pieces. Clayton was all about Clayton. Somebody had to be.

Giving the guy credit where credit was due, Clayton had found them a new pair of rooms in town, and the new landlord had a small shed on the side where Clayton could build his flying saucer if he so desired. By then Clayton was a sort of local oddity, if not an actual attraction. Almost a celebrity. He was tolerated by most and encouraged by some. The landlord smiled and the rent was paid. And Clayton got to at least pretend to build his flying saucer any time he wanted, just as long as he put all of his toys back in the shed every night when he was done. Fair enough.

Now Clayton's car was empty, and the shed was full. That made it easier to push, and Blanche appreciated that. And now Clayton was spending a lot of his time trying to make sense of all that he had in the shed and how he might actually build something from all of it. And could he? He would spend hours laying out parts, trying to make something like a flying saucer, not realizing that not everything he had came from the craft that crashed. To him, it was all alien technology. It had to be alien! Just look at it! What else could it be? Blanche was pretty sure that part there was Ford, but she said nothing. She just smiled and held tight to her purse.

Miss Miller was a tolerant young lady, but her tolerance for all of this was wearing thin. It had been a wonderful escape from her boring home town and a grand adventure on the road, and she was still not all that far from home. She could be back in a long day. An overnight bus trip west. She knew that by then, but then, there she was still. And why? Well, it *was* mildly amusing, and she did sort of want to see where it might all end up. Where Clayton might end up. And what sort of visiting hours they might have. She smiled at that, but not so much at him by then.

The shape he had laid out in the driveway in front of the shed was round. She had to give him that. He got the saucer shape right, at least. But it was way too small, no wider than the driveway leading up to the shed. This allowed him to put all of those broken pieces very close together, almost touching, in multiple circles with crossed supports. Almost well thought out if it hadn't been completely wrong. Now, she had no idea what it was *supposed* to look like, but she was fairly sure this wasn't it. Not sure why, but she was sure something was missing. Motors? Seats? Controls? She was making her own mental list when Clayton said he wanted to go look for more. For once she agreed. Good idea! Let's go right now! Her enthusiasm caught him off guard, but not for long. They ran for the car. It was a game, and the game was on! She even got him to help push the old car for once. What a guy! Let's go!

She had thought, in odd, quiet moments, about maybe faking pregnancy to get him to push the car more often, but no. It would be a tough sell. They never did anything, and he was too wrapped up in that whole UFO thing to do anything now. But he did just help push, so there was that. But was it a trend? Too early to tell, but she wasn't counting on it. She had her pushin' boots on. Still, what would he do if she told him? Might be good for a giggle just to see what he did. But not today. She was still too far from home and that last bus was already gone. And she'd need a small pillow. Maybe tomorrow. She smiled. Maybe later tonight.

With Clayton wrapped up in his own UFO build in Roswell, Arnie Benton had beat him back out into the desert earlier that day. They were both interested in the idea of a crashed UFO, but only one of them was taking it seriously. Benton was going on the theory that whatever it was, it was most likely not from... What was that planet Clayton said? Saffron B-12? Something like that. Arnie smiled. Wacky kid. But his editors liked the whole UFO story idea, and now they wanted photos. Of *what*? He had no idea, but he was pretty sure it wasn't in town. Back to the sand, camera in hand!

It almost didn't matter where he went for those photos. Any desert shot was a good desert shot, and what would any shot show? It would show whatever he said it showed. Arnie knew that, by then, most of the good debris had been found and taken, especially the big stuff the Army wanted. That went fast the first day, and he knew those guys were out late that night. Clayton came along after and had pretty much swept the sand clean. What he didn't find, other people gave him, and some of it was even from the crash! But not all of it. Arnie knew that, too. So whadda we got out here? A tree over there? Okay, we got a tree.

CHAPTER 12

Arnie parked his car, got out and checked his camera. Eight shots left on the roll. Make 'em count. Arnie pulled his hat down for the shade and made his way off the road and into the sand. Snakes? No snakes. Good. Just keep looking. Head for the tree. He looked up at the sun. Better shoot from over there. A minor course correction. He had all day and the desert to himself. No need to rush this, just get the shots, finish off the roll and head back into town. Maybe even get them mailed to the newspaper today. His editor would appreciate that. And look! Tracks!

The military truck tracks ran deep in the sand and straight for the tree. Arnie followed them, keeping one eye on the tree just to frame that first shot. Here? No, there. Yes, right there! Steady, steady, push. *Click*. Got it. Wind the film. Always wind the film. It gets weird if you don't. But then he thought about that. Maybe a weird double exposure would be good for this story. He should have bought more film. Arnie made it to the tree. It looked busy there. Yeah, he should have bought more film.

As he circled the tree, he could see the tracks everywhere, big truck tracks, smaller jeep tracks, and all sorts of footprints. Not all were military. Hey, *those* could be alien! (In truth, they were Blanche's.) Arnie found a spot that offered both the small alien footprints and the larger Army boot prints. Perfect! Check the sun. Shoot from over here. Yeah! *Click*. Got it! Wind. What else? Over there! Fire!

Well, an old campfire. Nothing to do with the crash. Arnie walked around it but didn't get near. No need to add his prints to this shot. *Let's see, pick up stick, move the old fire around, push the rocks that way... Sort of in a line... Yeah. That works.* Arnie pitched the stick and looked around. It needed something. Something. Anything. *That* thing. There was an old piece of rusted steel ranch trash half buried in the sand. Bigger than it looked. Bigger was good. Arnie dug it up and hefted the thing. *Ugh. Yeah, this'll work.* He judged his pitch and threw the steel. It landed in the thickest part of the old campfire. Take a good long look. No tracks? No tracks. Perfect. Get the shot. *Click*. Got it. Wind. Okay, now what?

With the idea that he would finish off the roll and mail it to his editor that afternoon, Arnie did a long walk around back to his car and shot some pretty good generic desert scenes, in case the editor wanted to get all artsy about it. Or maybe they could use them for another story later. He didn't care and it didn't matter. Back to the car, back into town, get the roll mailed and then call the newspaper. *Hey, we got a story here! It's headed your way today!* His editor was happy, and yeah, this was a story. They'd get the film developed, run some test prints and go from there. How soon? A couple of days. Maybe next weekend, the big Sunday edition if they want to make a big deal out of it. Arnie was told to stay in Roswell and stay on the story. And could he get some photos of those aliens? Sure, yeah, why not?

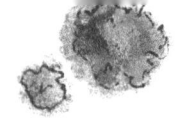

The ball was rolling a little faster every day. The newspaper in El Paso ran the story about the crash, the *UFO* crash, with Arnie's desert photos, in the Sunday paper and the wire service picked it up. Flying saucers in New Mexico! The lie began to spread. There was no stopping it now, as if there ever was. And there was going to be no stopping Arnie and Clayton, from the looks of it. Arnie Benton was "the reporter on the scene," even if he wasn't the only reporter in town and it wasn't really his scene. He was in from out of town, but it was his name on the story the wire service picked up, so now he was *the* reporter on the scene. The local newspaper guys were miffed, but they knew that's how it worked. His byline, his claim, his fame. His story.

Arnie stayed in Roswell, and for a time there, he was The King of Roswell. This was his big story now, and he was suddenly the expert in print on all things flying saucer. He was being all of that, and all without knowing how very hated he was by the locals. Word out: Arnie Benton was a lousy tipper. That was his other claim to fame. Clayton Whittaker, on the other hand, at least tipped well, even if he was living in Arnie's shadow by then. He didn't mind, seeing as how he didn't know.

Clayton never saw Arnie's big UFO story or the great artsy desert photos. Nor did Blanche, who would have recognized the location, the tree, and maybe panicked just a little over what Arnie might have found out there had he really looked. Arnie found nothing, but that never stopped him. He got the photos, he got the story and he got the fame. Clayton got the sunburn, but he never got the clue. At least he tipped well. Whadda guy!

Over on the military base, Col. Baden and Capt. Lewis were doing their best to try to keep track of the growing media frenzy over this whole crazy UFO thing. They were amused by what they saw, as it made their job so much easier if the newspapers did all of the work for them, but they still couldn't keep up. It was just too much too fast and most of it was too far away. They got a copy of the El Paso paper, of course, but after that, after it started to go nationwide, there was no way for them to know or see or tell where it was going to pop up next. But that was not a bad thing. This thing was catching on! Smiles all around! They saved the El Paso paper. Col. Baden had it framed and hung it in his office. Maybe they could get Arnie to sign it.

The only downside to the UFO story, for the Western Witch Project, was their reluctance to fly what they really did have. But why? Those big neutral buoyancy aircraft looked *just like* flying saucers with those big, round, disk-shaped gasbags. They could be the UFOs! But no. Maybe not yet. The whole idea, the whole UFO lie, was that they were hiding *one* crashed UFO, not that they had a whole flying fleet of them and had been flying them for a couple of years. It had to be about that single, exotic flying saucer crash, not the everyday monkey mundane. So no, they still couldn't fly the NBAs. Then again, maybe they should leave the hangar doors open? No, not yet.

Maybe tomorrow.

CHAPTER 13

IT WAS A TYPICAL WEEKDAY MORNING AT THE OLD LEWIS PLACE, which was very much like a typical weekend morning at the old Lewis place, just with everyone moving around twice as fast and an hour earlier. It was a work day and a school day and nothing like a play day. You could tell. Everyone got up early, and Julie got up even earlier. Breakfast was served on time, as it always was, and you'd better move it or lose it, Buck-O. And keep yer elbows off the table. Were you raised in a barn? Ashley looked over at her father, who knew to dread that look this early.

"I dunno. Dad, didn't we live in a barn at Fort Knox?"

"No, dear. It was just a shed. I wasn't an officer yet."

"See, Mom?"

Julie pointed at the table full of food. "Eat. Both of you."

And for a bit, they did just that. They ate in mostly blessed silence. Julie was thankful for that. Get them fed and get them gone. That was the plan. Eli took one quick glance between bites over at the clock above the stove and then he picked up his pace, nudging his daughter to do the same. If she missed her bus, he would have to take her to school, and then he'd be late for work, and no, not today. So eat. Ashley picked up the open box of cereal on the table and offered it to her dad.

"Space nuts?"

He had to look twice before he corrected her without smiling. "Grape Nuts."

"Uh-huh."

Ashley put the box back down and they both took a couple more bites. Julie smiled as Eli watched his daughter.

"So how is it at school these days?"

"Oh, I guess it's okay, but it doesn't pay very well."

"But they don't charge you?"

"Well, they do for the milk."

"I wouldn't pay it!"

"Tried that."

"Ah, yes, I remember that day now."

Julie tried to break up the act. "You two..."

"And your boyfriend this week is...?"

"Freddy."

"And have I met Freddy?"

"Nope, and you're not likely to."

"Ah, well, easy come, easy go."

"He said you were lying about the UFO."

Eli put his newspaper down and looked over at his daughter. Neither one of them was smiling now. Secrets were serious business with this family. That's what put the Grape Nuts on the table.

"You know what I do, and you know what happened. What does Freddy think?"

Now Ashley had to smile and giggle a little, but she still couldn't look up at her dad.

"He thinks you really *are* hiding a flying saucer."

"And what do *you* think?"

"I think if you are, it smells like bananas and monkey poop."

"Ashley!"

"What, Mom?"

Eli tried to hold on to what little control he had at that table.

"Freddy's a civvy, isn't he?"

"Kinda shows, doesn't it?"

"Kinda, yeah."

"Dad, all the Army brats know the truth, but all the civvies are being really stupid about that whole UFO thing. We're getting yelled at for it now. We never say anything, but they see the weird planes over the base sometimes. The UFOs."

"What about the chimps?"

"The brats know, but they know to never say."

"Good brats."

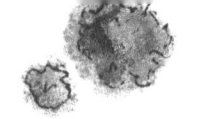

"But what do we do about that whole UFO thing?"
"Pretend the truth is the lie."
"'Scuse me?"
"Welcome to my world, darling daughter of mine."
"So I'm supposed to just tell them the truth?"
"But make it *sound* like a lie."
"And that's what you do?"
"All the livelong day."
"They don't pay you enough."
"Tell me about it."

Julie had to break up the little pity party. "Bus! Work! GO!"
"YIPE!"

With a quick glance at the clock over the stove, everyone jumped and ran. It was late! *They* were late! They suddenly had buses to catch, cars to drive, school, work, dishes to wash, things to do and places to go. The casual chat got slapped to the back, and now everyone was a blur. Well, everyone but Julie, who took her own sweet time about very carefully and casually cleaning up the whole messy breakfast scene at the kitchen table. She didn't have to catch a bus, and she had been at work for over an hour already. This was where she had to be, and she was already there.

Julie could follow the pounding footsteps and slamming doors all over the house as her husband and her daughter both made a mad dash for where they had to be five minutes ago. She knew they were running late. She had watched them run late, and she had let them run late. Then she told them they were late. They all had games they played. Julie won this one. She usually did.

"BYE, MOM!"
"BYE, DEAR!"
SLAM!

Silence... Nothing but golden silence in the house... Julie smiled at the front door.

"Goodbye and good luck."

Ashley ran like crazy, and she made the bus. Just. It was already there at her stop and loading. She got on just in time. Last in line. She made her way back to about the middle and sat down with friends. They had seen her run and kidded her about that. Late again! She kidded them about their runny noses, and they shut up. It was all fun and games after that. The bus ride was the best part of their day.

Eli had picked up his pace as well, but he wasn't nearly as strapped for time as his daughter might have been. He didn't miss his car. All he had to do to get to work on time was *not* do what he usually did every morning: Put the top down on the car. So he drove to work with the top up. No big deal. He could put it down after work and relax on the drive home. Maybe take the long way home. Yeah, that might be nice. He was already looking forward to that. It was a nice easy drive in the morning. No traffic. Maybe a snake or two, already out basking on the road in the morning sun. That made it interesting.

As her husband and daughter fled the home scene and got on with their hectic days, Julie Lewis was already deep into her day, and she was done with breakfast for that day. Everything was cleaned off, washed, dried and put away. On a weekday like this, it was simply going to be lunch for one at home, so there were no worries there. Nothing to plan, nothing to prep. She'd worry about dinner after lunch, which she didn't worry about at all. They all three had their constant weekday routines, and hers might have been the easiest of the three. After the busy breakfast routine, the apron came off, the hands got wiped and the house got a seriously stern looking over. A few things from the night before got picked up and put away. Then the phone rang. So soon?

Julie looked at the clock in the living room. It was too soon for the school to be calling about Ashley, and there was no way her husband could have to gotten to work by then, even in *that* car. Ah, but it might be his office calling to talk to him before he got to work. Fair warning or an urgent plea? Maybe a monkey got loose? She thought about that and smiled. This might be a fun day after all! She picked up the phone thinking, *Monkey, monkey, monkey...*

"Hello? Oh, hi, Cathy!"

It was not a monkey. Cathy Wilson was an Army wife just like Julie, married to Captain Jim Watson, one of the Mustang fighter pilots, but *not* one of the pilots involved in the crash of the NBA. Still, Cathy knew all about everything, and Julie knew they could talk about anything, so they did.

"So what's all of this about Eli hiding a flying saucer now? Did the monkeys get bored with the gasbags?"

"Oh, it just got crazy around here."

"And now Eli has a spaceship? Really? That must be fun!"

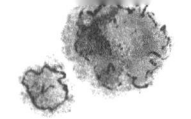

"Oh, no, no, no. Now he's *pretending* to have a spaceship."

"They never grow up, do they?"

"Not mine, no. How about yours?"

"Let me get back to you on that."

"Look, you know what they're doing out there, with the monkeys and all."

"Oh, yes, and I know he lost one in that bad storm."

"Yes, well, now people think what crashed that day was a UFO. A flying saucer."

"Complete with little aliens?"

"Well, of course complete with aliens. What else would a couple of burnt up monkeys in flight suits look like to the civvies?"

"Oh. Of course. I never thought of that."

"Well, somebody did. Big time. Now everybody thinks it."

"And your husband is good with that?"

"Oh, he's all about it!"

"So wait, now, you're telling me that there's no flying saucer, but Eli is going on like there is?"

"He's going on like there is, but there isn't."

"Okay, you lost me again. Back the bull up and try again."

"Eli is having to pretend that the Army *does* have a crashed flying saucer and aliens, but he's having to make it sound like it's all a big secret and he can't talk about it."

"Because...?"

"Because a silly little lie like that is much easier to hand out, easier than the big serious truth."

"Ah! But..."

"But what?"

"Where do the manned weather balloons fit in to all of this?"

"Good question."

"I thought so."

"That was the first lie they came up with to cover the crash and the bodies, but now I think they might be sort of real."

"Julie, I think they are very real."

"How so?"

"Baden asked Jim to check them out."

"As in, *fly* in one?"

"Well, he didn't *say* that. He didn't say fly, but it seemed to be implied."

"Oh, no, no, no, no, no."

"That's what I said."

"Eli told me if they launched one of those things, it could end up in Africa."

"*WHAT?*"

"They have no real flight control. They go up, and all they can do is vent gas to bring them down if it's safe to do so."

"In Africa?"

"Well, there is that pesky ocean between here and there."

"Oh, yes. That."

"Cathy, you do not want Jim to go up in one of those balloons."

"I'll be mentioning that to him. *A lot.*"

"You'd better. And Cathy?"

"Yes?"

"We need to push that UFO thing. Make it real."

"How do we do that?"

"Spend more time with the locals. Get the word out."

"Can do. And the word is?"

"We smile like we know something and say we can't talk about those UFOs, and then we let everyone else do the talking for us."

"I can do that."

"Just let them ask first, and look surprised when they do."

"I'm sure my hairdresser will ask."

"Are you still going to Barbara?"

"Oh, my, yes."

"Then this lie is as good as spread."

"Oh, my, yes."

They spoke after that about everything else. Everything but monkeys and UFOs. About their kids and the weather, and where they might be stationed next once this whole flying monkey thing was over. The Watsons were hoping for Japan. Someplace exotic. Julie was hoping for Oregon. Some place cool and cloudy. Both of them were over this whole empty desert thing. Cathy mentioned that she had an appointment with Barbara to get her hair done the next day, and she and Julie went over what she could and couldn't say about UFOs. (No need to mention monkeys or weather balloons at all now.) By the time they were done plotting and planning, the lie had a fine, full life all its own, and by the time Barbara got a hold of it the next day, it was going to be a tough lie to stop.

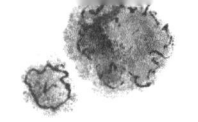

Cathy Watson hung up the phone with a sly smile. This was her game now, and she had her own good reason for making this happen: To keep her husband out of those crazy dangerous manned weather balloons. To keep him out of Africa. She hadn't liked the idea to begin with, and neither did he when he saw them all laid out in the NBA hangar on the base. There was no control in those things. You just get in, sit down and ride it out. A mannequin could do that. But if Cathy could help Julie push the whole UFO thing, maybe the wicked witches would be too busy playing *that* silly game to do the whole manned balloon thing. One could only hope, and she did. Cathy found her hat and her car keys. Maybe it was time to do a little shopping in town. And to spread the word for the team. Big smile. Go ahead and ask.

Julie was ready to do much the same, to spread the word, but from home. She didn't need to drive all over. Isn't that why we have phones? She sat there for a minute and looked at the phone. Hmmm. Who to call? Who needed to know? And who could be counted on to tell all to all? The Canasta Club! Of course! It was the perfect mix of Army wives and civvy women. And they never shut up. Oh, this thing is going global overnight! Or at least all over town. Eli will be so proud. And he'd better be.

Captain Eli Lewis was well aware of what he called The String of Pearls: The Army wives who all got together and talked and knew what was really going on all over the base. He got more information from them, from his own wife, than he ever did through the official base channels. Those memos were always late, and the ladies were always right on time. The UFO he didn't have was about to become famous. All it would take was a couple of very busy phone calls. Hello, Canasta Club!

The Army wives, The Pearls, all knew what could be said and what could not be said, and they knew what this was all about: This was all about the lie that needed to be said but said as the truth they couldn't say. They all got that. They were all experts in that. They were all women. Subterfuge was their other pastime, and the civvies—the civilian wives in town—were their intended victims. They would get this word spread like soft butter before lunch, before some were done with breakfast.

Clayton Whittaker had stayed up too late the night before, as he was still "building" his UFO. All he was doing was pulling all of those broken, burnt crash parts out of the shed and laying them out in the driveway, trying to make sense of the senseless, but he got to running late as he did that and ended up working in the dark, this time quite literally. No flashlight.

Blanche had watched him do this for a while, but then she found herself longing for a freshly painted wall of wet paint that needed watching as it dried, so maybe she'd go for a walk around town instead. He hardly noticed that she had gone. There were so many pieces now. And where do they all go? This piece must go here! (It didn't, but he put it there anyway.) Blanche had walked off while it was still mostly light, but no worries, Roswell was safe, day or night. And she wasn't going all that far. Only as far as the bus station. It was closer now to these new rooms, and closer was good. She could be gone in no time flat. But she wasn't gone. Not yet.

She strolled into the quiet bus station, bought a Coke and just sat there, all alone in the waiting room, thinking about the bus ride back home. Maybe she should buy a ticket tonight for a bus trip tomorrow. Maybe she should. She looked. Too late, the ticket window was closed. So maybe tomorrow. Sipping that cold Coca-Cola, she spied the big telephone booths. She had a choice. There were two. Men's and women's? She laughed at that, then looked around to see if anyone saw her laughing at the joke no one heard. No one there. No one laughed.

The women's phone booth (the one on the right) called to her. Maybe she should phone home. Call collect, just to tell them she was okay. To tell them that she was coming home soon. But was she? Now she wasn't so sure. She wasn't really stuck there in Roswell with Clayton, but was she really ready to go home and face *that* music? Maybe she'd just have another Coke instead. Sleep was so overrated. She got back in time in the dark to help Clayton put it all back in the shed, except for the parts she threw *behind* the shed when he wasn't looking. It was late, it was dark, and she was runnin' on caffeine and sugar. Better watch out! She was having fun. He never noticed. Smiles hide in the dark.

They ended up, late the following morning, at the small Tin Can Café over on the west side of town on Highway 70. This was just a little place for the locals, as most folks from out of town never saw it as they flew by on their way out of town. But it was a good place to stop if you saw it in time. They did. She made sure they did. *Veni, vidi,* ve eat!

After that late night of too much caffeine, Blanche was all soft and groggy as Clayton was wired 220. Apparently last night's "build" went well for him, and he was all about building that flying saucer now! It hurt to roll her eyes, so Blanche just looked down at her food, and why was it still there? Oh yeah, eat. Were the forks always this heavy? Would it be wrong to use two hands? She thought about that. She tried. That was dumb. Oh, well. They had taken a booth in the back corner, out of the bright sunlight. Blanche insisted. It was one of those days already.

With no one close, Clayton had only Blanche to annoy with his non-stop squirrel chatter about, well, the usual: Flying saucers, UFOs and what the government knew and had. And every time he told the tale, they had more than the last time. She wondered if the Army knew about how very much they had by now. It was tough to keep up. Maybe she should have taken notes. Would there be a quiz? She was pretty sure she could ace that thing by now. That was a complaint. She put ketchup on her cereal. Oops.

Even the lone waitress knew to give Clayton plenty of room to chatter away. She had other, quieter customers to deal with, but she did keep an eye on Blanche. She was not looking well. The waitress first thought, *That girl is pregnant.* Then the waitress looked at Clayton. Second thought, *Poor girl.* Was that guy on something? He was way too excited for that early in the day, and he never shut up. Never.

The waitress was, without thinking about it, looking for a big brown paper bag to put over Clayton's head. Maybe then he'd shut up and go to sleep. That would be nice. No bag. She looked. Then she looked at Blanche, who just shrugged and gave her an eye roll. *Yeah, Clayton. Whadda ya gonna do?* And was it too early for a Coca-Cola? Maybe that's what she needed right about now. She had to think about that. No, wait, too late.

Without anyone ever seeing him take a bite, ever do anything but talk, Clayton's plate was somehow clean. He had eaten. *When? How?* It didn't matter. He was done, and it was time to go. Just like that. Clayton paid the bill, and Blanche left the tip. The waitress quietly told Blanche to come back anytime, but she made sure Clayton didn't hear that. Blanche understood what she had meant and appreciated

CHAPTER 13

the rescue. Maybe later. We'll see how the day goes. He's got to sleep sometime, right? With one last eye roll, they were out the door and into the day. And he was *so* going to help her push that car this time. There was no doubt about that.

Clayton and Blanche rolled out onto Highway 70 just before Arnie Benton rolled into the Tin Can Café parking lot. And was that Clayton's old car just leaving? Arnie looked, but he couldn't tell. What if it was? Should he follow them and see? Ah, but what if it wasn't and he missed breakfast? Food first. And second. And third. Pretty sure he could catch them later if he wanted to. Right then, Arnie was thinking about catching the waitress at the Tin Can Café. He had been there before, and that was why he was there again now. Well, that and the food. Now it was her turn for an eye roll when he walked through the door. It was going to be one of *those* days. She knew that by then.

Clayton never looked back to see Arnie pull in as he pulled out. And would he even know Arnie's car if he had seen it? Probably not. It was hardly a UFO, even if it was a Studebaker. (A case could be made.) So Blanche and Clayton got away clean, and Blanche was taking in all of the scenery to see where they were, and where they might be going. They hadn't really talked much about that yet, but maybe they should. Then again, they were headed west. Toward her home. So maybe she'd just sit there and see how it went. And plot her escape.

She was ready. She had everything in one handbag and a small suitcase, and both were at hand. Well, at her feet. But they were right there, and if he stopped, she could be gone before he looked up. Abducted by aliens! Just like that! She laughed out loud. He looked up. Oops.

"What's so funny?"
"Oh, nothing."
"But you laughed."
"Did I?"
"Pretty sure."

Blanche made a point of looking all around. They were still traveling west at a good clip, but was that what they wanted to do?

"So where are we going?"

Oddly enough, now Clayton looked around like he had no idea how they had gotten where they were, or why. And he really didn't, on both counts. Blanche intervened and pointed to a small road off to the left. It was coming up fast. This might be fun.

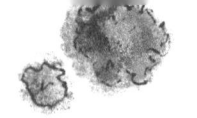

"Turn here!"

"*WAH!*"

Brake! Clutch! Gears! Steer! Clayton was a wild blur of everything all at once, and the car responded by lurching hard to port and nearly keeling over, but they made the turn. Once it all settled back down and Clayton was driving much slower, he looked back over at his random navigator who was still hanging on for dear life.

"Okay, now what?"

She honestly had no idea; she had simply picked the next turn and yelled for it. Ah, but now, once she took another look at where they were pointed, she knew where they were headed, and she smiled. This time she pointed straight ahead.

"Up into the mountains."

"What's up there?"

"A better view of down here."

With a bit of quick thinking, Blanche came up with both the plan for the day and an excuse for that wild turn. By driving up into the mountains, she said, they could look back down across the broad, flat valley and maybe see a pattern in the crash debris. Get the big picture, see what they might have missed. Now Clayton was literally bouncing up and down in his seat as he drove.

"*Yes! Yes! Yes!*"

Blanche was not amused.

"Just drive, drive, drive."

CHAPTER 14

WITH A QUICK BIT OF THINKING, BLANCHE WAS SUDDENLY the navigator for that day's adventure in the high desert. She had pointed out the turn, and Clayton had taken it. Now what? Now she had him drive up into the higher land, into the hills that weren't quite mountains, up on the northeast side of the base. Blanche smiled. It would be better in the hills. No need to push the car. An easy day.

As he drove, Clayton was spinning his head around, trying to take it all in. He wanted to see the military base to his left and whatever there might be to see on the right, over toward the long, drawn-out crash site. He couldn't see it all, and he was trying to see both at once. It got scary just to watch. The road wasn't all that wide, and Blanche got nervous about his driving. This was close enough.

"Just pull over before we fall over."

"Are we there yet?"

"We'd better be."

Clayton found a wider flat spot where he could park the car well off the road, and he made sure he set the parking brake. As funny as it would be to have the car that wouldn't start roll away, back down the hill while they were out snooping around, it might not be all *that* funny. He put a rock under the rear tire, just to make sure. Then they both took a good look around.

At that point, the road was more on the south side of the hill, with a great view of the military base even farther south, down in the basin. For a time, they both simply stood there and watched the base.

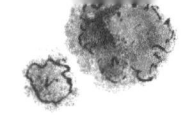

Airplanes, very normal airplanes, were taking off and landing. They were great to watch, but they were not what Clayton wanted to see.

"No flying saucers today?"

"Maybe they've got the day off."

That was supposed to be a joke, but Clayton didn't get it.

"Where do you suppose they keep them on their day off?"

Blanche took a good long look at the base. She was pretty sure she had seen where they kept *something*, she just wasn't sure what. Now, where was it from this angle? That hangar over there? Gotta be. She did not point, but Clayton did. At something else.

"They've got to be in that hangar there. The big one."

Blanche had to look again. What was he pointing at? Was *that* the hangar she had watched the day something had crashed? The day of the storm? She squinted. That helped. No, that was not the same hangar, but maybe Clayton was onto something there. That *was* a big hangar, and it was set out apart from everything else on the base. A sort of "let's put it here" afterthought. And it was huge. Now even she was wondering about that. And where was Clayton going? Down the hill?

"Let's get a closer look."

Clayton had started to make his way down the south side of the hill, toward the restricted military base. Blanche had thought they were going to go the other way, over the north side of the hill and down, to see about a view of the crash site. No? Apparently not. She let Clayton lead the way, knowing that never ended well. She looked all around first. It was perfect snake weather. So where were they? She picked up a stick and followed the leader.

"How many do you think there are?"

Blanche was still watching for reptiles and misunderstood the question. "What? Snakes?"

"*WHAT SNAKES???*"

"Oh, sorry, no. No snakes. What's the question?"

Now Clayton had stopped walking and was kind of hopping around, trying to see the ground all around himself all at once. Snakes? He did not like snakes. He did not like snakes *a lot*. It took him a minute or two to settle back down, and now, he was still too nervous.

"I meant the saucers. Flying saucers. In that big hangar. How many?"

CHAPTER 14

Blanche took another long look at the big building.

"Oh, I think all of them would fit in there. Don't you?"

"They've got to!"

Clayton, by then, was completely convinced that the Army had a whole fleet of flying saucers and that the base was simply crawling with little grey men. Aliens. And they only came out in the daytime because they glowed green at night, and that made them stand out too much. Of course it did. Blanche was pretty sure it was just the catnip talking, but then again, this guy was probably born crazy and raised nuts. And she got in that car anyway. She shook her head over that one.

"We've got to get a closer look."

"We've got to get binoculars."

Clayton stopped walking, turned around and got suddenly serious. "No. No binoculars. That makes us look like a couple of spies."

Blanche had to admit she was impressed with that sudden gust of reality. He was right. No need to look like spies. Without the field glasses, that were just a couple of kids out in the desert on a romp. Bird watching! Snake charming. No need to get shot for treason. Clayton kept walking.

"Let's try this way."

Blanche followed as Clayton took a stumbling turn and started walking to the right, along the side of the hill, and not simply *down* the hill. He wanted to keep what elevation he could. The better to see you with. Blanche took another good look around for snakes, double-checked her snake stick, and then took a squinty look at the base below them. It was busy down there today. Something going on? Would they really maybe see something today? And was there really something down there to see?

Blanche was not a believer. Not in UFOs, not in flying saucers or in little grey men that glowed green in the night. She also didn't believe in a lot of other things, but those were the biggies at the moment. Those were the ones she had to step over now. Still not as bad as snakes. She was pretty sure the aliens weren't actually venomous. And she was fairly well equipped for this walk in the desert. She had her hat, she had her stick and she had some water. She watched Clayton, walking up ahead of her. He had none of those things, and she wasn't about to share. And the day was getting warm. How long would he last?

As Clayton watched all around him for snakes and watched the base for UFOs (they were too far away to see the little grey men), Blanche, while still watching for snakes as well, had spotted four not so little men in green, and they were headed their way. Guards. Armed guards. They had been spotted. And they were about to be intercepted. Oh, this should be fun. Blanche knew if she took a right turn right then, she could be back up over the hill, on the road and gone before they ever got there, but where was the fun in that? She looked ahead. Clayton hadn't spotted the guards coming at them yet. She slowed down. It wasn't a race. She let the guards win.

To his credit, Clayton had been very right about those binoculars. That they did *not* have any was what kept this interception on a much lighter note than it might have been if they had been caught with such things in hand. Spies? No, they were not spies. Just a couple of kids too close to the base. But the guards were still armed. All four of them. Blanche watched the dance. Those guys had done this before, you could tell. One guard stayed down low, at the base of the hill, as one guard moved quick to get up ahead of Clayton as he climbed the hill. Another guard held back and was climbing up the hill well behind her. She lost sight of that one, but she knew he had to be back there. The fourth guard was coming right at her and being as obvious about it as he possibly could. He was all smiles and waves. She waved back, and she had to smile as well. Then came the thought: Did he maybe have a car? Hmmm...

"Good morning!"

"Hi!"

The closer he got, the better he looked. Blanche had to admit, there was something about a man in uniform. Especially this one. Was that why they sent him to her, or did he volunteer? Either way, she thought, lucky her. She looked up ahead. Clayton was almost out of sight and hadn't turned around yet. No sign of the guard ahead of him. What fun! She stopped, and *her* guard got close. She smiled a nice, warm hello smile. The guard had to at least pretend to be all business.

"You know you're kind of close to the base."

"The better to meet you with."

"I... Uh, yeah, but you might be too close."

"Is that even possible?"

The poor guy was happily flustered already. He never stood a chance. He pointed back to the soldier still waiting down below them at the base of the hill.

"My sergeant is going to think so."

"Well, we do need to keep him happy."

"Yes, ma'am."

"Blanche. I'm Blanche."

"I'm Sammy."

Sammy looked past Blanche, lost his smile and unshouldered his rifle. Without turning around, she could hear the stumbling, pebble-kicking footsteps coming closer, and she knew who it had to be. She kept her smile, though. Why not?

"And that would be Clayton."

Quietly, Sammy had to ask, "Dangerous?"

"Only to himself."

Sammy kept his eyes on Clayton and did not relax the grip on his gun. Blanche had to wonder if it was even loaded, but she knew better than to ask. The three guards that had climbed the hill all had rifles. Then she looked back down the hill. The sergeant standing down below them had a sidearm, still holstered. Pretty sure someone in that crowd must have a bullet or two. By then Clayton was right there, sort of out of breath, and she could hear more footsteps behind him, solid and heavy. That would be the lead guard in boots. She could see the other one now, hanging back behind Sammy. This was still his show, though, and she still smiled. But for how much longer?

"So how many UFOs you got down there?"

That only caught Sammy off guard for a second. He was watching Clayton and seeing the crazy in his eyes. He looked back over at Blanche. She seemed normal. He was trying to make sense of that and left the question alone.

"You got aliens, right?"

"We're all Americans here, sir."

Blanche giggled softly, and Sammy smiled at that. Clayton didn't get the joke. Blanche was pretty sure if he ever got a joke, the world would end. He was that clueless when it came to humor. And pretty much everything else. But he still had a car.

"I'm building a flying saucer."

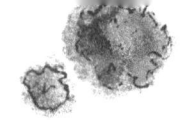

By then they were surrounded. There was a guard behind them, another behind Sammy and Sammy was right there, near Blanche, but not too close. He did not want to get all that close to Clayton. A wise move on his part. This guy was nuts. He could see that.

"Sir?"

"I'm building a flying saucer, rebuilding the one that crashed. I've got all of the parts."

Sammy took a casual step back, a move that did not go unnoticed by Blanche, who took a step off to the side, putting a little more distance between her and Captain Crazy. He needed his space.

"And do you plan to fly that thing?"

Clayton got serious. "Well, I still have to work out the details of the mass propulsion drive system. I'm not sure I have all of the parts for that sort of thing, but there's still so much more to find out here. Which is why we're here, looking for what we missed and hope to find so that it might fly."

There was a good long pause as all three guards did their very best to not laugh, and all three found that it helped a lot to simply look at Blanche instead. She wasn't crazy. Or ugly. It was the better view all around. The sergeant was still down there, arms crossed now, wondering what the heck was going on up above him. Sammy leaned over closer to Blanche. She didn't mind. He tried to not move his lips as he spoke.

"What's he on?"

She leaned toward him and whispered back, "Catnip."

Sammy stood back up straight and looked sternly at Blanche. This was his unspoken "Seriously?" look. Catnip? The crazy guy is on catnip? Was she joking? She just grimaced and nodded her head. Yes, seriously. He had never heard of such a thing, but there it was, and if she said it, it must be true. He looked at the other guards. They just shrugged. He looked down the hill at his sergeant, who looked at his watch and gave him the "Wrap it up!" sign. Sammy smiled. *Yeah, okay.*

"So how about we walk you folks out of the danger zone?"

"Are the aliens dangerous?"

Sammy adjusted the grip on his rifle. Blanche saw that.

"No, sir, I am."

Blanche pointed back up the hill, toward the road. "We're parked up there."

CHAPTER 14

"You lead the way."

Now, as much as Sammy would have liked to simply walk through the desert with Blanche, he also knew he had better walk behind Clayton. That guy was nuts, and he had to go. He was why they were all there. Sammy waved Clayton past him.

"I'll follow you, sir."

Clayton took the lead, thinking he knew where he was and where the car was parked up on the hill, out of sight above them. Blanche held back, and Sammy got his wish. They walked together in the desert and spoke softly.

"Catnip? He's on catnip?"

"He says it calms him down."

"He needs more."

"Tell me about it."

"You gonna be okay with him?"

"I guess."

"But you don't know?"

"He's mostly harmless."

"Mostly?"

"More noisy than anything."

Sammy watched Clayton stumble his way up ahead. What a goofball.

"We could hold him on suspicion of espionage."

"Do you really want to put up with that?"

"No. Do you?"

"Not for very much longer."

Sammy stopped and looked all around. So did Blanche and Clayton. They were all standing on the road now. On one very empty desert highway. Nothing there. No car. Sammy turned to Blanche.

"So where's your car?"

"Good question. Clayton?"

"The aliens got it!"

One of the other guards came up over the rise to their right and waved.

"It's over here!"

"The aliens moved it!"

Blanche and Sammy just looked at each other and laughed. It didn't matter if he heard. As Clayton fished the car keys put of his pocket on the third attempt, Blanche explained to Sammy that the car's starter was broken, and it had to be pushed. By then all three guards were there, and they all shouldered their rifles and nodded. They'd all push. She could relax. They had this. Sammy held the car door for her, something Clayton had never done. With three guards pushing, the car got started real fast. Blanche waved goodbye, and Sammy waved back, sorry to see her go but glad to see Clayton gone. Clayton, on the other hand, had no idea where he was going. After a while, he had to ask.

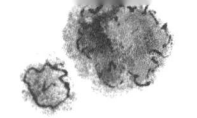

"So where to?"

"Not here. Just drive. At least make them think we're leaving."

"Good idea. But are we leaving?"

"Nope. Just driving around the base."

"Okay."

Blanche leaned out the open car window and looked up at the sky. It was getting late. She looked at the car's faltering gas gauge and rolled her eyes. She said nothing, but she knew where they were headed if they didn't turn around. They did not turn around. She watched the great barren desert scenery roll by, comfortable in knowing that this would not be her first night sleeping out in the open desert. She had done this before. But had he?

They got as far as the far side, the western side, of the military base, and were still up high in the hills and well away from it. The car had coughed once and then gone silent as the gas ran out, and they coasted as far as the top of the hill, where Blanche made him stop. There was no need to roll to the bottom. And hey, the view would be better up there! With that last bit of rolling inertia, Clayton took the car off the road and got it stopped.

"Gas."

"Yep.

"Not any?"

"Nope."

She smiled. "This'll be fun."

And for a time, it was. They got out and went exploring. Walking back to the east, they found that they really did have a grand view of the wide desert basin and the military base. It was all right there, all right down there, and all laid out for them to see. And now they were too far away for the guards to be a bother. Not that Sammy had been a bother. Blanche didn't mind that sort of bother at all. They watched the planes, all very regular planes, take off and land at the base, and it was so boring to see that there was no way Clayton could make any of them a UFO. They could very plainly see the planes. Just planes. But Blanche knew that scene might change at night, and they needed to be ready for that, too. And it might get cold. They might need a fire. She started collecting firewood.

Back closer to the car, Blanche cleared off a spot for a fire and sent Clayton off in search of more firewood. She resisted the urge to tell Clayton to make that he did not pick up any snakes. Funny, but no. They really would need more wood. No need to send him cowering in the car in fear. Yet.

By the time the sun set in glorious full color off to the west, they did have a fair pile of firewood and a nice little fire going. They had no food to cook, but maybe someone would see the fire and stop. That would be nice. No one stopped. No one even drove by. Then it got dark, and the stars came out and the universe smiled down on them. It was the desert at night.

For a time, they both just sat there and watched the stars and the moon and the airplanes. Well, Blanche watched the airplanes. Now Clayton was convinced that they were *all* UFOs. They had to be! That's why they flew at night! Blanche's eyes hurt from all of the rolling. She really needed to stop doing that. After a time, after the moon was well up and the world so brightly lit and beautiful, Blanche decided that she had seen enough and crawled into the car's back seat, made a pillow out of her hat, closed her eyes and was fast asleep, dreaming of soldiers.

Clayton stayed up for quite a while, studying the flight characteristics of UFOs, all of them trying so very hard to look just like airplanes, but he knew better. They were all flying saucers, and he saw them all! They did have a fantastic vantage point to see the show, and the base at night was a spectacle of lights, but time took its toll, as time always does, and sometime after midnight, Clayton fell asleep in the sand as their campfire was left to fend for itself. Right before the UFO came out. If only there had been some coffee in that car…

The word had come down from Col. Baden: Keep the NBAs flying. Keep them flight worthy, as the Western Witch Project was not over. However, hold the chimps. Find human pilots small enough to fit. Let's get their input on those aircraft. Oh, and let's fly them at night. No need to show them yet. The unspoken add to that: And if someone did see them flying at night, looking very much like a UFO, would that be so very bad? It would not.

With a little bit of work, the two-seat cockpits became single-seat cockpits, and the smallest pilots they could find were recruited to give it a try. *Hey, how tough could it be? Monkeys fly these things!* In all truth, once the order came through, the team was thrilled with the idea of finally getting some real input back from human pilots on these things. The monkeys had been decidedly reluctant to talk. One other change, as per Baden's orders, was to muffle those odd two-stroke engines as much as possible. Alien UFOs are not supposed to sound like Italian motor scooters.

By the time they were ready for the NBA night flights, the base had been ringed with small blue lights all around the edge, to give the human pilots some idea of where they were and when to turn. All they had to do was circle the base slowly at night. Just fly around inside the blue lights after midnight. And take the next day off.

The ground crew met at 11 p.m. to prep the NBA for flight that night, and it was a different NBA each time. They were in rotation to keep them all flight ready. Fuel tanks were filled, and that dangerous hydrogen gas was pumped into the big, round, silvery bag over the airframe. And yes, if you didn't see the cockpit and engines underneath the thing, it *did* look like a flying saucer. Everyone connected with the project was well aware of that now. And everyone connected to the project planned to use that now. What UFO? Oh, yeah, *that* UFO.

The pilot for the night had trained on the flight simulator and checked out the modified cockpit and controls. There had been plenty of time devoted to the training, and now it was time to fly. It was after midnight. It was flight time. The muffled NBA hardly made any noise at all, but they knew that would change, as the props would make more noise once they were up to flight speed. Nothing they could do about that, but the noise was odd enough to not sound like a motor. There was no need for a tow to the runway, so the NBA simply taxied out and took off. With all of that hydrogen and only one pilot, it could have *flown* out of the hangar. The pilot found it was harder to keep the NBA on the ground than to take off. That was going to be mentioned later.

Flying low and slow, the NBA took off into the brilliant, moonlit night sky and began a slow, easy circle around the edge of the base.

CHAPTER 14

The blue lights on the base borders made it easy to plan the turns, no need to get lost and get shot down. And everyone had taken a very serious look at the weather before they launched. No one trusted the weather wire anymore. It was a beautiful night. The pilot let the craft gain altitude with every turn. Higher, ever higher! Closer to the stars! The view was incredible, both above and below. Too bad Clayton never saw a thing, sound asleep in the sand. Blanche, on the other hand, saw the whole thing.

By the time the NBA got to the western edge of the base, it was up to around 2,000 feet above the desert basin, and with those muffled motors, all it made was a weird, high-pitched whine from the odd black props. Blanche heard the whine Clayton couldn't hear, woke up, got up and very quietly stepped out of the car to see what was going on. She didn't close the car door. That would have made noise. She gently pushed it to where it wouldn't slam, stepped away from the car and walked to the east to get a better look at the starry world above and below. Both were wonderful, and the UFO was a nice touch. She looked over at Clayton, sound asleep. She let him sleep. His head would have exploded if he woke up and saw that thing flying by, and she was *not* going to clean that up.

The NBA passed by her to the east, still overhead, but not by much. She waved. No idea why. Pretty sure they couldn't see her, unless aliens had great night vision like cats. She was also sure it wasn't aliens. Just another secret government project, out flying at night while everyone slept. Nothing to see here. Move along. As it went by, she saw a large, thick, silvery, disk-shaped gasbag with a crew cockpit, props and motors suspended underneath. Almost a flying saucer, but not quite. Still one of ours.

Then it hit her: *That's* what crashed. One of *those*. One of those secret round aircraft no one was supposed to ever see. And here she was, standing there seeing it. She took a step back, and then she took another. Did the crew in that thing see her seeing them? Oh, this might not go well at all. They needed to go! They couldn't go. They were out of gas. They were stuck there, and there she was, seeing the stuff she shouldn't see. Blanche looked all around, frantic now. There was no place to go, no place to hide, and the car was right there, for all to see. Especially from the air. And there was Clayton over there, sleeping though the whole thing. This was insane.

Where's the catnip?

CHAPTER 15

ASHLEY LEWIS WAS A JUNIOR AT ROSWELL HIGH SCHOOL ("Home of the Fighting Coyotes!"). It was a public school, but all of the Army brats went there, whether they lived on the base or not. And even though the brats never wore any sort of uniform, it was easy enough to tell who was who—the brats from the civvies. All you had to do was listen.

"Hey, Lewis."

"Hey, Madison."

The Army brats always called each other by their last names. That's how you knew who was who. It was an Army brat thing, but sometimes even the teachers, the civilian teachers, caught themselves doing it, as that was all they heard those kids being called. And that was okay. That was their name. The Army kids made no distinction between officers' kids and enlisted men's kids. Army was Army, and brat was brat. And they were the kids you never messed with. Just don't. And if you were able to get in close and just listen, you might hear stuff you didn't know.

"Hey, Lewis, your dad been to the moon lately?"

"Nah, I guess yer mom's out of town."

"Ouch. Those aliens much fun?"

"They're okay, but they fry up greasy."

"I guess."

Now, as wild as it got (and it did), they all knew that there were very solid lines not to cross when they were off the base and out in public. Especially at school. Those civvy kids were all ears. So no brat ever spoke directly about the Western Witch Project, and they especially did *not* mention monkeys in any way, shape or form. Not out loud, anyway.

It was dead quiet in the study hall that afternoon. So quiet you could hear a folded note being passed forward, from student to student until it got to Ashley. Her name was on the note. She never looked up, never looked back. She just quietly opened the note. It was a drawing. A cartoon. Of a monkey flying a rocket. "SPACE MONKS!!" was scrawled across the top of the page, and now she could hear footsteps coming. Big steps. Heavy steps. Teacher steps. She ate the note. Yes, really. The teachers were civvies, too.

"Miss Lewis?"

"Yeth?"

"What do you have there?"

"Nuffing."

"Are you sure?"

Gulp. "Yes. I'm sure."

"Food in class?"

"Have you *tried* the food in the cafeteria?"

Even the teacher had to laugh at that one, and Ashley got off with a smile and a finger wag. She got off easy. The teacher looked back down the row and saw the young man blushing in the back. Yep, it had been his note. And even though he maybe sort of got away with it, in that the note was not taken by the teacher, he also knew that he was dead meat the next time Ashley got a hold of him after school. Such was the price of artistic expression. The monkey was over the line, and even the idiot civvy knew it. But he drew it anyway. And now he would pay. Well, he'd pay later, when he least expected it.

If it was dangerous at school to mention the flying monkeys, at least the secret still seemed safe enough out beyond those walls. Newspapers all over the U.S. had picked up on the story about the UFO crashing outside of Roswell, but most of them were treating it as "novelty news"; that is, they were not taking it entirely seriously. And that was a good thing, as no one seemed to be asking, "So what was it *really*?" and no one mentioned the chimps at all. So far, that secret was safe.

The "flying saucer," a new phrase fast becoming quite popular when it came to novelty news, was somehow linked to the military base in those novelty stories, but exactly *how* it was linked to the base was left unsaid. The Army knew! That was implied, and when Capt. Lewis was quoted, as he so often was, those quotes were often seen as confirmation by denial. Exactly what he wanted them to be. His no meant yes. And are there any further questions? No? Yes.

The newspapers didn't get all steaming mad about the Army base hiding UFOs and aliens and not telling them, because those reporters all knew the times that they lived in, and if the Army was hiding something that exotic on a remote military base in the New Mexican desert, then there was probably a pretty good chance they might get into some very serious trouble if they said what it really was. As if they knew. Which they did not. So, UFO it was! Novelty news was the best news of all. No need to check *those* sources! Let's just run it!

And so it was that Roswell, New Mexico, became the de facto center for all things alien. It became a nut magnet, with Clayton Whittaker right there in the middle of it all. The Number One Nut! He was there first, and he was still there. Still collecting desert trash and trying to build a UFO. And a very large part of that town was hoping that he would. They all wanted to see *that* fly! (From a safe distance, of course.) And they all felt a certain degree of sympathy for that poor put-upon girl who was with him. She seemed so nice. So quiet. So sane. So ready to run screaming for the door. Everyone watched and waited. Any day now. Any day...

The local joke you never heard went something like this: Whatever it was that crashed out there, it crashed on the Foster Ranch. With so many people, local or not, wanting to see what they could see out there in the desert, the Fosters were very quickly over all of that and just wanted to get on with their lives, minus all the press and hoopla and weird crazy people walking around on their land. And so it was that the "flying saucers" got morphed into the "Sighing Fosters," as there was no way for them to keep everyone off their ranch, try as they may. And they finally gave up trying. What they did find, to their own small joy, was that it was great way to get rid of any broken ranch stuff they had on hand. Especially anything metal. Just leave it out there in the open and some nut would take it. Usually the same nut. Day after day. And all for free!

While the local Roswell newspaper had been kind to the Army base, and had let the story go, other publications, lesser publications, were not so kind and wouldn't let it go. Now, to them, anything that flew anywhere near the base had to be a flying saucer from another planet, and those little grey men were green now. And of course it was all a great big secret, and the Army knew all about it. They were in on it. They had to be. Of course they were. And all of this might have made Capt. Lewis's job that much easier, but somehow, it didn't. It wasn't supposed to be that big of a story, and now it was, and he was spending far too much time answering that ringing telephone and talking to those people, and didn't they ever give it a rest? No, they did not. For a very good reason.

With the war over, no one wanted to read about any serious news ever again. This silly "novelty news" was all the rage now, and the sillier the better. Too many saw it as harmless fun, a happy lie, but then, some people did take it seriously, and thought it was all very real. There were a lot of Claytons out there, and more than a few were making their way to Roswell by then. This was where it was at. The place to come and see and really be. Roswell was named The Flying Saucer Capital of America! Capt. Lewis was *not* pleased with *that* story. Certain newspapers were now reporting about all of the new UFO sightings all around Roswell. (There weren't any, but that never stopped them.) They linked them all to the Army base without actually blaming the base, knowing that there were lines not to be crossed in reporting when it came to the mysterious activities of the U.S. government on restricted military bases. They did report, and accurately, that the official spokesman from the base (Capt. Lewis) had not specifically *denied* the existence of UFOs. But did that confirm it? For too many, yes. Yes, it did.

The situation was getting close to out of control. They could see that by then. Capt. Lewis had a stack of newspapers on his desk from all over the U.S., and all with "Roswell UFO" stories in them. And these were just the ones they found or were sent. There was no way to find them all. It was too far gone. Capt. Lewis and Col. Baden took their time going through the newspapers. Some of those stories were all exactly the same, word for word off the wire, while others were obvious local write ups, and often completely different. There was no way to know who was going to print what, or why. Or next.

Capt. Lewis was not the least bit amused by this complete lack of control in all of the public information that was going out everywhere, the wild lies being passed off as the crazy truth, but by then, by that morning in that office, Col. Baden was actually laughing as he tossed the last newspaper aside and looked up at the captain, who looked so confused.

"What is so funny?"

The colonel picked up the last paper he had held and shook it at the captain. "Everything is funny! This is funny!"

The captain didn't see it. No smile there at all.

"How is this funny?"

"The lie! The lie is the truth now! We are winning!"

The captain pointed at the stack of papers. He still didn't get it. "How is this winning? We look like idiots in all of these stories."

The colonel lost his smile and got very serious. He also pointed at the stack of newspapers on the captain's desk.

"Because, my dear Captain, the word 'chimpanzee' appears nowhere in any article in any newspaper. Our secret, our real secret, is safely hidden behind a silly lie. And if the Russians think we are idiots, so much the better for us. Because we are most certainly not."

The captain took all of that in and began to understand the colonel's odd thinking on the subject, but he was still the one who had to deal with the press and the public. Still the one who had to look like the idiot that he was most certainly not. Capt. Lewis was the one who had to face those pesky reporters and that nosy public, all of them screaming for more information about UFOs and aliens, none of which existed, but the captain couldn't tell them that. He had to play the game. He had to keep the lie going, and that lie got bigger every day. He just shook his head. This lie had worked too well. There was no way to stop it now, even if they had wanted to. The captain pondered his own reality.

"Maybe I'll grow a mustache."

Now the colonel was confused. "Why would you do that?"

"So that I can go out in public unrecognized."

The colonel smiled. He knew *exactly* how to stop this one. Big smile now.

"Oh, ja! A mustache! Just the thing! They were very popular a few years ago. But just a short little one, like this, ja?"

The colonel held just two fingers vertically under his nose, and the captain flinched. He lost the battle that fast, and he knew it.

"No mustache."

"I didn't think so."

"Maybe a hat and sunglasses."

"You will be like a movie star!"
"I don't want to be a movie star."
"We are never quite what we want to be, but this is what we are now."
"What do you want to be?"
"I always wanted to fly."
"Why didn't you?"
"The war. It got dangerous to fly."
"Yes, it did."
"But you were never shot down?"
"Shot up, yes, shot down, no."
"Close?"
"Yes, once."
"But you made it back?"
"Yes, barely."
"Would you fly again?"
"Yes."
"Me, too. It would be nice now."
"Much less shooting."
"Ja."
"Maybe we should fly together some time."
"*Bitte.*"

The phone on the desk rang and both men jumped back and looked at it. Neither man spoke, and the phone rang again. After the third ring, the captain had to admit that it was his phone, and he picked it up as the colonel smiled.

"Captain Lewis here."

Col. Baden watched Capt. Lewis listen as someone else did all the talking. No expression. None. No smile, no frown. Was the captain even breathing? Tough to tell. Silent and still. Motionless.

"Thank you. Yes. Hold them at the gate. We'll be right there."

Capt. Lewis put the handset back down on the desk phone and looked up at his commanding officer. And then, for no reason at all, he smiled. Suddenly, this was funny. The colonel tried to smile back but couldn't. Not yet.

"*Was?*"
"This is our lucky day."
"Why?"

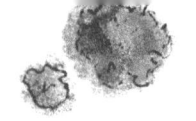

"That was the front gate. There's a crowd of civvies out there, all demanding to meet the aliens."

There was a three-second pause before both men broke into laughter so loud the rest of the office got worried and two people came over to ask.

"Is everything okay, sir?"

"Well, that depends."

"On what, sir?"

"Do you happen to have a Martian-to-English phrase book?"

"Sir?"

"We've got a mob of lunatics out at the front gate, all come to meet the aliens."

By now, Col. Baden was headed for the door and gave one serious order to the man standing there as he went by.

"Lock down this hangar. No one in or out until we get back. Yes?"

"Yes, sir!"

"Come along, Captain. Let us meet our admirers."

Capt. Lewis barely had time to grab his cap, but he did have time to drive the colonel to the front gate in his jeep. No need to show these people what he really drove off the base. And he was still thinking about a mustache, but not *that* mustache. On the way over, Baden told Lewis that he would handle it, and to watch and learn. That wasn't what worried the captain. It was the colonel's smile. Lewis was almost certain that Baden was unarmed, but not entirely. There was no telling which way this might go. Lewis looked down at the jeep's dashboard. Plenty of gas for the getaway. They were good to go. All they had to do was get there.

By the time the captain got the colonel to the front gate, there were at least a dozen people, mostly young men, all herded over to the side, outside the fence, and being kept in check and out of the road by two armed soldiers, and they were all quite animated in their demands. Lewis parked the jeep, and Baden jumped out, ready to deal with it. The captain watched the colonel walk fast out the gate toward the crowd. No gun, as far as he could see. That was good. Maybe. Lewis had to hustle to keep up. That man could *move!*

"*Hallo, was wollt ihr?*"

"We wanna see the aliens!"

"Which ones?"

CHAPTER 15

Capt. Lewis wasn't sure whether to laugh or cry at that. Baden had just implied that the base was hiding several different kinds of aliens. Come to think of it, as he thought about it, they were. Baden was German, and he knew of at least one Italian on the team under the hangar, one of the office staff was English, not to mention the Mexicans who kept the base running when no one was looking. So yeah, hey, which aliens you wanna see today? Now the captain smiled. The loudmouth civvy finally found his voice.

"The ones that aren't from here!"

"None of them are from here. That's what makes them alien."

The colonel looked past that guy.

"Is there someone else in charge? Anyone at all?"

By then, Capt. Lewis was taking a very close look at the crowd, looking for Clayton Whittaker. He was not there. He checked again. Still not there. That was not good. That meant these were all a brand new crowd of space nuts, and he was not pleased with that. The crowd was growing and getting out of hand. Lewis told the guards at the gate to call for more guards. And let's close those gates. The colonel had the guards hold the gate and not close it yet. He wasn't done yet.

"Listen closely. Our situation here is this..."

Eli Lewis, Captain, USAAF, could only stand back, watch, listen, and admire the artistry of a German in motion, playing to the adoring crowd. His crowd. Gorton Baden, Colonel, USAAF, gave the crowd of flying saucer enthusiasts (okay, yeah, nuts) the speech they wanted to hear, even though they never understood a word of it. Some of it was in English, some of it was in German, more than a few words were being made up on the spot and not a word of it made any sense at all. And none of it was true. It was a work of art, and Baden had the crowd completely mesmerized. He was waving his arms and pointing to places both on the base and off and telling them everything they wanted to hear without telling them anything at all. The captain knew he couldn't laugh, but it was tough.

"And thank you all for coming out here this afternoon. It is your enthusiasm that makes this great country what it is today. You are why we won the war, and you are why we will win against the Russians in the next one. Drive safe and always watch the sky. *Danke und auf wiedersehen!*"

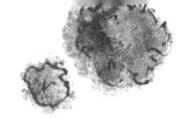

Baden gave them one very snappy salute, and those guys, all civvies, saluted him right back! Eli wanted to applaud but, instead, gave his commanding officer the salute he had just most certainly earned with that speech. The colonel turned around, marched back through the gate and gave the guards one quiet order.

"Now you close the gate."

Once the main gate snapped shut, Baden turned and waved at the crowd from the inside. They all waved back. As he walked past Lewis and toward the jeep, another quiet order.

"Now we go."

"Yes, sir."

It was only after they got back to their offices, under that hangar that was still in lockdown, that Baden had to give Lewis the bad news:

"We need a flying saucer."

And now it was Lewis's turn to go all German on the colonel.

"*Was?*"

Dinner that night at the Lewises' was all about battles recounted and who might have won. Unless you were Mrs. Lewis, then it was all about getting your wonderful husband and your darling daughter to actually eat something you spent all afternoon cooking. Especially that darling daughter, who hadn't taken a bite all night.

"Ashley, you haven't eaten a thing all night."

"I had a weird lunch at school today, Mom."

"And do I want you to tell me what that was at the dinner table, dear?"

"A piece of paper."

At that, Ashley's father put down his fork and looked over at his daughter. This just got interesting, and he already knew the next question to ask, even though he knew he didn't want to.

"And what was *on* that piece of paper you ate?"

"A monkey on a rocket."

"A monkey?"

"Well, yeah, but he said that's what everyone knows aliens look like. They look like monkeys."

"Brat or civvy?"

"Civvy. Sorry."

"How did he know?"

CHAPTER 15

"The civvy kids talk about the UFO you have that you don't have. Their aliens look like your monkeys. I don't think they know what they're talking about."

"But you ate the note anyway?"

"Had to. The teacher was coming for it."

"That's my girl!"

Julie Lewis was still concerned about the nutritional value of paper, even though her daughter had that daily fiber thing covered.

"You still need to eat something."

"I'll take her out for ice cream after dinner."

"Thanks, Dad!"

"Eli, that's hardly a substitute for dinner!"

"You can come along if you promise to behave."

"Oh. Well then..."

"And then maybe you two can help me figure out how to build a flying saucer."

Ashley was all grins and wiggles over that one.

"*Really, Dad??*"

Eli grimaced, smiled and shrugged, all in one smooth move. He was getting good at that.

"I'm not sure, but Baden said he wanted us to have one, so now I have to make one."

Julie was wearing her sly smile. The dangerous one. Eli looked up just in time.

"Piece of cake."

"Oh, no, thank you. We're going out for ice cream later."

"No, dear. Try to keep up. I know how you can build a UFO, and it might even fly."

"I'm all ears."

"No, you're not, and I'm glad for that."

"*MOM!*"

Eli tried to keep the conversation focused. "You had mentioned a flying saucer, I believe?"

"Eli, how many NBAs do you still have on hand?"

"Four ready to fly, one for parts, the sixth one is gone."

"Oh, this just got too easy. Simply take the cockpit and engines off that parts one and fly the big silver gasbag on a black wire tether from the same mounting points. You can weight down a deuce and a half to hold it down if you have to. Liberate a tow truck winch for the back of the deuce to raise and lower it."

"My dear, you're a genius!"

"Yes, and I want a banana split."

"You got it! Bananas all around!"

"I'm good, Dad."

"Party pooper."

"But we're still going out for ice cream, right?"

"Of course we are. Right after you and I do the dishes."

Eli Lewis kissed his wife, and his wife kissed him right back. Their daughter gagged, but the dishes got done and they did go out for ice cream. Julie got a banana split.

The next day saw Capt. Lewis directing the ground team to move the four functional NBAs over to one side of the hangar as the two almost-flight-ready manned weather balloons were both very carefully folded up and packed off to the *other* side of the hangar, leaving plenty of room in the middle (right in front of the door!) for the remains of the fifth NBA to become their first UFO.

In the middle of all of that, Col. Baden stopped by to see what was going on, and when the captain told him what was going on, he smiled.

"A very good idea."

"My wife's idea."

"Of course it was."

Now Eli wasn't sure if that was meant as a compliment or not, but at least he got the go-ahead to go ahead. Eli and the USAAF were now officially in the UFO business. Maybe they could shave a chimp to be the alien. That might be fun. Yeah. Right. *No.*

In truth, they had never done this before: They had never removed a gasbag from an NBA. There was a long "How to?" moment that day until they all decided to simply pump enough gas into the bag to bring it up to shape and off the floor, just enough to let them work under it to unbolt the cockpit and motors from the bag. No need to add fuel to the tanks, so less weight there. We can do this! Then the real question arose, no pun intended.

"So then, how do we get the gasbag back down from the ceiling?"

"Say what?"

CHAPTER 15

"What. Now, we unbolt the bag, the cockpit and motors all land there, and the bag goes straight up to the ceiling. So how do we get it back down?"

Everyone put their wrenches down and looked up. It was a good question, and the ceiling in that hangar was a long ways up. No one spoke until someone spoke, which happened a lot back then.

"We have to tether it first."

"To what?"

"It doesn't matter if the cable is long enough. If it goes up with a cable already attached, we can always bring it back down with that."

Capt. Lewis smiled.

"Take a buck from the Banana Bottle, son."

"Thank you, sir!"

By the end of the day, and after all of the other parts were carted off and hidden, the United States Army Air Force had its very first flying saucer. All they had to do was get it back down off the ceiling.

Good thing there was a cable.

CHAPTER 16

AFTER A LOVELY NIGHT IN THE DESERT (BLANCHE) AND A nasty night in the sand (Clayton), Blanche did finally convince Clayton to maybe raise the hood on his old car, should anyone ever drive by. And after she saw what *that* took, she knew why he hadn't even tried to do that the day before when they ran out of gas. It took both of them to get that beastly big hood up on that old car, and the first stick they used to try to prop it up broke. That was exciting! Could have lost an arm there.

With both of them using the thickest sticks they could find, they did get the hood up, and lo and behold, the next (and only) car to drive by did stop *and they had extra gas!* Apparently, Clayton, *some people* go out into the desert prepared. Who knew? Blanche made a mental note: Don't let him pull *that* stunt again. He did not look any better the next morning all covered in campfire crap and sand. And now the front seat was a mess, but mostly on his side. Ah, but they did get back into town. Finally. After a decent meal and a serious cleanup, they both felt much better. So much better that Clayton wanted to go back out into the desert again already. Blanche put both of her feet down on that one. *No. Not today. You'll stay here and play with what you've got, and with that trunk full of junk you just found.* Clayton smiled. Yeah, he could do that!

And so it was that after a night out in the desert, Clayton Whittaker spend the next day out in the yard, working on his flying saucer and trying to figure out that mass propulsion drive system thing, forgetting that he had made the whole thing up. It had to be based on Einstein's E=MC2, right? That worked pretty well around here a couple of years ago, didn't it? Or was it M=EC3? All he had to do was figure out how to convert mass to energy and not vaporize Roswell in the process. And how to build it out of a shed full of burnt and broken parts left over from the crash of a gasbag full of monkeys. Roswell was fairly safe for the time being.

Now you have to understand that, in what we might laughingly call the reality of that place and time, in that weird desert setting in the wild west, Clayton Whittaker had become something of a local hero in Roswell, if only because he got there first. He was, without even trying, the de facto leader and spokesperson for a growing crowd of flying saucer enthusiasts who were making their way to Roswell from all over the U.S., all because of those novelty news stories. And when they got there and they asked around, all the locals told them the same thing. "Oh, yeah, you need to see Clayton about that." And they did. Every time.

Before long, and to Blanche's mild amusement, Clayton had plenty of help that wasn't her when it came to anything flying saucer. All he had to do was open the shed door and he had help dragging stuff out, laying it out and pondering the great imponderables of a mass propulsion drive. Oh, and they helped put it all back, too. Blanche didn't mind that at all. It was the desert search scene that got really weird.

Despite that recent solo trip out into the sand that ended so very badly, more often than not after that they had plenty of company with them when they went out into the desert on a search. It would start, every day, over breakfast. There would be a nut or two wherever they went for breakfast, and they would all gather around Clayton to find out where he was going that day, and then they would follow. Tell others and follow. So now, yes, Clayton Whittaker, late of Irvine, California, did indeed have a cult following. Blanche didn't mind so much. They helped push the car. But it was still weird.

As she and Clayton would finish their breakfast every morning, these guys (it was almost always guys) would help push the car, and as they drove away, those same guys would all jump and run to follow in their cars. (Clayton never waited for them.) Once Clayton parked well out of town, wherever he planned to search that day, the guys would all park in a line behind and then follow him, in awe of his expertise and acumen. Not to mention his skill as a daring desert dweller. They were all city mice, too. Blanche, the one true desert rat in all of this, simply held back and walked behind the crowd, letting them do all of the work and find all of the snakes. By the time she got to wherever they were going, the snakes all had just about enough of that crowd. The guys were more than willing to carry all of that newfound junk to the car's trunk, but they did fill that trunk every day. There was no more room in the shed. Blanche was pitching stuff out the back when no one was looking, but still, the pile grew. And grew. And as long as the rent was paid, the owner didn't mind. The same might be said of the entire town of Roswell. Flying saucers were the new cash cows.

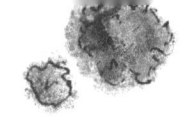

Since all of Clayton's followers, all of those wacky UFO nuts, were all in from out of town, they were more than welcome to stay in town, just as long as they all remembered to bring their wallets. And for the most part, they did. (The few that didn't went home first.) Boarding houses and hardware stores, restaurants and clothing (boots!), everyone needed something, and Roswell had most of it right there. Even snakebite kits for the very nervous. Those were going fast. As long as they spent money, they could stay. The locals were happy with that, even if they did laugh a little when the saucer nuts weren't looking. And sometimes even when they were. Their money was good. But were they?

All of these new guys, and a few new girls, did keep the sheriff busy. He wasn't so sure he liked this new crowd, and he made a point of trying to meet every one of them, if only to say hello. A handshake can tell you a lot about a guy. Especially if your watch is gone right after that. As soon as he got a name, he checked that name. No poster? No invite from the FBI? Yeah, you can stay. With Clayton Whittaker, the leader of the pack, the sheriff went as far as to spend the dime to make the call all the way back out to Irvine, California, Clayton's home town. It was worth it for the laugh. The local Chief of Police was truly amused.

"You've got Clayton Whittaker out there?"

"Yes, sir, I believe we do."

"He made it all the way to … where?"

"Roswell, New Mexico."

"That boy shouldn't cross the street alone."

"Well, he's here now. Is that going to be a problem?"

"Not for me!"

CHAPTER 16

"What about for me? Does the young man have a record?"

"Oh, he was never all that good at anything, let alone crime. He's mostly harmless."

"But not entirely?"

"Only to himself."

"I'll keep that in mind."

"And when you get tired of him, just point him back our way."

"I'll be sure to do that."

With the sheriff busy checking records, the local car shop was busy with small repairs and fender benders. Seemed those space nuts had some small trouble driving on planet Earth. Must have been the gravity. Got 'em every time. They were forever bouncing into ditches, off of rocks and sometimes each other. Nothing too big or too bad, but just enough to make the local shop really happy and very busy. Now the locals had to plan their mishaps to work them into the shop's busy schedule. But the money was good, and no one dared complain. Even the doctor and dentist were doing well. The local large animal vet saw no change. There were no new horses in town.

The space nuts (that's what the locals called them) had a sort of daily routine, all based on wherever Clayton ate breakfast and dinner. And because of that, he and Blanche were often given a "best friends" discount wherever they ate if the crowd ate with them. Clayton never quite figured that out. He really thought they were all best friends. Blanche pegged it and said nothing. Cheap food was cheap food, and who was she to complain? More often than not, Clayton handled the bill. Nice guy. A dim bulb, but a nice guy. And the food was good.

The big plus for Blanche when it came to the crowd was the car. That is, she seldom had to push the car anymore. There was always someone else, usually several someone elses, all ready, willing and able to give that old beast a shove. So all she had to do was sit there, smile and wave as they drove away. So that's what she did. That was not a problem. Nice. She could get used to that.

With the parts piling up in the shed, Clayton had put the word out: He needed more drive parts. Something powered that UFO, and they needed to find it. Those mass propulsion drive systems still had to be out there, somewhere in the desert, just waiting for them to pick them up and bring them back and finish this flying saucer! To that end the search was on, but of course they found everything but. With the real motors from the NBA having been picked up by the Army's ground team on the first day, whatever "motor parts" they found after that most assuredly were *not*. And did that stop them? It did not. Now *this* became the new game in town, and it seemed as though everyone wanted to play.

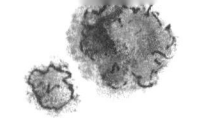

There was, in the small town of Roswell, New Mexico, a certain small faction of young men all about the same age as the space nuts that were not nearly as amused as the rest of the town with these new young men around. While they were hardly any real competition, they were seen as an intrusion. And they were also seen as fair game. In this early part of the Cold War, spies were all the rage, and so it only made good sense to send in the spies. Their spies. Locals listened, and locals heard. And what they heard was "motor parts." The space nuts were looking for "motor parts." They were all pretty sure they could make that wish come true. Just as soon as they stopped laughing.

Over time, over the ensuing weeks, all manner of broken, rusty and tragic motors that had been pitched out anywhere near Roswell over the years were all rounded up and carefully put *somewhere* that those space nuts might find it. It was almost like recycling, long before that word came around. Now, the fact that none of those nuts would know a motor from a mothball made the game almost too easy, but that didn't stop the locals from playing. And it sure did clean up all those other ranches! Long nights were now being spent out in the desert, carefully arranging old parts of everything in new and interesting ways. And what if they maybe did accidentally build a mass propulsion drive system out of all of those old parts out there? Hey, maybe then all of those space nuts would fly away! *What else ya got? Come on, let's go look out back.*

Blanche saw the difference, the change in the haul. Now it looked as though they had found all they were going to find of whatever had really been shot down out there in that storm, and almost all of what was coming in now was older stuff. Just junk. Real junk. Old motor parts and pump parts and farm machine parts. Nothing aircraft, and certainly nothing spaceship, but it was all still getting picked up and brought back, and where were they going to put all of this stuff? Quietly, in odd moments, Blanche did her best to throw away what she could, but it was a losing battle. The nuts were winning. Something had to give.

Out in the middle of the White Sands basin, out in the open desert that passed for an Army base, inside the tall fences topped with blue lights, there was an aircraft hangar you never saw. Hidden at ground level by the other buildings all around it, one hangar, and all that was in it, was being protected by everything else on that base. That was where they kept the UFO. Or so they say.

In the days following Col. Baden's meeting outside the gate with the space nuts, the order was given to make what they did not have: A flying saucer. A real one? Real enough. It had to float, if not fly. And they found that they could do that. They had just the thing, with a little work and a great big truck. The ground crew had attacked the remains of their fifth Neutral Buoyancy Aircraft, their parts donor for all of the others. It didn't fly, but it had exactly what they needed: That big gasbag up on top. It was silver, it was round and it looked like a flying saucer. All they had to do was get it off the rest of the NBA under it without losing it. Without it flying away. Oddly enough, that thing flying away would be a bad thing. Go figure.

With Capt. Lewis overseeing the slow, deliberate process, it was a very serious operation, even as funny as it was. They were making a UFO! They were gonna fly a saucer! Did that make them all aliens? It got weird until the captain cracked down on the whole alien shtick. Earthling or else! *Yes, sir.* They got on with it, and to their credit, they did not lose the one part they needed. The big silver gasbag, semi-inflated but securely tethered, did *not* float away. Go team! Col. Baden was impressed.

"So we are ready for gasbag testing, ja?"

"Well, it's either that or we wait for the next bad election."

"Better to have bad elections than none at all."

"We are almost ready."

"Show me."

With Capt. Lewis leading the way and the ground team standing back, Col. Baden was led around all that was left of the fifth NBA—nothing but piles of loose and random parts on the hangar floor and that big silver bag of explosive hydrogen rocking gently overhead, tethered to the ground by steel cables to tow truck winch spools. Baden was nodding his head at everything he saw.

"The spools go on a truck, ja?"

"We have a truck coming this week. All four spools will fit in the back, and the truck is strong enough to hold the weight."

"What color?"

"The truck?"

"Ja."

"They never said. Olive drab or khaki."

"Make it dull black. Everything. Even the cables. Nothing shines. Invisible at night."

"Yes, sir."

"So when it is done, you can drive it around and let it fly above?"

"Yes, sir, that's the plan."

"Make sure the truck makes no noise at all. Many mufflers."

"Yes, sir."

Baden stopped walking and said nothing for a long minute.

"Can we give it a noise?"

"What do you mean?"

"What does a flying saucer sound like?"

Capt. Lewis had no answer to that one, and he looked at his crew. Shrugs all around. No one knew, but he did have the right answer for the colonel.

"What do you want it to sound like?"

"Something high-pitched. Something like *we-you-we-you-we-you*."

The crew stood stock still and silent. No one dared to move or speak. They had no idea what to do. The captain thought this was wickedly hilarious for no good reason, but he knew to not smile. He didn't dare.

"We can make that happen."

The risk was worth it for the looks on their faces. The ground crew was now jumping around behind them in a total panic, and they all had no earthly idea how they were going to do that. The tour continued as Baden looked at everything except the ground crew. The ground crew didn't know this had been Baden and Lewis's idea of a great joke. They were both in on it. Lewis thought he might mention that to the crew later. Or maybe not.

"How far can you take it?"

"To the edge of the base and outlying land in every direction. The truck is all-wheel drive, and there are unpaved roads inside the perimeter fence."

"Don't drive too close to the fence. People will see the truck. Keep the truck hidden as much as you can."

"Yes, sir."

"And let me know when you are ready for the first flight. I want to see."

"Yes, sir."

Back at the door, Col. Baden turned around to address the still-panicked ground crew. He just couldn't resist.

"You are doing a very good job here. Keep up the good work, and don't forget: *We-you-we-you-we-you!*"

And with that, the colonel was gone, the ground crew was freaked out and the captain was laughing so hard he had to hold on to something. It had been a good day all around. Before the mob could attack the laughing captain, he did have to wave them off and explain the joke that no one thought was funny even after they got it, except for one guy in the back, who hadn't said a word until he finally did.

"Yeah, we can do that."

That quiet statement got the captain's undivided attention, and everyone else stopped, too.

"What did you just say?"

The guy had to think about it as he moved his hands over invisible things, and his eyes never left his hands, but then he spoke again.

"We can do that. Hook a microphone to an amplifier, the amp to a speaker and put the microphone in *front* of the speaker. You get a high-pitched scream we can control with the volume knob on the amp. We can put the whole thing on the back of the truck and control it from the cab. We can *we-you* all night long."

"Son, take a buck from the Banana Bottle."

"Yes, sir!"

The captain then addressed the entire ground crew.

"And let's let this be our little surprise for Col. Baden when the time comes, shall we?"

"*Yes, sir!*"

Through all of this, and right from the beginning, the local newspaper, the Roswell Daily Record, had been both professional and polite on the subject of the original crash, the weather balloons and the whole strange UFO weirdness that had followed. They had reported the news based on the facts, they had not divulged any military secrets, known or guessed, and then they had moved on. To them, the story was done, and that whole UFO thing was not news. Not even novelty news. It was sad comedy and a sad commentary of the state of affairs in America so soon after such a horrific war. But that was just the local paper.

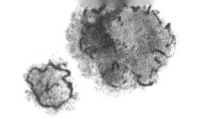

Out-of-town reporters, like El Paso's Arnie Benton, were a lot more aggressive and not giving up so easily. There had to be a story here, and that story had to be UFOs! Flying saucers! Little men from outer space! It was either that or go home, and Arnie did not want to go home. If he could stay there on the story on the newspaper's dime, it was like a working vacation with cute waitresses! There just had to be a story here. All he had to do was find it. Or make one up.

Now, in truth, Arnie Benton knew there was no UFO. He knew *something* had crashed, but whatever it was, it was a government thing, a *secret* government thing, and they were not about to let out any more information than the no information that they already had. Had the Army made up the thing about the UFO? Arnie wasn't so sure about that. He had heard Clayton go on about it long before anyone in uniform denied the claim as if they were lying. That got complicated, but Arnie was still sure the lie was the truth. There was no UFO. The waitress at the Tin Can Café, however, was very real, and Arnie was hoping for a story there he could tell later. But not in print.

Arnie knew he needed photos. Maybe not of a UFO, but certainly of *something*. Almost anything. Preferably military. All he had to do was get on the base with a camera, and he could drag this paid vacation out a bit longer. But how? It wasn't easy. The gate guards were all edgy now, and no cameras allowed. He could maybe sneak in hidden in someone else's car trunk, but the last time he tried *that*, the driver kind of forgot about him and that did not end well for the trunk.

To his credit and amusement, Capt. Lewis was more than willing to talk to Arnie anytime he called. Arnie didn't make a pest of himself, but he did call every few days or so, just to catch up and chat and find out what was new in the green alien world of UFOs and flying saucers.

"And what's the difference, anyway?"

"Pardon me?"

CHAPTER 16

"Well, Captain, we talk about UFOs and flying saucers as if they are two different things, so maybe I need to ask. What's the difference between a UFO and a flying saucer?"

"Oh, that's easy, Arnie. If you see something flying and you don't know what it is, that's a UFO, an *Unidentified* Flying Object. It could be anything, you just don't know what it is right then."

"And a flying saucer?"

"Oh, those really stand out. You know what those are every time you see one. Have you seen one of those yet?"

"Well, no, I don't think so."

"You really should."

"Which ones do the aliens like to fly?"

"Oh, they like the flying saucers, Arnie. That's what they like."

"And what else do aliens like?"

"Hot dogs and Ping-Pong."

"I don't doubt that for a second, Captain."

Arnie Benton, ace reporter for the El Paso Times, had the high ground all around the military base all checked out. He knew every view. He knew where to go to see the sights, day or night. If only there was something to see. He also knew every airplane in the Army's vast collection, along with every other airplane they might possibly fly into that base when they thought no one was looking. And now he also knew the difference between a flying saucer and a UFO. And he knew he did not want to see a UFO. He wanted to see a flying saucer. That much, he knew.

It got to the point where Arnie had given up on trying to get on the base and instead spent his days sleeping as much as he could to stay awake at night, up on the various overlooks he had mapped out to keep an eye on the base, and on all that might fly there at night. He was convinced that if they *did* have anything worth seeing, it might only fly at night. This was definitely costing him quality time with that cute waitress, but if he landed this big story, he and the waitress might just run away. They might just have to. He tried to explain the whole thing to her but ended up just tipping heavily. That worked, too.

The toughest part was not keeping to a schedule. That is, Arnie tried to go out on random nights to random locations, with no set pattern for either. It was not as easy as it sounded, but would it pay off? He *did* see things at night, strange things, but so far, under the

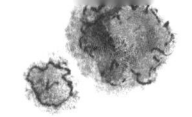

captain's definition of things, they were just UFOs, not flying saucers. Still, he tried. He persisted and he knew:
All he had to do was pick the right night.

CHAPTER 17

AS THE PROGRESS REPORTS FROM THE BRAND NEW FLYING Saucer Ground Crew were coming fast and furious, and those reports were all very positive (even the secret *we-you-we-you*), Capt. Lewis and Col. Baden were meeting more often, at least once a day, and more often than not in the captain's office, as it was closer to the stairs up to the hangar floor. Baden was still worried, though. He paced the small room as he spoke.

"How soon, do you think, before the first flight?"

"By the end of the week, certainly."

Baden thought about that, looked at the calendar on the captain's desk, then frowned and shook his head. No. Now the captain frowned as well, even though he had no idea *why* he was frowning.

"Wait. Do not fly yet."

"Why not? We're ready. What are we waiting for?"

"We will wait for the first day of the month. Next month. That is your first flight."

"*Because*?"

Now Baden looked up and smiled that sly smile. He was up to something again. Already. Still.

"Let us see how many people might be paying attention."

"How so? To what?"

"You take out your flying saucer for the first time, big and bold, shiny and silver, on the first night of the month, and then you fly it again the following night on the second."

"Okay... And then?"

"And then you fly it again on the fourth, on the eighth, and then on the sixteenth of the month. But only at night."

"And after that? After the sixteenth?"

"Then you must wait for the first again, of the next month, as there is no thirty-second of any month. Do you think our friends will catch the mathematical pattern?"

Capt. Lewis smiled at the genius of the thing.

"I'll make sure that they do."

That gave the ground crew team a couple weeks of down time between the last flight of each month and the first flight of the following month, but they all had other things to do. They would keep busy. Baden was still walking around Lewis's office, looking at things and still thinking. Always thinking. And questioning his own reasoning. And frowning again.

"Only five flights a month. Will that be enough?"

The captain gave it some thought.

"What about flying on prime number nights?"

"Let us see: One, two, three, five, seven, eleven, thirteen, seventeen… Too many already."

"You're right, we want it to be seen, but maybe not seen that much. Maybe on the squares?"

"One, four, nine, sixteen and twenty-five?"

"It's still a logical math progression that can be caught, and it's more evenly spaced throughout the month."

"I like it! Make it so."

"And just like that, we have a flight plan!"

"A schedule. The same every month. Make sure."

"What about bad weather?"

"We do not fly in bad weather. That lesson we have learned."

"Yes, we have."

Baden was still, in his mind, going over the far too many small details of what should have been a very simple thing. Just go fly a big gasbag over a heavy truck. How tough could that be? Somehow, it all got complicated long before the first flight. How did that happen? Little by little, the problems got solved and, one rule at a time, the rules got laid down. They would only fly at night, well after dark, but start at different odd times each night. Ah, but always well before midnight, so as to start on the correct day of the month each time. Yes, that date would be important. On the squares! They would learn.

CHAPTER 17

Know when to watch. Capt. Lewis mentioned square dancing, and the colonel did not get that one at all. He'd explain later.

Also important, and Baden was right: Don't let anyone see the truck. Paint it dull black, and drive without lights. Could they do that? Drive around the base at night with no lights at all? Capt. Lewis decided to let the ground crew try to do it with just the truck (no flying saucer) before they flew the bag over it. No need to wreck both. He needed to test his crew for their night vision, to find the best drivers for this. Maybe a couple of them.

They decided on using several different "flight" routes all around the base, but as had already been mentioned, never too close to the fence. Hide the truck! Different routes, different times, different nights, launch the bag at different places, and fly it at different altitudes each time. This was not a parade. Or was it?

"What about lights?"

"No lights."

"I mean shining on the bag? To make sure it shows up."

Baden had to think about that.

"Let us see how bright and shiny it might be without any new lights. The base has many lights. Maybe too many already."

Capt. Lewis had to think about that. When was the last time he had walked around the base at night, just to look at the lights? Too long. It had been too long. He would walk around it that night. Just to see. He had to know. What else did they have to figure out?

"What about photos?"

"We don't have to take any photos. Let *them* take their photos."

"Do we *want* them to take their photos?"

"We are *counting* on them to take their photos. Very blurry ones."

Baden smiled at that.

"Do they get to see the aliens?"

"We might let them think that they did."

"Not ground crew in flight suits?"

"No, no, no, no... Well, maybe. But can we paint black windows on the silver bag?"

Capt. Lewis stopped smiling. That was a tough question.

"That might not be so easy. Paint doesn't like to stick to that silver fabric."

"So you repaint after every flight?"

"We might have to."

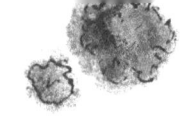

"Let's try that and see how it works."

"Fair enough. That will be a good test, good to know how it goes with paint."

"Just paint black windows. No aliens in the windows, waving."

Now it was the captain's turn to smile. "Are you sure about that?"

The colonel smiled as well. "I am sure for now, yes. Maybe later. We shall see."

They both laughed at the idea of having aliens waving at the windows, but then the captain lost his smile first. Was all of this really worth it?

"Gorton, do you really believe we can make people believe this? That we have a flying saucer?"

The German frowned at that question and looked right at his friend and fellow officer.

"People will believe anything you tell them if you tell them just enough."

"But not too much?"

"The same simple, easy lie, over and over. They will find their own truth in it every time."

"Even flying saucers?"

"Why not? It is a simple lie. Easy to believe if you see it."

"But we never let them see the lie up close?"

"No, never. They never get to *touch* the lie."

"Because...?"

"Because if you touch the lie, you feel the truth."

"So we don't want this thing to get loose."

"No, never. Never loose, never too close. Let them see it from afar, but never touch it up close. Can you do that?"

"Ja."

"Good man."

Capt. Lewis knew that he and his ground team still had a lot to do to get that silver gasbag and big truck ready for the first night flight. Now he looked at his own desk calendar, and he was thankful for the new flight schedule. Ready by the first of the month? Yeah, they'd be ready. He would make sure that they were ready, even if he had to paint those windows himself. That might be fun.

The sprawling military base outside of Roswell, New Mexico, for all of its size, was not entirely self-contained. Not everyone who worked there lived there, right on the base, and not everyone who

CHAPTER 17

worked there shopped there. There was a sort of "Army general store" on the base, the PX, or Post Exchange, but it didn't have everything. They never do. Sometimes you had to shop in town. And sometimes you wanted to shop in town, just to get off the base. It was like going on vacation, but everyone still spoke English. Mostly. Well, some. *Que?*

With a day off from school and nothing to do, Julie figured her daughter deserved a "Girls' Day Out," and with Eli safe at work (as far as anyone knew), Julie Lewis took Ashley shopping in town. It was going to be a fun day, and that it was, right from the start. They had gone dress shopping first and shoe shopping, of course, and they even pretended to do a little jewelry shopping (just window shopping), but then it was time to get serious and hit the grocery store for the real shopping. That was why they were there. The PX on the base had good prices but a limited selection. Ah, but if they filled the car in town today, they'd eat like queens for a month! Hooray! And so they did.

The mother-daughter team of Julie and Ashley tackled the grocery store with their usual busy "investigative shopping" style. "What's this?" What's this?" became the common bond and rallying cry between the two of them, aisle after aisle and item after item as they made their way through the grocery store. They wanted to see everything and buy most of it. What fun! Well, it was fun until it got even funnier and "What's this?" became "Who's that?" Of course they were not alone in the store. It was a big public store in a wide open town, and there were plenty of other people in there, both staff and customers, stocking shelves and shopping. And then there were *those two* right there. Yeah... Those two... That guy...

Julie had seen them first, up ahead, as they had turned into the aisle, but said nothing to Ashley right away. She'd see them soon enough, and then there was no telling how that might go. What she might do. Julie could hardly wait. A small smile arrived on her lips and stayed there, waiting as she watched. Any moment now. The young lady of the couple in question seemed normal enough as she watched her, but that young man, my goodness, what was wrong with him? Was he drunk? No, maybe not drunk. Perhaps he was challenged. Dropped as a baby? Maybe twice. Julie Lewis was, of course, watching Clayton Whittaker and Blanche Miller, who also happened to be doing a bit of grocery shopping in the store on that day. Even the saucer nuts have to eat.

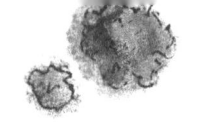

Ashley had seen them, of course, but for once she had said nothing at first. Then she started to watch them more, intrigued by The Guy That Never Shut Up. Now she couldn't look away. In a way, he was shopping much like she and her mother were shopping; he was looking at everything, and at some things twice. He'd pick something up, look at it, show it to the girl, look at it again and then put it back. Or maybe put it in their basket. (They hadn't even bothered with a cart.) There were only a few small things in their basket by then, and they were in the middle of the store. Halfway through, no matter which way they were going, if they were going anywhere at all. Ashley wasn't so sure. They hadn't moved. And he hadn't shut up. Good grief.

They could not possibly be locals. He couldn't. With another look, the girl could be a local, maybe. She had the boots for it, and those boots were used. Ashley pegged her as a desert rat, but what was she doing with him? How could *that* have been the best she might have done? Were all the cowboys gone? And, after she thought about it, *where* had all the cowboys gone? They probably ran from that guy. Maybe that guy was her brain-damaged brother. Yeah, that had to be it. It was a pity date. And what was he going on about? She had to get closer. She had to hear what he had to say. Ashley smiled at her mom and held up a hand.

"Be right back."

"Be careful."

"Oh, yeah."

There was no doubt where Ashley was going. Julie had been watching the same two young people up ahead of them in the aisle, the same non-stop guy, for just as long, and she wondered just as much: What was wrong with that guy? And did he *ever* shut up? Julie simply stopped walking and pretended to look at small bags of rice. Fascinating!

Ashley worked her way up the aisle, picking stuff up, looking at it, and then putting it back down. Was there anything there she really did need? Not so much, no, but she had to at least *pretend* to be shopping, just as though she was fooling anyone. She was not. Well, maybe she was fooling Clayton, who paid her no attention whatsoever, even when she was right there. Blanche, on the other hand, had seen her coming, knew why, and just smiled and winked when she got there. *Welcome to the floor show, kid.* Clayton was looking the other way and saw nothing. As usual. But now Ashley did get to hear the running monologue. To her dismay.

"We've got to figure out what they eat. What their metabolism runs on. They can't be like us. They can't eat like us. We need to know why they are here, where they came from and where they are going next. This must just be one stop along the way for them. They never stop, you know…"

Blanche said silently to herself, "Tell me about it."

Ashley, stopped behind Clayton, was wide-eyed and speechless. She had no idea what she was going to hear, but that certainly wasn't it. Wow. Yeah, this guy was seriously damaged goods. *Put him back on the shelf, girl!* Ashley put back whatever she was holding (she had never bothered to look at it) and had to run back down the aisle before she started laughing so hard. She hid on another aisle until *that* giggle attack was over. Her mom waited patiently and smiled softly. This really was amusing at a safe distance. Then came the silent dawn in her mind as she watched Clayton. "I wonder if Eli has met this one?" Ashley said much the same thing when she got back from her attack.

"Oh, I can't wait to tell Dad about *this* one!"

Julie looked over at her daughter who was all grins and wiggles over the nutcase in aisle three. Julie put a silent finger to her lips. *Don't let the nutcase hear you, dear.* But then she added, "I worry that your father is meeting too many like that already."

"What's to worry about if they're just crazy?"

"Crazy can be dangerous."

The fun slowly drained out of the conversation, and the smiles left first.

"How?"

"When they find out they're wrong."

Ashley did think about that for a moment as she thought about the looney up ahead in the pasta aisle. Then, still serious and still watching him, she had the answer.

"How would they know?"

To either his credit or his demise, Clayton Whittaker had never actually *known* himself to be wrong. Not as a kid, not then, not now, not ever. It was his one outstanding charm, to always be right.

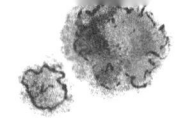

Whether he was or not. And now, to his completely unappreciated advantage, no one could quite say for sure. Flying saucers? UFOs? Aliens from another planet? In the summer of 1947, there was still that wonderfully remote possibility that he was right about all of that and they *were* here and that *was* what crashed on the Foster Ranch outside of Roswell that day. No one could say that it *wasn't*. Could they? So he had to be right. Didn't he? Well, he thought so. And no one could get a word in edgewise to say otherwise. So he was right again, as always. As far as he knew.

Blanche Miller, on the other hand, was considerably more skeptical about the whole celestial situation. She had found bits and pieces of this and that in the desert that had led her down a very different lane entirely when it came to that mysterious crash. But since Clayton was kind enough to give her lift out of town when she needed one, and foot the bill for most of the adventure, she wisely said nothing, nodded her head and hid the evidence. But she knew what she knew. And she knew what it was not. But it sure was fun to watch.

There was no doubt in her mind that Clayton and his wacky band of followers were seen as the welcome comic relief in that small town in what might otherwise have been a dull summer, indeed. Take away the flying saucers and little grey men, and there wasn't much going on in Roswell any time of year. It was a nice small town, but it was still a small desert town, and not much different from the one she was from. At least Clayton was from the big(ger) city. Blanche did wonder about that. What might that be like? California? It was like a dream to her. Maybe she could get him to take her there. That might be interesting. This certainly was, for what it was.

It was fun for her to step back and watch the locals deal with the loons. To watch people when they saw Clayton for the first time, as that girl had in the grocery store. Blanche knew there had to be a hundred questions, but there was no way for her to ask. All the girl could do was get close and listen in awe and wonder. And then run away and laugh. It always ended like that. And why hadn't Blanche run away and laughed? That was a very good question, and one she kept asking herself. No answer yet. Still looking for that answer. And still smiling in awe and wonder, too.

CHAPTER 17

But what if Julie was right? What if it got dangerous? Blanche had not heard that conversation, but she had wondered about the same thing over the time she had spent with Clayton, and especially by then, with that whole flying saucer thing. What happens when he finds out he's wrong? Does he just go home? Does he remember to take her home as well? Or does he get dangerous? She had not seen a dangerous side to the man, but that didn't mean it wasn't there. Maybe no one had dug deep enough. Maybe this would. Maybe she should. But not today. And probably not tomorrow.

Just as Julie and Ashley had taken their haul from town back home, got it all sorted out and packed away, Blanche and Clayton took their small bag of groceries back to their rooms, and she did a fine job of making dinner for two on one hot plate. She called it Rice Surprise. Clayton looked at it. Then he looked at it again.

"What's in this?"

"Well, rice."

"I can see that. What else?"

"Let's see... Ground beef..."

"Yeah..."

"Carrots..."

"Uh-huh..."

"And artichoke."

"*Artichoke?*"

"Surprise!"

Now, California boy that he was, he knew what an artichoke was, and he didn't really mind it so much in his dinner, but then again, he had to be the Clayton, and he picked at his food until it was cold as he told her everything he knew about artichokes and agriculture. Blanche sat there, eating her rice surprise while it was still warm and wondering how tough it might be to get horse tranquilizers in Roswell. That would be a nice surprise. And maybe tomorrow's surprise. *Surp...*

It was going to be a quiet evening at home for everyone that night, including Arnie Benton, as everyone elected to *not* go back out into the desert that night, or even just walk out in the yard and look up. The little grey men were on their own. Have fun guys! Fly safe! But it was a beautiful night, clear and deep and full of stars, with just enough airplanes to keep it interesting at first and then, after midnight, a shooting star or two to spice things up. And there were always a few people up and out, watching the sky and wondering now: Was anyone looking back? And if no one on Earth was looking, maybe one or two of them waved at no one in particular up there. You know, just to be friendly.

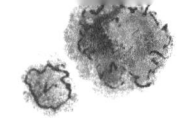

If nothing else, the news out of Roswell that summer *did* get people thinking about the big picture. The *really* big picture. Were we alone in the universe? Was there anyone else out there? Would they ever come here? And *why* would they come here? What alien in their right mind thought Roswell was a cool place to hang out? Maybe they were lost. They had to be lost. Maybe they should have taken a left at Albuquerque. *Better luck next time, guys.*

If it was all fun and games in town that week, life on the base, life *under* the base, was neither, and it was getting out of control. The chimpanzees had been cooped up in their compound under the NBA hangar and had not flown for far too long. They knew something was wrong, and even with the new chimps to get their community's number back to right, they were all still nervous and annoyed. That made it dangerous to get near them, and Capt. Lewis had no desire to have to explain *those* injuries to anyone at the base hospital no matter what sort of security clearance they had. Col. Baden stepped in, but only figuratively, He didn't want to get near them, either. They met in Capt. Lewis's office. That seemed safe. No monkeys there.

"They want to fly."

"As do we all, Captain."

"Should we risk it?"

"Not yet. We need to show something very different now."

"We could turn them loose in town. That would be different."

Col Baden just stared at the captain. He wasn't sure...

"A joke, yes?"

"Maybe. Who wants to know?"

Now the captain smiled, and the colonel smiled. Yes, it was a joke.

"What if we took them for a ride?"

"In a plane?"

"Too dangerous. They would want to fly the thing."

"In what, then?"

"In a car."

"Just drive the monkeys around? Would they like that?"

"Beats just sitting at home and eating bananas."

"Ja."

"We could suit them up as if they were *going* to fly, but then simply drive them all around the base in a car, let them see the real outside world again."

"A closed car? No one sees?"

"Yes, of course."

The colonel thought about all of this, and while he didn't smile, it did make him think.

"Or not."

"No car ride?"

"No car ride. Jeep."

Now it was the captain's turn to stop and think.

"An open jeep? But people might see them."

"And at a distance, ja, and what will they see? Small, human-like, long-armed forms in space suits. And what will they think? Think!"

"They will think they are seeing … aliens!"

"Ja!"

"Ha!"

Now the colonel waved an arm at the captain.

"But not too much too soon and not too close. Pretend to be hiding them as you are not."

"Pressure suits and flight helmets?"

"Ja?"

"One at a time?"

"One in each jeep. Only one."

"And not too close to the fence. Just far enough away to catch interest without detail."

Baden thought about it some more.

"Human drivers in surgical gloves and masks, so as not to infect our alien friends."

"And to keep their identity a secret as well."

"Ja. We still have to deny."

"But we still want them to ask."

"Ja."

"When?"

"First thing tomorrow morning. One only. Then let us see. And captain?"

"Yes?"

The colonel wagged a warning finger at the captain. "No laughing."

"Ja."

CHAPTER 18

IT WAS FLYING TIME. IT WAS LATE IN THE DAY, AND IT WAS THE first day of the month. The ground crew team that had worked so hard to turn the remains of a Neutral Buoyancy Aircraft into a flying saucer were ready to make that happen that night. They had also started calling themselves the Space Cadets. Capt. Lewis didn't mind that so much, but Col. Baden didn't get the joke. The captain planned to be there for that first flight, but the colonel did not. Something about "frowning a line" in town. The ground crew didn't get that joke, and the captain didn't bother to translate. He just smiled. Good for Gorton.

Now in truth, this first flight was not exactly their first flight. They had tried this inside the hangar before they planned to do it outside. Of course they had. They made sure they had. They made sure it worked before it had to. The dull black truck, with holes and gaps where all the lights had been, was backed into the hangar, the cables were all attached to the round silver bag, the bag was gassed and they did drive the truck slowly back and forth, as much as they could, inside that closed hangar. They practiced raising and lowering the bag as well, just to make sure that went well. So far so good. They were ready to fly. Right after dark. Right after dinner. Let's eat!

The ground crew, The Space Cadets, all ate as a group at the base commissary and, had anyone asked, they were the bowling league! And after they thought about that silly excuse, they also thought it was great idea, and maybe they would be The Interplanetary League! They mostly tried to eat quietly, but it was tough not to laugh at everything, whether it was funny or not. They were glad to all get back to the hangar, where they could laugh anytime they wanted and no one would ask questions they couldn't answer. That went better for all concerned.

They knew what they had to do, and they had done it before. Just as they had tested their "flying saucer" within the confines of the hangar, that was how all of the real flights would start—inside the hangar. The huge disk-shaped gasbag from the NBA had been laid out flat at the very back of the hangar. The hangar doors were opened just enough to allow the odd black truck to back in so very silently. All you heard were tires squeaking on the smooth concrete floor. Cables were played out from the four spools in the back of the truck and carefully secured to the bag. That was not as easy as it looked, as the bag, empty, was not light. That took some serious team work, but they got it done. Double-checked? Check. What next? Gas the bag and wait for dark. Not just First Star, but true night dark. How do you tell? You bring a book.

This had been a small argument early on: How do you define dark? After sunset, yes, of course. And for this, after First Star, as the western sky was still light for quite some time after sunset. So, then, when? Someone suggested a book, but that was laughed at. Don't be silly. You can't read a book in ... the ... dark. *That's it!* When we can't read a book outside, it's dark! They had already figured out how to turn off all of the outside lights around their hangar and outside all of the buildings around them, so it really *would* be dark out there at night when they rolled out. (No need to advertise where they were.) After that, it all came down to which book. There was, of course, an easy, hands-down winner in that contest. The book on hand had to be H. G. Wells's "War of the Worlds." A copy was procured and kept safe in the hanger, just to tell when it was dark. When the driver for that night couldn't read the text as he stood outside, it was time to fly. It was dark. Let's go!

It was after dinner, the sun was down and the First Star had been sighted. With that, the gasbag was slowly being filled, and by the time the driver couldn't see the text, the book was put back and everyone was ready. So was their flying saucer. With the cables pulled in, the silver bag floated gently over the truck, looking as though it might lift it. They had certainly thought about *that* possibility, and wisely elected to only drive out with the fuel tanks full.

There was no need to risk odd flying-truck sightings out over the town. Funny, though.

With full dark, the big hangar doors were silently rolled back (they had oiled them), and the truck was fired up. Was it running? You had to stand close to the front to hear the fan and belts. Take three steps back and it was silent. Exactly what they wanted. And there were no lights. Literally. All of the lights on the truck had been removed, even the dash board lights. No. Lights. The driver took his time about this, as there had been lights in the hangar, and now he had to acclimate to the dark and drive with no lights. And yes, he had been practicing that, too.

The word had been put out on the base that they were testing a new night vision system. You might see a truck with no lights at night. Then again, you might not. Do *not* shine a light at the truck you can't see. On that base, that was not an unusual request. Just another one of many. The truck (and the drivers) had all been practicing after midnight, driving slowly in the dark, getting a feel for the truck and the base, an idea of where they could go and where they could not go. By this first flight night, they were ready to go. Everything was. It was time.

Slowly and silently, the truck rolled out of the hangar as the flying saucer hovered so ominously right over it. No one said a word. It was an incredible scene, now so very real and maybe a little bit scary. Yeah, that looked like a flying saucer! And the fact that it dwarfed the big Army truck made it look far less than friendly. The driver and his co-pilot gave a thumbs up, as did the winch crew in the back. Capt. Lewis was standing there, outside the hangar, and returned the thumbs up with a shiver despite the heat. He suddenly remembered being the man in the pilot's seat and giving that same thumbs up to his ground crew before each flight. It hadn't been that long ago. Seemed like just yesterday. He whispered what he had heard.

"Safe return."

No, they weren't flying a bombing mission over Germany in the heat of a great war. No one was going to shoot them down. They would all get back alive. But still, he remembered. And he remembered that not everyone had that luxury of a safe return back then. It was not a given just two years before. And now? Hey, they'd be back in no time. All safe and sound. The captain walked back inside. He didn't look back. He had seen enough. Maybe a little too much.

CHAPTER 18

The "launch" was hidden from view by all of the other buildings around the NBA hangar. That had been the idea all along, that no one ever saw where the NBAs were kept, and no one ever saw them go in or out of any building. They were just suddenly there. Or not. Now, that same secrecy by design was helping them launch these "flying saucers" with the same level of hidden sneak. As the dark black truck rolled away, the winch team was ready, but no, they held off. They did not start to unspool the saucer, to let it fly high, until they were well away from the buildings. They had time. They had all night. The truck made a turn and was gone from sight. The hangar doors would be closed until they got back. Everything else in there was still a secret.

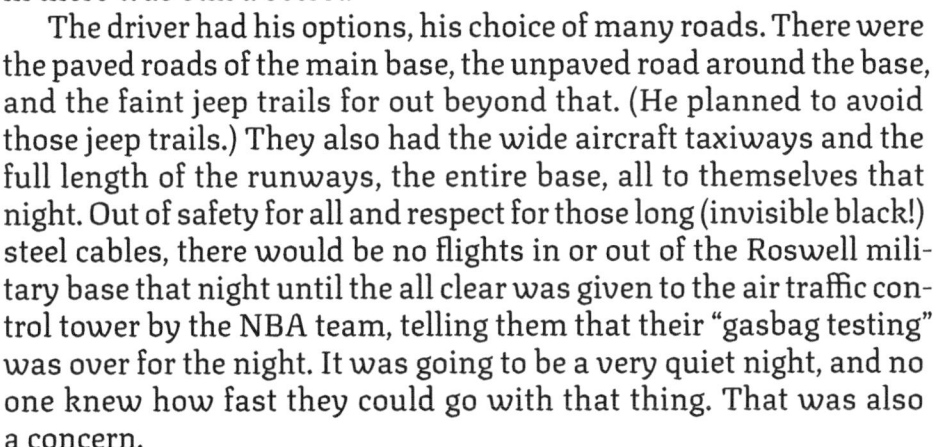

The driver had his options, his choice of many roads. There were the paved roads of the main base, the unpaved road around the base, and the faint jeep trails for out beyond that. (He planned to avoid those jeep trails.) They also had the wide aircraft taxiways and the full length of the runways, the entire base, all to themselves that night. Out of safety for all and respect for those long (invisible black!) steel cables, there would be no flights in or out of the Roswell military base that night until the all clear was given to the air traffic control tower by the NBA team, telling them that their "gasbag testing" was over for the night. It was going to be a very quiet night, and no one knew how fast they could go with that thing. That was also a concern.

Since all of the "flight testing" had been done (had to be done) inside a closed hangar, there was no way to know what might happen when the truck tried to tow the gasbag that might actually lift the truck if they went too fast. Oh, several of the engineers on the Western Witch Project tried to do the math, tried to compare the weight of the truck to the weight of the NBA, but it got iffy once you added the cables and crew and at that unknown ground speed with maybe a bump or two. There were too many variables. They were all pretty sure that the truck weighed more than a nuclear bomb, but no, not entirely sure. Their best advice: If the truck goes airborne, slow down. *Yeah, right. Thanks guys. Big help there.*

The truck did not go airborne. By the time they had added the four winches in the back with all of that cable, and very full fuel tanks, it weighed a lot more than a normal NBA, and still more than any nuclear bomb. So there should be no odd bounces or weird air time over the humps. Then again, with no lights in the cab, they had no idea how fast they were going. The driver wisely elected to hold it to a comfortable third gear idle. That seemed fast enough. He'd be sure and check the speed (whatever it was) in broad daylight (and without towing the saucer) the next day.

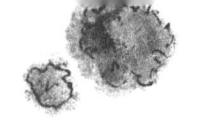

Slowly, carefully, after they cleared all of the hangars, the winch crew started to let out cable, all as a sort of synchronized dance to make sure the fake flying saucer above them rose flat and even as a real flying saucer might. The bag itself gave them some wiggle room in that, so it did just sort of rise up silently over the base, and they had it flying high, all spooled out, before they made their first turn. And to their credit, they did not fall over in the turn.

That had been a real concern as well. Would the gasbag drag the truck over on its side in the turns? There was no wind that night, but they did have to change direction. The base did not go on forever, and they did have to get back to that hangar eventually, so they did have to turn, and everyone held their breath when they did. Were the wheels still on the ground? The driver and co-pilot leaned out the cab and looked. Yep. Still on the ground! So far so good. They turned and they did not fall over. Quiet smiles in the dark. Funny how they were all being so very quiet.

They were miles from the closest fence, the truck was silent, and they were all whispering as if they could be heard in town. The crunch of the tires in the sand was the loudest noise around, the only noise they heard. They whispered when they spoke. And man, was it *dark* out there! How was anyone going to see this thing if they couldn't see this thing? Just drive. They drove.

Back at the NBA hangar, Captain Eli Lewis was asking himself much the same thing. Where *was* that thing? He found himself walking around outside in the dark, pacing back and forth, trying to see the big silver flying saucer out there, somewhere, but where? He knew the route that they had planned to take, but had no idea by then where they might be on it, so they could be anywhere, but where were they? Where *was* that thing? He walked, he looked, and he saw nothing. So how were they supposed to show off a flying saucer if no one could see it? This just got frustrating. All of that hard work for an invisible flying saucer. Except that it really wasn't all *that* invisible. Someone saw it.

CHAPTER 18

But he almost didn't see it. Ace reporter Arnie Benton had planned on *not* going out into the desert that night. What he had planned involved a certain waitress and several local establishments in hopefully prompt order. To that end, pun intended, Arnie arrived at the waitress's restaurant with flowers, only to find ... no waitress. He looked around again. Still no waitress. No waitress? How could that be? Now he was completely confused before dark. Not a first, but still annoying. She had to be there. All he had to do was ask, right?

"Where is she?"

"Not here."

"Yes, I can see that. But where?"

"Home. Sick."

"How sick?"

"Too sick to be here."

"Home alone and sick?"

"Nope. Not alone."

"Who's helping her?"

"That would be her husband, the professional wrestler."

Arnie waited for the laugh and the punch line, but there was none. The flowers began to droop.

"You want me to put those in some water?"

Arnie handed the nice lady the flowers, with instructions. "Yeah, face down."

And so it was that Arnie Benton had a nice quiet dinner in town *alone* and no plans for the evening. May as well go out into the desert and look for, well, whatever might be out there. He was thinking more along the lines of an insomniac rattlesnake, but an unpleasant scorpion might do just as well. He had seen better days, and it wasn't even dark. Pretty sure it could get worse if he worked at it. He drove out to Rattlesnake Ridge. Sure, why not? Maybe he'd get lucky.

By the time he got there, got parked and got out, yeah, it was dark. Really most sincerely dark, that far out of town. The stars were coming out faster than you could count them, there was no moon up yet, and the night was crystal clear. And really dark. Maybe he'd walk off a cliff. He gave it a shot and walked off the road and into the rocks and scrub, unwittingly walking toward the military base. Toward the overlook. But he stopped before he got to the cliff. Force of habit. He stood stock-still on that big flat rock, silently thinking,

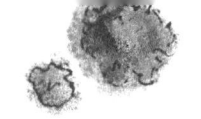

Here, snakey, snakey, snakey. No snakey. And no scorpions. It was just Arnie Benton from El Paso here, and whatever that was over there. In the air. And what *was* that over there? Arnie looked again, and then almost *did* walk off the ledge as he stepped forward to get a better look. Whoa!

With a sudden mysterious reason to live for at least five more minutes, Arnie took a cautious step back, looked around for snakes he couldn't see, stomped whatever that was under his foot with his boot and then walked back even farther away from the ledge, all the time focusing on that silent, floating shape with no lights that appeared to be hovering out over the military base. It was too far away to make out any detail, and the whole thing was so very dark, but there *was* something over there. Wasn't there? Something flying? It was moving. He could see that. He could see it move. It was moving south. And it was flying higher now. Silhouetted by the stars as it was ... a disk. A really big disk. Sort of saucer-shaped. And it was flying...

Slowly, ever so slowly, Arnie did the math in his head. And then he held his breath for as long as he could so the flying saucer wouldn't go away. As he watched, unblinking, the great shape caught a stray ray of light, and the silver flying saucer flashed for that instant in the deep night sky, its shape revealed to the hapless and helpless reporter. He responded as you might expect, as you might respond. He screamed.

"THERE IT IS! THEY DO HAVE ONE!! I KNEW IT!!!"

After a quick and dangerous stumble in the dark, Arnie got his act together as quick as he could and tried to not die out there. ***This*** was the story! ***This*** was why he was there! This was why he should have brought a camera. No camera. He stopped and thought about it and looked back toward the road. Nope, it wasn't in the car, either. But then, even if he had his camera, how would he get a shot of that? Black on black in the deep night sky? Yeah. No. Nuts. All he could do was watch and not blink and try to see the thing as it flew slowly south, away from him, high over the base, picking up and reflecting stray lights now and then to reveal that shape. That saucer shape. Arnie Benton was watching a flying saucer. Reporter that he was, and without taking his eyes off the thing, he pulled out pencil and paper and began to draw. It was all he had.

CHAPTER 18

All it took was a flying saucer to turn the distraught Don Juan into a blithering, happy idiot, laughing like a lunatic as he sketched what he saw as it flew away, farther away, and then... Wait, no, was it turning? Was it coming back? Was it coming back to pick him up and take him away to, what did Clayton call it? The planet Bingo B5? Hey, as long as he could file his story first, yeah, sure, let's go for a ride! Arnie stopped sketching and just stared into the deep night sky, trying so very hard to make out any detail, anything he could, about that flying saucer that was coming his way. Maybe he should stick his thumb out? Did they even have thumbs? And who else was watching this thing? He looked around. No one else there.

Arnie tore his eyes away from the flying saucer and looked down at the dark military base and the land all around. There was nothing else moving for as far as he could see. And if it was tough to see the flying saucer, he was certainly *not* going to see anyone else out there. Not even Clayton Whittaker, who *was* out there but never saw a thing. If Arnie was having a bad day at first, Clayton was just finishing his bad day with a very long walk. How bad was it? It was so bad that he never bothered to look up and never saw the flying saucer almost right overhead. Yeah, Clayton's day was that bad.

To say the day had started out well enough for Clayton and Blanche might be misleading. For Clayton, every day was about the same, neither good nor bad, but simply all about flying saucers and UFOs and did it ever end? Blanche was beginning to see that now—it did not ever end. She was going to be stuck in Roswell until the aliens really did show up, and even then, she was pretty sure that Clayton would want to stay for the wrap party once the aliens had conquered the world. She did not want to stay. She was ready to go but had already missed the morning bus.

Now here they were, back out in the desert, and there he was, picking up pieces of old broken ranch equipment, convinced that it all came from the planet Booboo 28. Blanche was over it. Over all of it. But she still had to watch her step out there because, you know, one bad step and there goes your ankle and you might say...

"*OW!!!*"

He never looked up. She did her best bad ankle hobble, and he never looked up. Oooooo... That settled it right there. Had he come running, he might have had another chance. But no, he didn't. Too late now. His fate was sealed, stamped and mailed. First class.

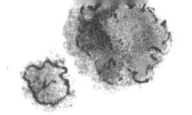

"CLAYTON!"

Now he looked up, but it was still too late.

"Help me!"

The idiot looked back down at the trash at his feet. Pick it up or not pick it up? He looked back at Blanche. She was wavering, and he thought she was waving. He walked over to her anyway, but he took his sweet time about it. She noticed *that*, too. That just made her mad.

"What's the matter?"

"I've twisted my ankle; I can't walk. You're going to have to help me to the car."

The idiot looked back at the trash in the desert. He really did. She wanted to slap him.

"*Now.*"

"Um, okay."

He was a lousy crutch, and all she could think was, it was a very good thing she was *not* hurt, as they would have never made it back to that old car if she was damaged and he had to help. He was that useless in a crisis. She knew that now. Good to know, even if she didn't need to know it any more. And before the idiot could ask, she told him, "I'll drive. You'll have to push."

Now Clayton was all concerned for his car.

"Can you even drive a stick?"

Blanche had reached her limit for stupid about three seconds before and almost gave it away with her next line.

"Let's find out."

Clayton dumped her ever not-so gently in the driver's seat, but it was up to her to get herself positioned as she needed to be. *Thanks for the help there, Clayton.* All he did was stand there. She had to close the door herself. And still, he stood there.

"You know to put it in second, right?"

"That's forward and up, right?

"Yeah."

"Okay, got it. Then I turn the key like... Where's the key?"

"Oh, sorry! Here."

As usual, Clayton had to fish around in his pocket for far too long before he came up with the keys, and at least he made sure she had the right one. There were all of two.

"This one?"

"Yeah, that one. The other one is the trunk."

CHAPTER 18

Blanche put the right key in the ignition and turned it the right way without thinking. She double-checked the gear shifty thingy. Second gear? Sure. Gotta be. She looked out the window and smiled at the village idiot still standing right there.

"Okay, ready!"

Clayton walked around to the back of the car and tried to push, but the car wouldn't budge. Ugh.

"Push in the clutch!"

She couldn't resist that one last joke.

"Oh, yeah! Okay! Sorry! Try again!"

Blanche pushed the clutch, Clayton pushed the car, and he kept pushing the car until he was almost out of breath. The car was rolling right along. What was she waiting for?

"Let the clutch out!"

Blanche was wearing a wicked smile that Clayton never saw. With both hands on the wheel, she let out that clutch. The car lurched once, fired up and roared away out across the open desert and out of sight as Clayton Whittaker just stood there in the road, out of breath and confused. What just happened?

Blanche Miller knew how to drive a stick shift all along. Of course she did. She learned how to drive a stick shift at age 15, in a truck—her father's big, old, flatbed Ford. That made her daddy proud. She never looked back that day in the desert outside of Roswell. She ran the old car up through second gear, dropped it into third and made tracks like a road runner. She stopped once for gas but knew to not stop the car. (She set the hand brake.) She stopped one more time to throw out all of the trash in the trunk and made it back to Winslow by midnight. Her daddy was very glad to see her, but not so glad to see that old car. It was not a Ford.

Clayton Whittaker, late of Irvine, California, had stood there in the road outside of Roswell, New Mexico, for a very long time as it all began to sink in. Then, as the sun beat down, he turned around and began the long walk back into town. It was dark by the time he got there, and almost midnight by the time he got back to his rented room. All he could do was flop across the bed. He was done. And he had never looked up the whole way back, not even once. He never saw the one thing he wanted to see.

He never saw the flying saucer.

CHAPTER 19

CLAYTON DID FINALLY GET TO SLEEP THAT NIGHT, BUT IT WAS only out of a bad combination of total exhaustion and complete depression. He had no idea why it had all gone so very badly for him out there in the desert that day, what he had done to deserve such a horribly unfair fate, or that she could even drive a stick. Who knew? And now here he was, no car, no friend and seven hundred miles from home. Could his reality possibly get any worse? Of course it could. He woke up with the morning sunlight streaming in, hot on his face. May as well get up. He stumbled through the shower and then put the same clothes back on again before he staggered out the door in search of food. He wasn't about to try to cook his own breakfast that morning. New Clayton Rule: No more Rice Surprise. From now on, he wanted to *know* what he was eating. Or at least be told first. He made it to the closest restaurant without falling over. A small victory right there. Go team.

The man who walked too much the night before made it through the restaurant's front door on the second try, only to find himself immediately accosted by waving arms and shouts of "Hello, Clayton, over here!" from some loud guy in the back. Clayton squinted and tried to focus. Yeah, that hurt. Who was that? Oh yeah, that reporter. Arnie? Second New Rule: Arnie had better be buying. Clayton plowed his way through the tables and chairs and people, over to his one and only friend on planet Earth, pulled out a chair and almost missed it as he sat down. Arnie hesitated. Was Clayton drunk? Arnie sat down and backed off. Maybe he'd better pace himself with this guy. Clayton looked like crap. And not the good kind you put on your garden. Ew.

"You okay there, cowboy?"

"Yeah, no."

"Late night?"

"Long walk."

"You wanna talk about it?"

"No."

And then Clayton told Arnie all about it. Everything he could remember about the day before, ending with the car, *his* car, roaring off over the horizon and his long walk back into town, and how very late at night he got home and how he was still tired the next day and hungry and where was breakfast and so what? And then, for once, Clayton shut up. He just sat there and stared at the empty table in front of him. It was Arnie's turn. Out of respect for his distraught friend, he leaned forward and spoke as quietly as he could.

"I saw it."

"Good for you. Tell it I said 'hi.'"

"Clayton?"

"Yeah, what?"

Arnie spoke slowly and distinctly to make sure his friend heard every word correctly. "I saw the flying saucer last night."

And that's how you get time to stand still. Arnie didn't move. Clayton couldn't move. If anyone else moved in the restaurant just then, they were being mighty quiet about it. Everything had stopped as Clayton processed the information. Clayton started to feel himself come back to the world around him, and he leaned over, closer, just to make sure he heard that right. He squinted.

"Say that again, slowly."

"I got stood up yesterday."

Clayton was not amused by this change of subject. "Yeah, a lot of that going around these days."

"So I went up to Rattlesnake Ridge."

"Understandable. Who wouldn't?"

"After it got dark, really dark, something came out down below and flew over the base, really slow."

"A small plane?"

"Too big to be a small plane, too slow to fly, no lights."

"A cloud."

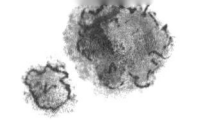

"A silver flying saucer. It had to be. I saw lights bounce off of it. I saw the shape. I saw what it was. What it had to be. It was a flying saucer. It flew high up over the base, made a big slow loop all around the thing, then came back down on the base and it was gone."

Clayton was still trying to be very skeptical about this, and not simply jump up and scream, which is what he would have done if he had the energy. He did not. Not yet. Maybe after breakfast. And where *was* that waitress? He looked around, then back at his friend, who was still close.

"You sure?"

"Here, look."

Arnie pulled out his sketches from the night before and put them on the table in front of Clayton, who picked them up and turned them around as he looked at them. Which way was up? Clayton made a face. Arnie corrected that for him.

"Like that."

"Wow."

"And it was big."

"How big?"

"I don't know where they keep it big."

"Maybe it's dimensionally transient."

"Huh?"

"Maybe it changes shape."

"Yeah, that's gotta be it."

Clayton looked all around again. Who was looking? No one was looking. Not yet, anyway.

"You sure?"

"I'm sure."

Now, there was no doubt that this fascinated Clayton, but it also made him mad. The one night he could have seen the flying saucer, and he did not. And why not? Because he was busy walking back into town. And *why*? Because *she* took his car. It was all *her* fault. Wherever she was. With his car. The idea that maybe he should report his car as stolen had not yet occurred to him, nor would it in time to find it. The desert was a very big place, and Clayton was getting madder by the minute, but not about his car. He missed the flying saucer!

With the sketches still on the table, Arnie and Clayton talked about the flying saucer, and what Arnie had (and hadn't) seen out there the night before as breakfast showed up and disappeared. Other people in the restaurant heard them, and chairs were scooted over as the gang grew and ideas were shared and compared. They were suddenly the most popular guys in town. That Arnie had seen it, and what he had seen, was never questioned, even if it had made Clayton mad that it had been Arnie, and not him, who saw it first. Clayton was going to see it next time, he was very sure about that. He would make very sure of that, even if he had to live up on Rattlesnake Ridge. In the meantime, everyone else had questions for Arnie that should have been his. That didn't help.

"How big?"

"Bomber big."

"How high did it fly?"

"Oh man, I dunno… A thousand feet up? Tough to tell."

"How fast?"

"Not fast at all. Slow. Very slow. It just kind of hovered over the base."

"Could it have been any kind of airplane?"

"Not going that slow. It just sort of floated. Maybe stopped sometimes."

"Make any sort of noise?"

Arnie stopped and had to think about that. *Had* he heard anything? *Did* it make any noise? The more he thought about it, the more the thought that maybe it did, but he was puzzled by his own answer to that one. Quietly, as he still thought about it, he made the noise he thought he had heard.

"*We-you-we-you-we-you...*"

Clayton saw his chance with that one.

"Yeah, that's the mass propulsion drive system. That's what they sound like."

Two tables away, a couple of young guys got up, waved to the waitress, left some money on the table and ran for the door as quietly as they could, never looking back. They didn't dare. They were laughing too hard to stay any longer and hear any more. They had been on the ground crew the night before. It was nice to know that their work was appreciated. Better go tell the captain.

Clayton was getting more alert, and he focused on the subject now. He was fed and watered and ready. Yeah, he was mad that he had missed it last night, but he was *not* going to miss it tonight. No way, no how. He leaned toward Arnie. The game was on.

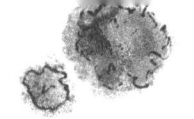

"You got a camera, right?"

"Well, yeah. *Reporter*."

"And you got film in that camera, Mister Reporter?"

Arnie had to think about that and then he frowned as he remembered.

"No."

"Some reporter you are."

Arnie stood up, looked around and addressed the crowd in the restaurant. "Is there a camera shop here in town?"

What happened next was a stunning display of group improv comedy. Without any one of them knowing that the question would be asked, or that they should all work together on the answer, they all worked together on the wrong answer, and it was comedy gold.

"Yeah?"

"No."

"Maybe."

"Used to be."

"Hey, there's one in Albuquerque!"

"Yeah, Albuquerque!"

"You can't miss it!"

"Just take a left when you get there!"

"Yeah! Go right to the left!"

Arnie spun all around trying to listen as everyone kept answering, having no idea he was being played. Yes, of course there was a camera shop in Albuquerque. There was also one two blocks away in Roswell, but no one mentioned that one. Not even the owner of that local camera shop, who was sitting right over there, laughing harder than anyone else in the room. Then it was up to him to bring it all back down to earth. He waved at Arnie.

"Son?"

"Yes, sir?"

"Do you have a tripod for your camera?"

"Well, no."

"How about a bulb shutter release cable?"

"A what?"

"I see."

"See what?"

CHAPTER 19

"Well, you know, good daytime photography is tough enough, but at night it's a whole different beast."

"So what do I need?"

"Superfast film, a camera with a good tripod, that shutter release to hold the shutter open and a subject that doesn't move."

"Whoa, wait, what was that last one?"

"You're going to have to hold the lens open for quite some time out there in the dark like that, so nothing can move if you want it to show up."

"But the flying saucer..."

"It moves, doesn't it?"

"Well, yeah, but not fast."

The old man just shook his head. This was not going well for Arnie.

"If you got the perfect night shot, everything on the ground would be in focus, the stars would be streaks of white and the flying saucer would simply not be there at all."

Clayton, in his enthusiasm, completely misunderstood the situation.

"They're invisible to film! I knew it!"

The old man looked at Clayton, trying to figure out if he was joking or not. He was not.

"I, wait, no, oh, never mind..."

The man paid his bill, left a generous tip and got out of there as fast as he could. The rest of the crowd got back to the breakfast at hand, and just like that, Arnie and Clayton were left to their own devices and whatever was left of their breakfast. There wasn't much left. Arnie looked at his wristwatch and jumped up.

"So you wanna go to Albuquerque?"

Clayton was no longer amused and picked at his food. "No."

"Rattlesnake Ridge, tonight, after dark?"

"Yeah, I guess."

"Okay, gotta go, see you there!"

Clayton gave a hollow wave without even looking up. "Bye."

Arnie bolted out of the restaurant and was long gone before the waitress came over for his plate and cup. She leaned in close to Clayton. It was nice. She smiled really good. Like bacon. He smiled until she spoke.

"Your friend forgot to pay."

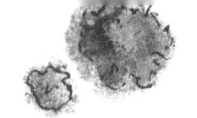

Clayton simply, silently, put his head down on the table and everyone left him alone, even the nice smelling waitress. Someone else, out of pity for the waitress, covered Arnie's tab and tip, but did not pay for Clayton's. He was still there. He was on his own, and he knew it. After a while, and after a fresh cup of coffee, he was feeling a bit more upright, if not all right, and motioned for the waitress. She came right over. He looked as though he still needed help.

"Yes, dear?"

"Train station?"

"Right down the road, same side as us. I'd say you can't miss it, but you can. The sign's gone. Just follow the tracks. They go right to it."

"Thank you."

"Anytime."

With the waitress gone again, Clayton emptied the coffee cup, stood up and began to fish money out of his pockets for the bill. He didn't seem to have a wallet but kept the loose bills in one pocket and the loose change in another, and the small UFO parts in both. After a bit, he ended up with several very different piles of small things on the table: A wad of small bills, a pile of loose change, a collection of UFO parts and the bag of catnip. Then he just stood there and stared at the table before he turned around and walked away. He left it all, even the catnip. It was time to move on. Like so many others before him, he never looked back.

Once the waitress figured he was really gone, she went over and sorted through it all. There was more than enough to cover his bill and a very generous tip. She smiled at that, but what was all of the rest of this stuff? She had to go get a trash can for all of the UFO parts, and then she opened the small bag. No idea what *that* was but it had to go, too. Straight into the can. Gone. The table got scrubbed and reset. *Next!*

Meanwhile, the two Army guys in civvies who had been there for the start of it had decided to go back to the base on their day off to spread the good news. They knew the captain would want to know. And they wanted to tell him!

"*We did it!*"

No one in the hangar had any idea what those two were talking about, but it was worth it to listen just to take a break. Tools were put down, and everyone walked over closer, but not too quickly and not too close. They still didn't know *what* they had done, and was it contagious? They were wary. The guys were happy. Somebody asked.

"What ... did we ... do?"

"The saucer! They saw the flying saucer!"

The ground crew in the hangar went wild, cheering and dancing around, before they had to settle back down, gather around and ask for more.

"Who saw it?"

"Some reporter."

"Did he get photos?"

"No, he made sketches."

Everyone looked at each other. *Sketches? Okay, sure, why not?* The two guys who had been there in the restaurant that morning were still thrilled by it all and explained what they had seen and where they had seen it. Nods all around. Everybody knew that place.

"Guys?"

The team settled back down to listen.

"Here's the thing: No one in that restaurant ever questioned what he said he saw. He said he saw a flying saucer fly over this base last night, and everyone in the restaurant believed him."

"WE DID IT!!!"

"And we'll do it again tonight."

As they had been talking, Capt. Lewis had come up quietly behind them and had heard everything. By then he was all smiles, and his big question had been answered. Yes, that flying saucer *could* be seen in the dark. Good to know, but he had to know more.

"Did he say where he had been to see it?"

"Up on Rattlesnake Ridge, sir."

"Hmmm."

"Sir?"

"It might be good to know how visible this thing is from right down here in the basin. At ground level, looking up."

"Yes, sir."

"How about, tonight, we spot some ground crew around outside the base in civvies and private cars to keep an eye out for flying saucers, you know, just in case."

"Yes, sir, will do!"

After that, it was a house party in the hangar as the ground crew, the Space Cadets, knew that their work had been seen the night before, and by golly, they'd make *sure* it was seen tonight as well! Everyone picked up their pace as plans were made for some of them to get off the base early, before the launch, and find spots out around the outside of the perimeter fence to see what they might see.

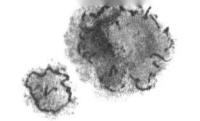

As they made those plans, Capt. Lewis had gone back down underground, to the offices below the hangar, to confer with Col. Baden and tell him the good news. The colonel had planned to watch the flight that night, but now, maybe from off the base. He could be one of the spotters. The captain tried an old question a second time.

"But should we shine a light on it?"

"Why? He saw it."

"From a high vantage point."

"Let us see what it might look like from below, but no, not tonight."

"Fair enough."

"And where will you be tonight, Captain?"

"I'll be right here."

"Very good. One of us should be."

As all of this played out in and around Roswell, Arnie Benton had made his mad dash for the camera shop in Albuquerque, having no idea that it was a 200 mile drive. One way. And for what? He had no idea what he was going for, but he got there in time for lunch. The waitress there, not being in on the joke back in Roswell, did give him the right directions to a camera shop, but once the gentleman behind the counter began to understand what Arnie wanted to do, he knew hopeless when he heard it. And he figured Arnie for a total nutcase. Best to humor the loon. A roll of Kodak Tri-X film was laid on the counter.

"This is the fastest thing we've got."

"Will this do the trick?"

"Do you have a tripod?"

Arnie looked around, and the clerk took that as a no. A tripod got laid on the counter.

"Cable release?"

Arnie shrugged, and one got added to the pile.

"This'll do it?"

"It's a start. It will give you a chance to practice."

"What if I don't get another chance?"

"Welcome to the wonderful world of outdoor photography."

"Whadda I owe ya?"

CHAPTER 19

As Arnie had left the restaurant in Roswell in such a hurry, and everything in there had quieted back down to the usual dull roar, the rest of whatever followers he and Clayton might have had did the same thing, all of them getting up, leaving quietly and saying less. It was a silent exodus. Clayton never looked up, never questioned whether their enthusiasm had been real, or if had he just been played for a fool by the crowd. By then, it didn't matter to him. Flying saucers or not, it was time for him to go home. He knew that now. Clayton stepped outside, squinted into the late morning sun, got his bearings and began to walk. Again. And his feet hurt already. He missed his car. He looked up and ahead, looking for the train station. No sign? Yeah, that figures.

The leader had no followers now. Clayton Whittaker walked the streets of Roswell alone, lost in his scattered thoughts with only a vague idea of where he was going. He caught sight of the railroad tracks. There. Follow the tracks. They lead to the station. It was the building with no sign, but somehow, he knew. Through the door and in. Was this the place? There was a ticket window over there, on the other side of the waiting room, and there were people waiting. Yep, this had to be it. Unless it was the bus station. He looked again. Tracks. Yep. Ticket window.

"L.A."

"You're just in time. That train is due in within the hour. Maybe sooner."

"Lucky me."

The man behind the counter gave Clayton a ticket and took his cash. It was an easy transaction. Clayton was reminded to not get too far away, as the train was due soon and would not wait if he wasn't there. Not a problem. He wasn't going anywhere else. His feet hurt too much to go anywhere else.

Now, in truth, Los Angeles wasn't home for Clayton, but it was close enough that he could take a bus down to Irvine from there and not have to walk much more. He was over walking. He was so over walking that, as he paid for his ticket and looked for a seat, he decided that he was *not* going to walk back to his rented room and pack. Just leave it. Along with all of that junk in the shed, his flying saucer. He was done. He was tired. He sat down hard and did not look up. He didn't need to. He could hear someone talking loudly behind him—one side of the conversation. They had to be on the phone.

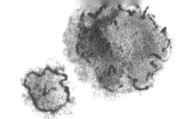

"*Yes*, feed the bird."

"*Yes*, feed the cat."

"No, do *not* feed the bird to the cat."

Clayton just shook his head. No one ever closed the doors on those phone booths any more. Why even bother with them? And should he call home and tell them he was coming? He saw no reason to make that effort. It would be a big surprise, as opposed to a nice surprise. And where's the train? No train yet. He sat up and sniffed. That smell. He knew that smell. Coffee. Coffee? Where? With a slow look around, he saw the small lunch counter all the way over there, and as he looked that way, the smell was stronger. Yes, coffee. That's exactly what he needed. Because he was done with catnip. What had he been thinking? Coffee. Yes. His new thing. He made the effort.

"Cuppa."

"Yes, sir, coming right up!"

Silently, to himself, "And I'll pay you extra if you never say another word."

Two strong cups later, with plenty of sugar and a dash of cream in each, Mister Clayton Whittaker, late of Irvine, California, was finally back on Earth. Look out, world. Big smile. Dangerous smile. No more catnip for this boy! Clayton was wide awake now, all sly smiles and a dangerous man. That's when the young lady walked right in and sat right down. And yes, her hair was long. Clayton smiled and hailed his good friend behind the counter.

"Coffee for the lady."

"Yes, sir!"

The steaming cup got set down in front of her, and the waiter pointed to the man who had bought it. She looked over, and she smiled. Nice smile. He offered a smile of his own.

"Oh, thank you."

Clayton looked on the floor behind the young lady. Three suitcases. In the distance, he could hear the train. This was going to be close. Good thing he had that second cup. He was ready, but was she?

"Headed to L.A.?"

"Yes."

"I'm from L.A."

CHAPTER 19

She looked puzzled. "Then what on earth are you doing in Roswell?"

"Going home. Have you been to L.A. before?"

"My first time."

"You might need a guide."

Now the young lady gave Clayton a serious look over, top to bottom. He looked more like a desert rat by then, but hey, he *said* he was from L.A. And he didn't look *that* bad.

"I just might."

The train whistle, so very close by, cut off the rest of their warm conversation. The young lady gulped down her coffee, Clayton paid the bill and left a tip, and without asking, he reached down and swept up the two larger suitcases and stepped back to follow the girl to the train. And to the ends of the earth, if need be. She didn't seem to mind. She snagged her makeup case, and they ran for the train.

And so it was that Arnie Benton spent the night on Rattlesnake Ridge all alone.

CHAPTER 20

IT ALL CAME DOWN TO THE SQUARES, THAT IS, THE SQUARE dates of the month: The first and fourth, the ninth, the sixteenth and the twenty-fifth. Those were their scheduled flight nights, and from what the outside ground crew, their spies on the ground outside the base, could tell, yes, people *were* starting to know when to go see the show. The ground crew also learned very quickly to always have a man up on Rattlesnake Ridge. That was where the action was, and it quickly became the best party in town. But only on certain nights. Everyone knew that now.

The oddest part of it all was the monkey drives. The team was still trying to keep all of those chimpanzees happy without them actually getting to fly, but was driving them around in flight suits close enough? It did help, and it didn't take long for the chimps to know that "flight suit" meant "drive" now. And they did like that. It did help. There was also a quiet little betting pool going on how soon they might have more monkeys without having to actually buy them. Tell no one.

With the flying saucer "gasbag test flights" over the military base at night going so very well, and the chimpanzees all happy with being driven around the base posing as aliens from time to time, everything seemed to have settled down to a dull routine around Roswell, and dinner at the Lewises' fell back into its own routine. But it was never dull. Eli just sat there at the dinner table and watched his wife, who finally picked up that she was being stared at and gave him The Look.

"What?"

"Oh, nothing."

"Oh, no. I know that look. It's something. *What*?"

Eli hesitated too long, adjusted his position in his chair, looked over at his daughter, who looked right back at him, and then he popped The Question.

"So how do you feel about Nevada?"

"I hear Las Vegas is nice."

Eli smiled at that, a sort of in joke, but then he frowned. A lot. Julie saw that, too.

"Not Las Vegas."

Julie never blinked an eye and never looked away. "What else is there?"

"They call it Paradise Ranch."

Big fake smile on the wife now. Ashley was paying attention but said nothing.

"Oooooo, sounds lovely!"

"Yes, well, they almost called this place Forest Lake."

"But..."

"My point exactly."

"Eli, are we being transferred again so soon?"

"Not exactly."

"Uh-huh. So what, exactly, are we being?"

Julie's husband, Captain Eli Lewis, told her that maybe the whole fake flying saucer thing was too successful, and now the base that they were in outside of Roswell was too popular and too public for what they were trying to do with the Western Witch Project when no one was looking. Now everyone was looking, and more people were looking all of the time. Roswell was getting bigger faster, and too many people were seeing too much. The chimpanzees were still the big secret on that base, and that big secret still had to be kept.

"Even though you drive them around dressed as aliens?"

"We were told to back off on that."

"I would imagine so."

Eli shrugged. "And now we're being told that the Western Witch Project may be moved out to Nevada, where there's literally no one around."

"No town?"

"No town."

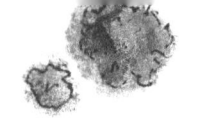

"No people?"

"No people."

This is where Ashley finally had to speak up. "No school?"

"No kids. Sorry, Ashley."

"But what about me and Clint?"

Eli gave his daughter a scrunchy look. Even Julie was looking at her now, but it was her father who had to ask.

"What kind of name is Clint?"

"*Dad!*"

Eli did a quick frantic look all around (and under) the table. Was Clint there? He was not. *Whew. That was close.* Eli smiled. Ashley did not. Then it was Julie's turn.

"What about *wives*?"

"I'm not even sure about that. This is about as remote as it gets, on purpose."

"So we'd get to stay here while you go out there?"

"Something like that."

Ashley thought about it some more, and now she was all grins and wiggles over that one.

"So I'd get to stay here with Clint?"

Eli gave her another look. Then he looked around again. "Have I ever *met* this Clint?"

"Well, no..."

"And *will* I ever meet this Clint?"

"Not if you move to... Where was it, Mom?"

Now it was Julie's turn to give her husband a look. Yeah, That Look.

"*Paradise Ranch*, dear. Your *father* is going to Paradise Ranch. While we stay here in Pitsville, USA."

Eli was faking incredulous, but still had to smile. "Pitsville? Really?"

"Oh, I made that up."

"I thought so."

"You don't want to know what we really call it."

Ashley blurted it out without thinking. "The Horny Toad Corral!"

Eli was suddenly not the least bit amused by that name. "*WHAT?*"

"Cowboys, dear. It's all about the cowboys here."

"And Clint!"

Eli had to frown at his daughter. He didn't want to, but it was called for.

CHAPTER 20

"And is Clint a cowboy?"

"He wants to be!"

"I'll just bet he does."

Julie tried to bring her husband back in line. "Dear, about Paradise Ranch?"

"Look, would it help if you knew it was officially known as Area 51?"

Actually, no, that didn't help at all, but Julie lied, "Oh, yes, that makes it *so* much better. So when do *you* go?"

"I don't know."

Dinner got quiet after that, as everyone had something to think about. Eli was thinking about having to move without his family. Another remote assignment. May as well be overseas again. His only consolation was that, at least this time, no one would be trying to shoot him down. Julie was not happy with losing her husband to the Army again. Those war years were bad enough, even if, this time, no one would be trying to shoot him down. They both took some small comfort in that. Ashley was just happy that she found a great new way to bug her dad, and now she knew that Mary Ellen at school was right, imaginary boyfriends were the best! Yay, Clint!

It was late summer in 1947, and it was New Mexico. The days were hot and sunny, and the nights were, well, maybe slightly less hot. Yes, it does cool off at night in the desert, but also yes, it's still nice to have a fan going if you want to sleep. No need for a blanket, and it's okay to sleep on top of the covers. Almost required. So they did. And no need to turn in early. Let's wait for night, and for however close to cool it might get. With the lights out at ten, that was as cool as it got, and they dealt with it. With a fan, of course. And if the power goes off? Yes, well, if the power goes off at night, it takes your precious fan right off with it, and you will notice a thing like that in New Mexico in the summer at night. So did Eli. Right quick like.

"Power's off."

"Hmmmm...?"

"The power is off. The fan is off."

"Hmmmm."

Eli looked out the open window. He did not like what he couldn't see. And he couldn't see anything.

"The street lights are off. It's not just us."

"I paid the bill."

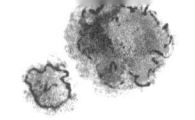

By then Eli was up on his feet and very carefully making his way over to the window. The stars were the brightest things out there.

"The whole town is dark."

Julie was sitting up in bed by then, but she stayed in bed. There was no need for them to collide in the dark, and she could hear him walking around, stumbling over stuff in the bedroom. Where was he? And what was he doing? No way to see, no way to tell. She stayed where she was. It seemed safe there.

"What about the base?"

"Good question."

Julie could hear her husband getting dressed in the dark now, shirt, pants, shoes (what, no socks?), and then she heard what she did not want to hear: The drawer in the nightstand on his side of the bed was pulled open, and something very heavy was pulled out. He had his issued sidearm. That beast, the M1911. She heard the safety click off. This just got serious. She didn't dare move.

"I'm going to look around outside, you'd better get dressed."

"Yes, dear."

She waited until she heard the front door open and close before she got out of bed and got dressed. What time was it? No way to tell. Late. After midnight? It had to be. And where were her shoes? Oh, these will have to do. But they certainly do *not* match. Maybe no one will notice. And where was Ashley?

Before Julie was going to go outside, she was going to check on her daughter. She wanted to make sure she was safe, and more importantly, she wanted to make sure she didn't get shot. That gun was a dangerous thing, and Julie had a healthy respect for it. She had seen what it could do and did not want to see that again. Ever. Julie stuck her head into her daughter's bedroom.

"Ashley?"

"Hmmm?"

"The power's out, dear."

"Hmmm."

"Just stay in bed. Your father's out on patrol, armed to the teeth."

"Don't forget to duck, Mom."

"Thank you, dear, I'll try to remember."

Carefully, in the total dark of deep night, Julie made her way through her own dark house by memory and was pleased with herself for not actually walking straight into a wall along the way. She smiled at that. She found the front door, opened it as quietly as she could and stepped out to greet the waiting universe. It was magnificent. She forgot to close the door.

By the light of the Milky Way, that brilliant streak across the night sky, Julie Lewis could see her husband standing in their front yard, heavy pistol in hand, as he, too, could only look up and admire *everything*. It was all there, the entire universe was right there, looking as though you could reach up and touch it. He almost tried. He started to, but then he put his hand back down. A brilliant shooting star streaked across the night sky, vanished and took their night vision with it for a minute or two. By then, they were standing side by side.

"They say that's good luck, to see a shooting star."
"Only if it doesn't hit you."
"Does close count?"
"Only in government work."
"Then that was good luck. Should we have made a wish?"
"I always do."

Hands were held in the dark. The night was beautiful, the stars were perfect, but everything on the ground, all around them, was so very dark. There was no power, no lights to be seen anywhere in town. No ground glow at all. Not even on the base. Not even the blue lights on the perimeter fence. That was what worried Eli, that the whole base was out, too. The captain put an arm around his wife. She didn't mind. He felt her arm wrap around his waist. That was nice.

"So the whole town is out?"
"Sure looks like it."
"And the base? How does that happen? I thought the base had its own power."
"It does. That's what worries me."

Julie had the answer first. "This is intentional. They are doing this on purpose."
"To what end?"
"To hide something in the dark."
"To hide what?"
"To hide *that*. Listen..."

Eli didn't hear anything at first. He would be the first to admit that his wife had ears like a fox, and she could hear things that he would never hear, but now, this? What did she hear that he could not? He stepped away from her, as if that might help, and did a slow circle in their front yard, head up, trying to pick up what she could hear. Nothing. Nothing. Nothing. **Something**.

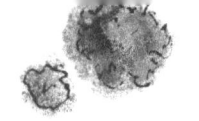

At first, it wasn't so much what they heard as what they felt. Not a noise, but a sort of low-resonance vibration in the atmosphere. If they turned just the right way, faced toward the southwest, they could feel the air from that direction trying to move them back, push them back with a deep force. It was something big. Something very big. And it was getting bigger. Closer. Louder. Much louder.

"Eli?"

Julie sounded genuinely worried about that low noise as they both looked toward the source they couldn't see. Whatever it was, it was getting closer. Eli just shook his head at the question she hadn't asked. What was it? He didn't know. He kept looking, kept trying to see it, but there was nothing to see in that great dark night. There were no lights, no reflections, nothing to bounce off the thing. They had learned their lesson too well. He had taught them how to hide.

They knew what it was, what it had to be; it had to be an airplane. But a very large airplane, and like nothing they had ever heard or seen (or not seen) before. Between the two of them, Eli and Julie Lewis had heard enough different airplanes that they could listen and tell you what it was before they saw it. It had been a game of theirs for years. He flew them and she knew them. And they were very rarely wrong. But now? This? Neither one could even guess. Julie gave up first.

"What is it?"

"No idea."

"Is it even one of ours?"

"I sure hope so."

"What if it's not?"

"One of ours?"

"What if this is how it starts?"

Eli had to think about that. Were they witnessing the start of a Russian invasion? In the middle of the night? In Roswell, New Mexico? Eli shook his head, but he wasn't so sure. He went with all he had.

"Why would they start in the middle?"

"Because who would expect that?"

CHAPTER 20

Eli looked over at his car. How much gas did it have in it? Half a tank? How far could they get on that? And which way would they go? Then he looked at his home, all dark and silent. They'd have no time to pack. There were no bug-out bags. All they could do was run. Grab a few things and run. Don't forget the daughter. Grab the daughter and run. To where? He just shook his head, unseen in the dark. He had no idea where to run if they landed in the middle. And from the sound of it, that's exactly what they were doing. They were landing. He could see that now.

If he stood very still, Eli could see stars being blocked by something large as it came in to land out of the south. Had it come from the west, over the mountains? Maybe so. Did Julie see it? He pointed, but he wasn't so sure. All they could see, if they knew where to look, were the stars going dark as the aircraft passed under them. There wasn't much to see, but they sure could hear it. Eli watched until he was sure it had landed. No stars were blocked now, and the sound spooled down. It was on the ground. Taxiing. Still no lights. The low sound, the idle hum, went on for some time. Where were they taking that thing? To Phoenix? Then it stopped. Silent. No warning.

The silence, in that darkness, was overwhelming. There was nothing to see and nothing to hear. The world spun, the stars moved and another bright shooting star cut the night sky in half.

Julie whispered, "Missed me, missed me."

Eli kissed his wife, and they walked back inside, hand in hand, as the lights of the town began to come back on. Their fan was running again by the time they got back in and shut the front door. Neither one said a word. Julie checked on Ashley, who was back to sound asleep by then. Good for her. Lucky girl. Eli and Julie went through an abbreviated version of their bedtime routine, still with no idea what time it might be. Julie checked her alarm clock, just to make sure it was still set, even if she couldn't see it. They still had a workday to deal with, and very, very soon. May as well try to get some sleep. Just one more kiss. Good night again.

Not a word was spoken about the night before over breakfast the next day. Ashley, even though she *had* spoken to her mom in the middle of that odd night, had no recollection of the event at all, of the power going out, or of anything making any noise whatsoever. It was a non-event for her. Lucky her. Between Eli and Julie, they both looked as though they had been up all night, which they sort of had, but neither one was brave enough to mention it to the other the next day. That was wise on both counts. Even Ashley knew better than to make fun of them, as she did *not* want to know what those two had been up to last night. Ew.

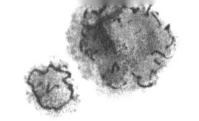

Eli drove very carefully to the base, looking at everything as he went. He saw no sign of any Russian invasion; indeed, he saw no sign that the power had gone out the night before, or that anything was any different at all. By the time he drove through the main gate, he was half convinced that he had dreamt the whole thing. Except he knew that he hadn't. And he was still wary about it. Why did everything look so very normal today? Something was up. Something was going on. Something had to be. But what? The driver was waiting in the captain's office, hat in hand. So was Col. Baden.

"Sir?"

"Yes?"

"As soon as you've had your morning coffee, sir, we've got something for you to see today."

The captain looked over at the colonel, who already had his cup. That cup got raised with a smile. Yeah, he was going to need more coffee for this. He looked at the driver and smiled.

"Let's find two cups."

"Yes, sir!"

After enough coffee for all three of them to run in top gear for the rest of the day, they made their way back to the surface and to the waiting sedan. Not just a jeep, but something nice. Something for officers. The driver held the doors for them. Much appreciated. As they drove across the base, the captain looked at the colonel, who just shook his head. Not now. Not here. Not yet. Understood completely. The driver's clearance was questioned. Capt. Lewis looked around. Where were they going? They were almost out of base. Except for that hangar there. The really big one. Was that where... Yep, that was where they were going. The driver pulled up and jumped to open the doors.

"I'll be waiting for you out here, sir."

"Thank you."

"*Danke.*"

The driver pointed to a small windowless door on the side of the building. There was an armed guard next to it. The guard opened the door, the car door was shut behind them, and the two officers

CHAPTER 20

went inside. A curtain had been hung around the inside of the entry, keeping anyone outside from seeing anything inside. As Capt. Lewis pushed that curtain aside to walk through, his world changed forever. The hangar, that one big room, was full of the largest aircraft Eli Lewis had ever seen. It filled the hangar and was all brilliant, polished aluminum. No wonder they had to turn the lights out. It was blinding to look at in daylight. And even right there, at the door, they were already standing under one wing.

"*Oh.*"

"Ja."

"You knew about this?"

"Only a little. You?"

"I heard rumors."

The colonel smiled at the captain and nodded at the craft.

"The rumors are true."

Slowly, carefully, the two men began to walk around the giant aircraft. It towered over them as no other machine ever had. The captain hardly knew where to look first, and what he might see next. The colonel followed behind him, and took it all in as well. This was going to take some time. They might be late for dinner, but with good reason. This was a B-36. The very first one.

Knowing that the bombs were getting bigger quicker than the airplanes were getting faster, the Western Witch Project had been created to give the U.S. an expendable delivery system for those bigger bombs. And while that was going well, the U.S. was also working on faster aircraft to outrun those bigger bombs, and this, the B-36 Peacemaker, was that plane. Capt. Lewis had heard the rumors, of course, but he had been kept out of that loop. As with all secrets, not everyone needed to know. All he had to do was train the monkeys, and that was all he did.

The captain counted six turbo-prop pusher-prop engines, along with four jet engines. Those big wings were full of engines, and there was no doubt that this thing could *fly*. By the time the captain had made his way all the way around the hangar, with the colonel right behind, they had seen the largest aircraft they would ever see. They could reach out and touch it if they wanted to. The captain, when the colonel wasn't looking, did just that, if only to make sure that it was real. It was, and the colonel had to ask:

"So what do you think?"

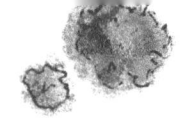

The captain was completely overwhelmed by the size and scope of the thing. This aircraft was massive, far beyond the scale of anything he had ever seen, let alone flown. And now what did he *think* of it?

"I think it's the most beautiful thing I've ever seen."

"Ja."

And as he looked at it, as he couldn't take his eyes off of it for fear that it might disappear, Capt. Lewis realized more about what it was, and what all it meant to him. He didn't know whether to laugh or cry. His expression must have puzzled the colonel.

"*Was?*"

"We can send the monkeys back now, can't we?"

The colonel didn't answer right away, but then, slowly, without a smile, he nodded his head.

"Ja."

Eli Lewis, Captain, USAAF, understood exactly what he was looking at now: His retirement. This plane, this big, beautiful, aluminum giant of an airplane, gave him the out he didn't know he wanted until he found himself looking at it in that locked hangar. And then he wanted it very much. The captain slumped and almost fell. He was suddenly more tired than he had ever been in his entire life. The colonel was concerned for his friend.

"Are you alright, Eli?"

"I can retire now."

"Yes, you can."

"The war is over. I can go home."

This puzzled the colonel, as he had never heard the captain speak of home before.

"And where is home for you?"

"Florida. I'm from Florida."

The two men began to walk back toward the door, or at least toward the curtains that hid the door. Or maybe not. Were these even the right curtains? They both looked around. No idea. Worth a shot. With one last look at the largest airplane on earth, they pushed the curtains back, stepped through the door and out into the bright desert sun. Their driver was waiting. It was the right door. The car was opened for them, they got in, and it was time to go back to work. The colonel was intrigued by the idea that the captain had been from

CHAPTER 20

Florida. A nice, warm place, but not a desert. Warm, but with water! Gorton Baden smiled at his friend.

"So, you go back to the beach now?"

"The beach? No, my family lives on a small river in the middle of the state."

Baden seemed disappointed by that. "No beach?"

"No, no beach. Just a prefect, quiet little river, the Silver River, just east of Ocala."

"O-calla?"

"Just a small town. We call it 'Slow-Cow-ah.'"

"And you like that?"

"Yes, I like that. It's quiet, the fishing is good, and that is where I'm from."

"So now you go back."

The captain sat back and smiled at the thought. "Ja. Now I go back."

EPILOGUE

THE FULL MOON ROSE SLOWLY, BIG AND SOFT AND ORANGE, through the trees at the edge of the clearing, out beyond the small clapboard home. It was a typical Florida home, just one floor and with that comfortable wide porch all the way around, a sort of outdoor living room all around the house. There was a green swinging bench by the front door and plenty of chairs for friends. They had stopped by earlier, but the visitors were gone by then. It was late. The one light that was on, the bedroom light, went out, and it was dark. Comfortable, quiet and dark.

"Happy?"

"Yes, you?"

"Very."

"You don't mind the peace and quiet?"

"Not at all. Those jets made the base too loud."

"Yes, they did."

"Quiet is good."

"Yes..."

Julie and Eli Lewis, USAAF Retired, had just settled in for a nice quiet night, a relaxing night of deep sleep and sweet dreams. He felt he had earned that. He had gone through the war and he had put up with monkeys and he had invented UFOs. And now all he wanted to do was fish, after a good night's sleep in his own bed in his own home with his own wife. The windows were open, the breeze was gentle and the world was silent all around them, right up to the moment that it wasn't.

EPILOGUE

"*WWWWAAAAAKKKKKKKKK!!!!*"

Eli Lewis came very close to falling out of bed as he sat up so fast he almost fell over. Whatever that was, it was big and loud and close, and was that loud thing, whatever it was, in the room with them? He lunged for his gun, still kept right where it always was, as he stopped to feel the bed shaking. Why was the bed shaking? And why did his wife have her head buried in her pillow? Why was she laughing so hard the bed was shaking? This wasn't that funny yet. Was it?

"What *WAS* that?"

All Julie could do was wave one arm high over her head, as she was still laughing too hard to speak. Eli put the gun back down with a loud clunk.

"*W W W W A A A A A K K K K K K K K K ! ! ! ! WWWWAAAAAKKKKKKKKK!!!!*"

Whatever it was, there was more than one of them. Eli picked the gun back up. It was never too early for a little late night hunting. But now his wife was waving both arms and trying to speak. It was tough, as hard as she was still laughing, but the words finally came.

"No, dear, don't shoot!"

"WHY NOT?"

"Well, because there's too many of them, for one thing."

"Too many of WHAT?"

Julie wished, with all of her heart, that she had turned on a light by then, just to see the look on her husband's face when she answered that last question. No time now. All she could do was imagine that look as she answered that question.

"Monkeys!"

"*WHAT?*"

"We're surrounded by monkeys here now!"

Julie collapsed back onto the bed, laughing too hard to sit up, as Eli got up and went to the open bedroom window. The screeching went on at odd intervals, but with the noise in the house, the monkeys had moved farther away. Eli was still holding his pistol. It was still loaded. He was not laughing. It was a dangerous combination.

"Put the gun down, dear. We're outnumbered."

Julie managed to get out of bed, walked over and hugged her husband. She knew it would come to this, but she never had the heart to tell him. Now she had to. She led him back to the bed, and they both sat on the edge. She made him put the gun away. He was still confused.

"Monkeys?"

"Yes, monkeys."

"Why are there monkeys?"

"You can blame Tarzan."

"Not funny."

And that was all it took to get Julie laughing again, because yes, it *was* kind of funny. It was kind of very funny. Once she could speak again, and before Eli could say anything else, Julie explained that while Eli had been away at war, Hollywood had stopped by and filmed Tarzan movies in the woods along the Silver River east of Ocala, all around his old home. It had been very exciting for the locals at the time, but after the production company packed up and went away, the locals noticed that they had left a few things behind: The monkeys. A lot of them. Eli was not amused at all by any of this.

"You have got to be kidding me."

"*WWWWAAAAAKKKKKKKKK!!!!*"

All Julie could do was point out the window at the source of the noise and collapse again with laughter on the bed. Eli stood back up and walked over to the window. All he could do was stare off into the noisy night.

"We've got to do something."

"What would you do with them, dear?"

"Blast them all into space."

ROSWELL REVISITED

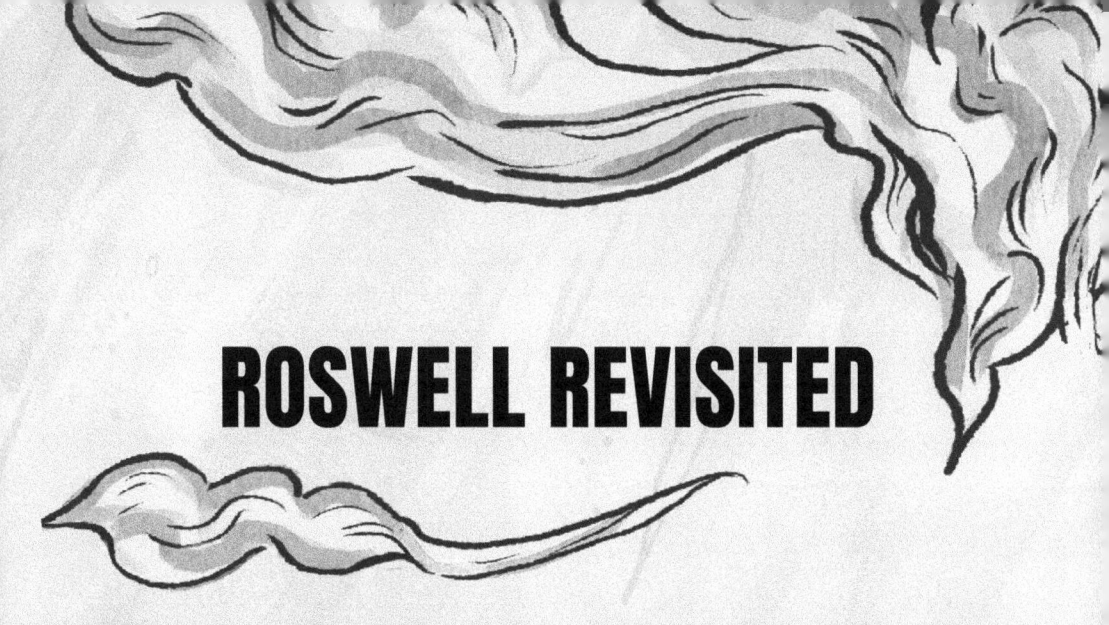

ROSWELL, NEW MEXICO, THAT QUIET LITTLE DESERT TOWN near the Roswell Army Air Force base way back in 1947, is now a bustling modern city of some 50,000 people seventy years later. And yes, if you stop by, you can still see some mention of those odd events of the summer of 1947, as they really did embrace their image as "Flying Saucer City." There are still those who believe and still those who don't, and the city welcomes them all. Their money's just as good as yours.

As for what really happened outside of town when no one was looking back then, well, time does hide a great many things, and so does the desert. But if you know just where to go and which way to look, far out of town on a quiet night, you might still get a whiff of bananas and monkey poop.

Just sayin'.

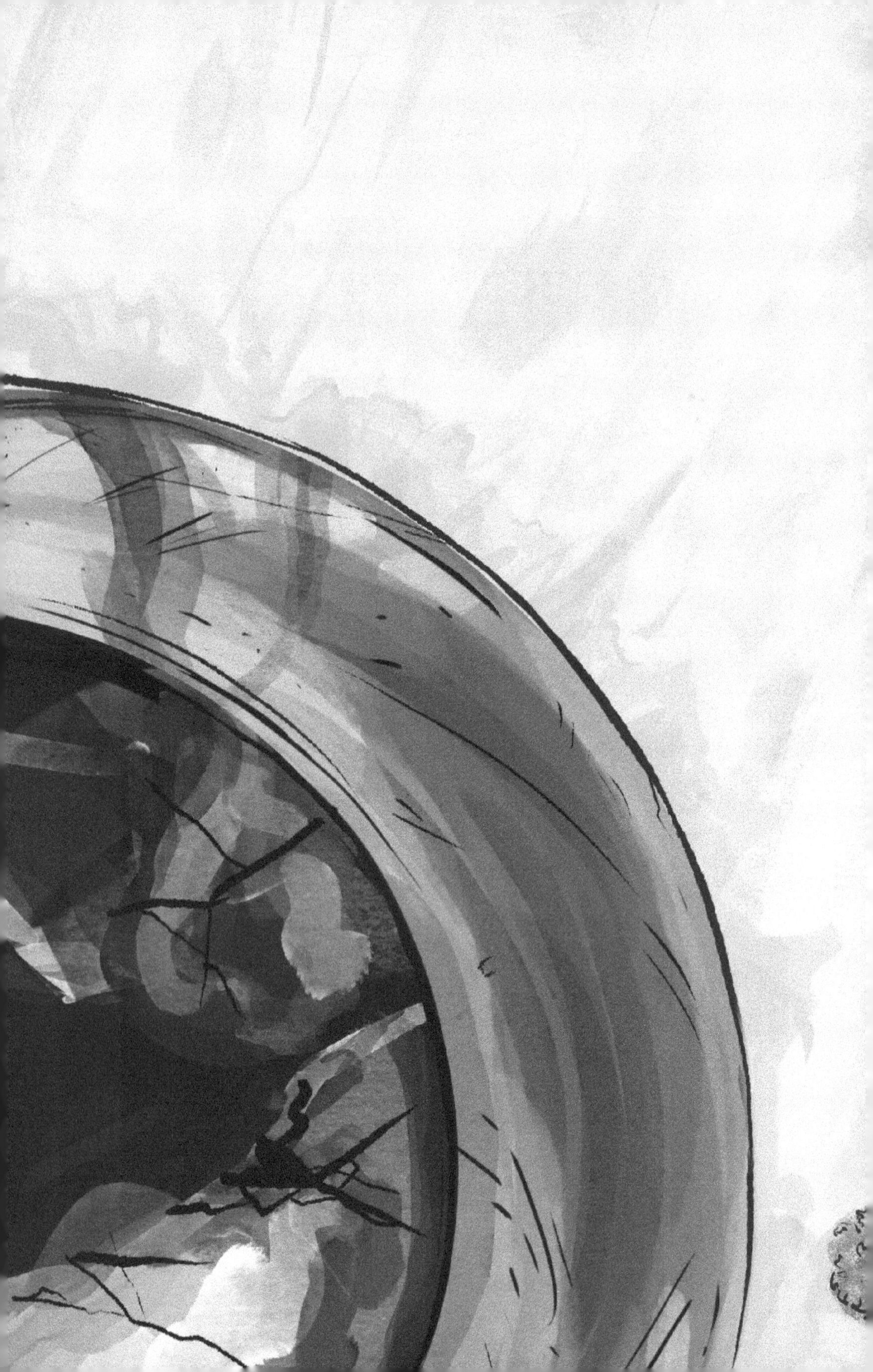

AUTHOR'S NOTES

I USUALLY START OFF MY AUTHOR'S NOTES BY BLAMING someone else for what I've just written, for the source of the story or the idea, but you know, this one is entirely my fault. I've been kicking this idea around for years, and it was finally time to put it in print. Sure glad I did, it was a lot of fun. And it might even be true. No one who read the premise could tell me that it wouldn't work, and everything I had read tells me that it would. But did it? Was this what really happened back in 1947? Let's leave it at this: If I disappear, you'll know I got it right.

As for who's who, there's only a few. I pictured the great actor Tommy Lee Jones as Captain Eli Lewis, and you should, too. The name came from a young man named Eli at Paradise Pickers in Pinellas Park, Florida and my father's first name was Lewis. Julie and Ashley, the mother and daughter in the story, are in fact a wonderful couple that work at the Lakeland Antique Mall over in Lakeland, Florida. I am honored to have them in my story here. I hope they are, too.

What about the rest of them? Colonel Baden, Clayton, Blanche and Arnie? All made up from whole cloth, as they say. I had no one specific in mind for any of those characters, but they were all a lot of fun to write. I hope you enjoyed them as much as I did.

Two very real people: My editor, the incredible Maggie Talbot. I will always thank her, and I will always be amazed that she wants to read what I write. This is my 23rd novel and my 49th book. Talk about yer glutton fer punishment! Wow! Thank you, Maggie! And of course, M'Lady Lisa, the absolute focal point of my life when it's not flying monkeys.

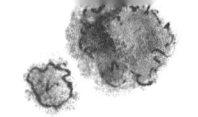

That's about it from here for now. I still have to go back and re-read Chapter 20 and all the rest that I wrote after that before I send it off to Maggie tonight, but let me tell you about tomorrow:

I'm going to Disney World!

Woo-hoo!

Chip Haynes
Tampa, Florida
January 11, 2019

CHIP HAYNES

CHIP HAYNES IS AN ARTIST, WRITER, CYCLIST, AND JUGGLER living in Tampa, Florida. In 2009, New Society Publishers of British Columbia, Canada, published "The Practical Cyclist, bicycling for real people" and "Wearing Smaller Shoes, living light on the big blue marble." In 2010, Satya House Publications of Hardwick, Massachusetts, published Chip's "Peak of the Devil, 100 questions (and answers) about peak oil." Two out of three won awards and picked up some really cool endorsements. So there. From there, Chip had had just about enough of telling the truth and took up writing fiction instead.

Chip still dabbles in fiction and poetry when he's not out pedaling in shorts and sandals.

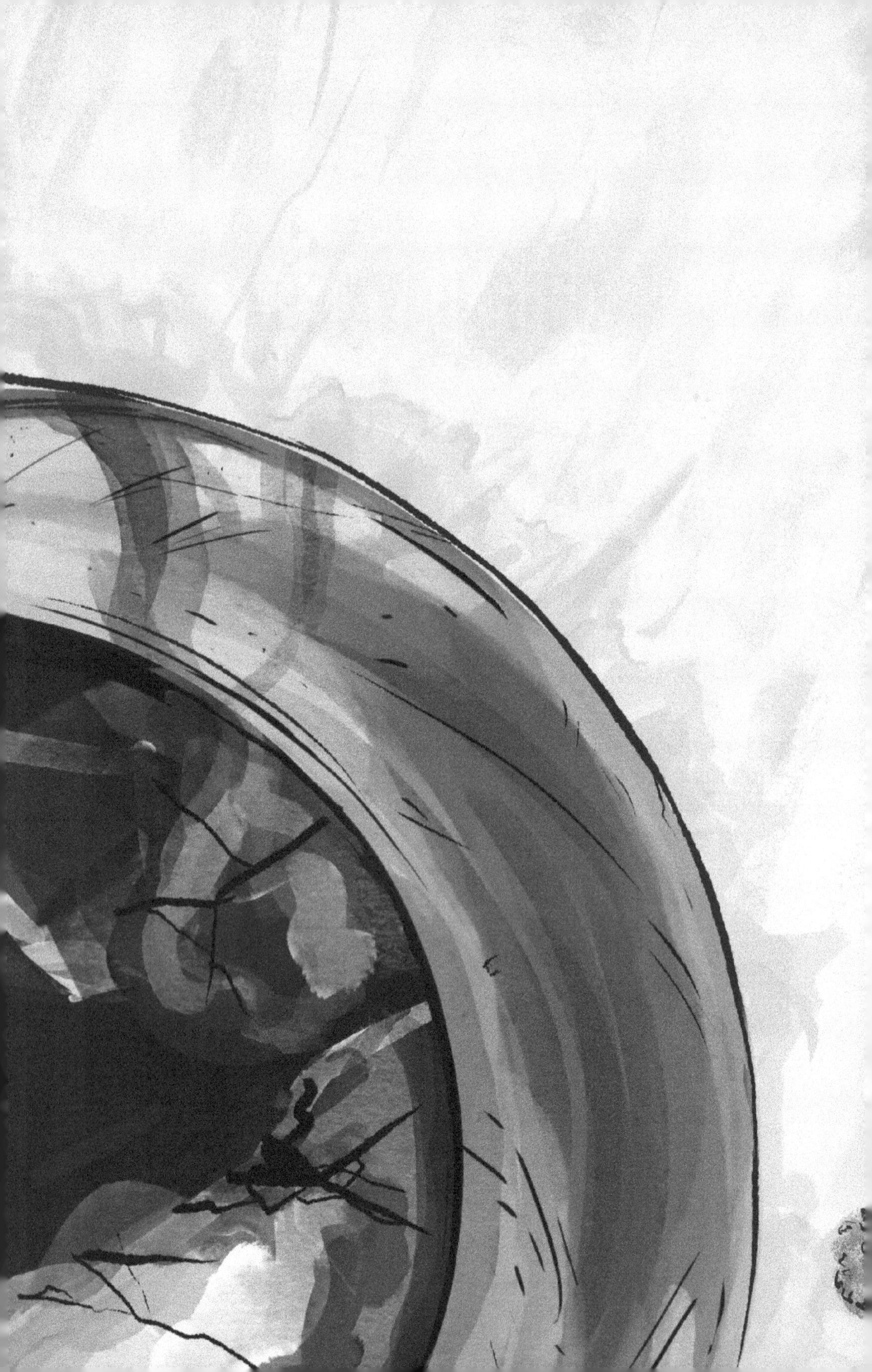

Discover more at
4HorsemenPublications.com

10% off using HORSEMEN10